SEEDS

Comes the Shadow

SEEDS OF EDEN

Comes the Shadow

PREFACE

FIRST BORN (Book 1)

Eden

Eden was once the home and Mother Planet for the Edenites. A planet, rich in everything imaginable but they took from it until it had no more to give and only when the planet began to die, did they realize what they had done. By then, it was too late. Now uninhabitable, their population dispersed among the sister planets and throughout the star system. It took them hundreds of years to find suitable life sustaining planets for all of their people.

Earth was discovered by the Edenites in their search for suitable life sustaining planets. It was chosen as a seed planet. Its new population transplanted onto the planet and waking one day to their new world, only to them it was just another day.

When the Edenites returned, they found the inhabitants on Earth were doing to their planet what they had done to Eden. Something had to be done to prevent this. They made their decision. Now, the clock was ticking.

Mathew, a child placed on Earth to an Edenite family already living there and waiting on his arrival. They were well prepared for him. Now, finally of age and a young man, his parents leave Earth. Mathew to be on his own, except for his android teachers and a master computer called Trainer. Will he overcome the tremendous odds against him? Will he be enough? Will the humans listen and can he survive long enough to convince them? The adventure begins.

SEEDS OF EDEN (Book 2)

Second Seed

Mathew was brought to earth years earlier as a new born to be raised like a normal human by his Edenite parents. His parents were called away on a new assignment. Mathew began his assignment by entering the secret base where he would begin his real training for his assignment on Earth. On a short break from the base he was shot and left for dead by killers. He later woke to find he had been repaired and was now part android. His physical abilities greatly enhanced, he was soon able to continue his mission.

The secret base lies beneath his home. Run by the giant super computer known as Trainer who has access to all the communications and computer systems on earth that use public or private communications systems. Trainer is assisted by aides. Androids so human like you can't tell they're not humans.

Mathew begins his first mission by taking a field trip to get to know his surroundings and capabilities. Almost as soon as he starts out, he finds himself intervening to save the humans from killers, robbers and kidnapers. His methods of intervention soon bring unwanted attention from the local and governmental authorities. It's not long before a full scale manhunt is underway to locate him, but can they catch him?

Brad Bowen is the leader of the FBI's tactical team assigned to locate and capture Mathew. Their paths have crossed and now they are teaming up against new terrorist cells. Brad is not aware he is the bait the military is using to try to capture Mathew.

Will these two, together, be enough to stem the tide of destruction the human race is bringing upon the planet? Can they convince the others to help them? The adventure continues.

SEEDS OF EDEN (Book 3)

Prince of Bara

The Edenite plan to change the way humans treat the planet Earth and its resources is showing promise. Brad Bowen, former team leader of a FBI special ops team and four former military members, now recovered from their enhancement surgeries, are pushing to recruit more team members to work alongside them in the fight against terrorism and extremism.

Construction of an entry point for Edenite equipment at the Area 51 base in Nevada is underway along with a new training center and rehab facility for the new recruits. Technology sharing with the military has begun.

Brad and his team are enlisted to assist in the battle against drug operations at sea, as well as freeing hostages.

Mathew is on his way to the planet Bara, where he will face off against those who would destroy the very ones he has been sent to protect. He is unaware of the forces and the prophecies that will shape his arrival and his future.

As the battles begin and the prophecies unfold, will he have the ability to win them and meet the new challenges he will face? Challenges that he has no control over. Challenges that will soon change his life and the lives of those he loves, forever.

INTRODUCTION

Mathew is now on the planet Bara, having succeeded in saving the royal family from the Pache war machine and now joining with the android warrior Lord Logan to find the source of a killer virus now infecting his new family and the people there. They must find the source and secure a vaccine before all those infected, including his princess bride and the Queen perish.

As their search begins, centuries old prophecies come into play that require all of Mathew's skills and abilities. Each one a fulfillment of a peoples hopes and prayers and only something that Mathew himself can solve.

Brad Bowen, former team leader of an FBI special ops team is now in charge of Earth operations. He and Mathew successfully recruited four former military team members, who in turn recruited two more teams from England and Europe. Now they must face off with home grown terrorist groups determined to kill those they believe are now tools of the Edenites, or as they prefer, aliens.

Construction of the entry point for Edenite equipment at the Area 51 base in Nevada is well underway along with a new training center and rehab facility. Technology sharing between the Edenites and the military has begun.

As new adventures and battles begin and as more prophecies unfold. Mathew faces changes and challenges he has no control over. All too soon he discovers his life and the lives of those he loves are being forever changed and he has no way of stopping the changes.

Contents

For Monica

Friend, Confidant and Wife.

Thanks for being a part of this Journey with Me

For the Literary and Artistic support

The Artist in you providing another awesome book cover

No Journey Would Be Complete Without You

Chapter 1 – Search for a Cure

Prince Mathew and Lord Logan continue to meet with Commander Borne onboard the spaceship Eden Phoenix. They are reviewing the satellite recordings taken of the other continents on Bara, while searching for the source of the bird plague that came with a freak storm from the south of their continent.

Large black colored birds with white heads and red wing tips were discovered after the storm passed and anyone coming into contact with the birds was taken ill. Many have died and more are seriously ill with no prospects for living without an anti-viral serum.

To make matters worse, both the queen and princess were infected and are presently incased in stasis chambers onboard the ship to slow the progress of the virus.

There are two continents south of theirs. One a rocky desert terrain that backs up to forested mountains. The other a group of islands with one smoking volcano.

As they study the satellite recordings, they take note of the animal life and the apparent lack of human like existence on the desert continent. After careful study, they have determined there are trails made by animals or something else but they are unsure as to the exact makeup of what is making the trails. They are waiting on the results of other recordings taken at night with infrared technology, which will indicate heat sources, a sure indicator of life.

They study the visual recordings for the islands, noting the extensive tropical forest growth which tends to block their view of life forms on the islands. The volcano appears to be active though not violently so. Here again, they are waiting on the infrared recordings.

They do not want to go rushing into anything without background information. They could likely disrupt a culture far below theirs or even more advanced but they feel that is unlikely or they would have heard from them before now.

They have come up with a plan which involves limited interaction. They will locate the birds and upon securing any live specimens, put them in net bags and send them up into the atmosphere to be picked up by a cloaked vessel which would immediately transport the birds back to the Phoenix.

As they continue studying the visual recordings, increasing the zoom to get a closer view, they sight something they hadn't seen earlier. Within the mountains they discover large nests made up of limbs, sticks and large leaves and obviously built by something very big. In one nest they find a large nesting bird or something akin to one. It is similar to the giant birds of old on earth and Eden and could have come before man.

Scattered about the nest and on the cliff edges are what appear to be bones from prey they have killed. Among the bones are what appear to be humanoid skulls? As they look closer, they can see that the skulls are either human or humanoid in makeup. Smallish in appearance and likely that of young humans or a similar small humanoid like animal. That could explain why they are not seeing life signs in the daylight hours.

As they continue scanning the video clip, they find nesting nearby, a bird similar to the one they are looking for. Perhaps it's a scavenger bird and feeds on whatever the big ones leave behind. It is very similar to the ones they are looking for and the discovery gives them a place to start.

Soon, one of the vessel techs arrives to inform them the recordings from the night flyovers are ready for viewing. They bring up the recordings on their monitors. The amount of heat sources springs out like fireflies in the night. There are all kinds of life signs. They appear to be going in and out of what appear to be caves as the heat signs continuously appear and disappear. The heat sources are in small groups near what they assume are cave openings but as they follow the heat signals, they can see that not far from the openings are other heat sources that appear to stay in position or only move ever so slightly. It's as if those heat sources are watching the heat sources near the caves.

They continue to watch as one heat source moves further away from the cave and within minutes is set upon by multiple sources lying nearby. As they watch, the one heat source dims and slowly goes out. Obviously, something or someone has killed it.

This is, they agree, most definitely a dangerous place to live as is evidenced by what they have seen so far. They wonder what type of life sources they are seeing. As they watch other scans, they note there are heat sources in the desert as well. They don't appear to move very fast but rather in a steady almost orderly fashion and they often appear to move in a line. Every once in a while, they seem to just disappear into the ground or a cave. Almost as if they dug into it or have become one with it. It was baffling, not being able to see exactly what was happening.

Next, they begin studying the scans of the islands. Like the mountain areas, they find many heat sources. Some are indicative of animals and in some locations there appear to be groups of humans or humanoids. There are also fires or fire pits. The island with the volcano appears to have many rifts in its surface where the molten lava can be seen in the dark.

They discover something else. There are many heat sources in the oceans surrounding the islands. Some singular but many in groups as if they were in the water or perhaps on boats. They came to that decision based on the fact that many were lined up as if sitting in a boat or something similar. In one of the scans, a large heat source appeared to disrupt a smaller group of them. Like something had struck a boat or something.

The heat sources were scattered in the water and moving towards what appeared to be nearby land but most or all disappear. An indication they had been consumed by the larger heat source.

Mathew thought of the giant fish he encountered on the white continent and suggested that might be something to consider as an explanation of what they saw on the scan. After viewing the night scan of the islands, Mathew went back to the day scans. He reduced the zoom to get as close a look as he could. After careful study, he thought he could make out some non-natural fixtures near the water's edge on one of the islands, possibly the ends of boats tied up or even houses on stilts. Upon further scrutiny, he found what appeared to be a manmade structure on a barren spot near one of the volcano vents. It resembled a stone edifice perhaps an altar.

As he studied it even closer, he discovered there were posts lined up around it with what appeared to be humanoid skulls on the tops. Could this be a sacrificial place? Were the humans or whatever they were, that far in the dark ages? Only a physical investigation would tell them. As he was about to turn from the scan, something else caught his eye. He looked closer. There perched on one of the skulls was a bird. By all appearances, it was just like the ones they were looking for. Now they had two sources to look for the birds.

Chapter 2 – The Group

At the Area 51 base, the two teams from Europe were finishing up their question and answer session with Terry and his team. All of them had been through the pros and cons regarding the transplants. For some, like Graham and Wallace, there would be no issues with which or how many limbs they wanted transplants for. For the others, the decision was theirs and their alone. They had six hours to make their final decisions.

Colin spoke up. "I've made my decision and the sooner we can get on with the operation, the better I will like it."

"And what have you decided?" Terry asked.

"I want them all. The legs of course but I also want the arms."

"You're sure of that?" Terry questioned. "You know you can't undo it."

"I know," Colin replied and he hesitated for a moment then continued. "In my mind I see two possibilities. One with less and the other with more and I don't want to be in a situation where I would ever want to say I wish I had more. It won't affect my quality of life but it might affect someone else's, so I opt for all of it."

Adrian spoke. "Well you've helped me make my decision. When you put it like that, it all makes sense. I'm in for all of it too."

"Me too," Nigel replied.

Bailey wheeled her chair over to Martin.

"How you doing, little cousin?" he said.

"Just fine, now," she replied.

She turned her chair to face the others and in particular her teammates.

"Okay guys," she said. "Listen up. This is one time when you have to make your own decision and I don't want anyone to say I told you to do it but just so you know. I am opting for the whole thing. Nobody here will think any less of you regardless of what you decide to do but whatever you do, keep it even."

"What's that mean, Bailey?" asked Carlos.

Well, any of you can function pretty well with only one arm transplant if that's what you choose but I'm telling you now, you can't have a fast leg and a slow one, so if you want to be able to jump over buildings in a single leap, you gotta go for the two meal deal."

The whole room burst into laughter. After a few moments, Victor spoke.

"We know where you're coming from, Bailey and like you, I'm going for the whole thing."

"Me too," Francois announced.

"And I," Damien echoed.

"Count me in," Alexander replied with Frenchy chiming in, "me too."

"That only leaves me," Carlos stated "and I'm in for it."

"I guess that makes it unanimous," Terry stated.

He walked over to the fridge. Opening it, he began pulling out cans of beer. Handing one to Martin, he said, "Pass them around."

As soon as everyone had a beer in hand, except for Graham and Wallace who had straws, Terry raised his and said, "A toast to two new teams and a new beginning for all of us."

"Here, here," the group replied.

As soon as they finished their beers, the doors opened and med techs entered the room. It was a signal for Terry to speak as they began to wheel Graham and Wallace out of the room.

"Ladies and gentlemen, right this way please" and he led them out of the room to their own rooms where they would be prepped for the operations.

#

In a large bunker in Montana, a group of men were meeting. They were known as 'the group' by locals. Up to no good, most people said. No one really wanted to know as long as there wasn't any trouble and several local deputies were part of it, so all the more reason no one thought much about them.

They might have thought a little differently had they been party to some of the meetings held recently. Today's meeting was special. They had a special guest, a former member of their group who moved to Maine several years earlier. There, he started a similar group also known as the group.

The subject today was the state of the union, meaning the speakers particular opinion of the state of the union. He brought along with him, some special weapons he felt would up the ante on their as yet unwaged war on those they felt were bringing their country down to a level they felt they could no longer live with.

Roger, as his companions called him, began his speech by telling them that it was now obvious that their president, most of their government and many of their military leaders were under the influence of aliens. The same aliens they spoke of as offering new technologies to the government.

"It should be obvious," he stated to everyone there that this was not rational thinking and those people that thought that way were under the influence of others.

He continued his rant by stating they only had to watch movies like V and GI Joe to understand what was at stake here. It was, he was certain, the beginning of the total loss of their society as they knew it and only a matter of time before everything they believed in was taken away.

"Already," he said, "they are passing laws right and left that banned organizations like ours. It was only a matter of time before the authorities began collecting their weapons and soon after, they would all be enslaved to the government or at least what they thought was their government but was in fact something entirely different. It was time to start taking matters into their own hands.

"I've done my research," he stated, "and there are weaknesses in their armor we can exploit. If we don't act soon, it will be too late."

One of the men in the audience raised his hand. Roger indicated he could speak.

"What do you recommend we do?"

This was what Roger had been waiting for. The man asking the question had been coached by Roger and knew exactly when to speak up. There would be several more times when he would interact with Roger before the evening was up.

Later, as the evening was winding down and so was Roger, it was deemed time to show the group the latest toys in their arsenal. At his suggestion, they followed him outside to his truck, a late model ford with a bed cover. Roger raised the bed cover and lowered the tail gate. Inside the truck bed were three military gray aluminum boxes that just fit across the width of the truck.

"Boys," Roger boasted. "You're gonna love this," as he opened up the first box.

At first, some of the men were not sure what they were looking at. Then after a few seconds of closer examination they realized they were looking at a shoulder fired missile launcher.

"Where the hell did you get those?" one of the men asked.

"I've got connections," Roger boasted. "People who support what we stand for and aren't afraid to stick their necks out to prove it."

"So what you got in mind?" another man asked.

"Boys," he said. "We are gonna shoot down an eagle and a couple of war birds as well."

"An eagle," another man stated. "Why the hell we gonna use that to shoot down an eagle? I can do that with my rifle."

"Not the bird, my friend," Roger stated bluntly.

"I'm referring to Eagle One, the man."

"Shit, Roger, your referring to the president."

"He ain't our president. Not any longer. He's one of them now and we have to put an end to him and all his military cronies."

"What you got in mind?"

"A young friend of ours is a congressional intern. He has the inside skinny on the presidents' movements and will let us know his travel plans and we can make our plans accordingly. Any one of these little babies can take his plane or helicopter down."

"It sounds simple enough if we can get away with it," one of the men remarked, "in fact, too simple, so why hasn't somebody tried it before now?"

"Their either scared or stupid," Roger replied, adding, "I'm not either."

The men spent another hour or so going over the pros and cons of Rogers plan and where the best place to try and pull it off would be. The group now in the killing mood, discussed alternate plans they felt would work if the opportunity presented itself. They all agreed that the most rural setting was to their advantage. Now it was just a matter of waiting for the optimum time and place.

Chapter 3 – The Sacrifices

Mathew and Logan spent hours going over their plans for recovering one or more of the birds. After much discussion, it was agreed that Logan would go for the birds in the mountains and Mathew would work on the island. Logan's initial attempt would be to approach the mountain nest in a cloaked hawk. He would attempt to snare one of the birds and if nothing else, get a good look at the terrain in that area.

Mathew, on the other hand, was going to launch off a hawk just before daylight. Taking a skimmer down to the edge of the volcanic island and conceal it near the shore where he could summon it if needed. He would then make his way inland wearing his armor and cape. He would arm himself with a sword and his throwing knives and stars. He wanted to avoid using his personal weapons unless forced to but that was dependent on what he encountered. He would try to bring down one or more of the birds by wounding them, which might require him to use the splinters. Afterwards, he would bag them and send them up for the Hawk to collect and return to the Phoenix.

It was early morning the next day when they put their plans in action. Logan wanted to be ready at first light hoping the birds would still be in the roosting mode, giving him a better chance to catch one or more. Marine pilot Brady was to position the hawk near to the nest they spotted earlier. Logan brought a pole that extended out and had a snare on the end of it. He planned to lower the ramp and snag the first bird he saw. There would be a short space of time when the ramp was lowered that they would be visible but they had to risk it.

As they approached the nest, Logan and Brady could see there were several large birds in the giant nests. Among them were the hatchlings. It was early and none were awake yet but they would be stirring soon once the sun came up. Those hatchlings would be clamoring for food and the parents would begin searching for it. Just as they hoped, there were several nests near the giant bird. Nests with the black birds they were looking for. Brady moved the Hawk into position while Logan prepared to lower the ramp. He attached a safety line in case something startled one of the large birds and they had to quickly move out of the way.

Once Logan was in position he lowered the ramp. He was ready and extended the pole outwards snagging the first bird he saw. He quickly retracted the pole into the hawk and took the bird out of the snare. About the time he got it into a bag, it started squawking. Logan made an effort to snag another but before he could get the pole out, the nearest birds were in flight.

"Raise the ramp," Logan ordered as he moved back from the opening. "Take us around to see if we can spot any others."

By now, the clamor of the departing birds disturbed several of the giant birds and they too were making noise as they hoped around their nest areas. Brady took them around the large out cropping near to them and not seeing any more nests moved further down what appeared to be a valley. They remained in the cloaked mode. As Brady was swinging the Hawk around to go back into the nesting areas, he caught sight of something that made him pause.

"Lord Logan," he said.

Logan was still occupied with securing the bird in the bag and hadn't yet returned to his seat in the front."

"Yes, Brady," he replied.

"You need to see this, Sir."

"Coming," Logan said as he made his way to the co-pilots seat. "See what," he began to say, and stopped.

There in the valley was a statue. It was a statue of a man and a Houn. The man stood beside the Houn with his left hand resting on the Houns shoulder. It was almost an exact likeness of Prince Mathew and Shadow. From where they were positioned, they could see what appeared to be people in front of the statue. They were laying something before it. There were others there who had spears and appeared to be guarding those before the statue. Then off in the brush, Logan could make out what looked like humanoids but were more apelike. They stayed in the brush but it was obvious to Logan they were a threat to those around the statue.

As they looked on, one of the ape like creatures flung a large club in the direction of those near the statue. It narrowly missed several of the men with spears who appeared to be shouting at the others to come away. They quickly began a fast march back toward the cliff face some distance away. This appeared to enrage the apes who began screaming and gesturing at the humans.

Logan instructed the pilot to take a position so they could see where the humans went. It took them less than a half hour to make it

back to the cliff face. They followed a well worn trail and from a distance, Logan could make out what appeared to be some kind of settlement in front of the
cliffs.

There was a stockade and what appeared to be guard houses mounted on it. He could see that the gates were opened to allow the humans in. As they looked on, he observed a large group of the apes were approaching the stockade behind the humans. They held back but it was obvious they were a threat and had they chosen could have probably taken those in front by their force of numbers.

They moved closer to the encampment getting near enough to see inside. It was not very large but within it was a large garden and a few animals that might be for slaughter. There was not a lot of people inside or at least not that many appeared to be about this early in the morning.

"Let us go," Logan stated. "We will discuss this with Prince Mathew and Commander Borne."

They departed passing back over the statue and headed directly back to the Phoenix.

#

Mathew exited his hawk just before light. He left marine pilot Glen at the controls. Another marine was onboard to help retrieve any birds he sent up. He took the skimmer down near the water's surface then moved toward the island. The water was nearly as smooth as glass as he glided over its surface.

Approaching a small beach area, somewhat hard to make out in the dark, he noticed the beach appeared to end in an outcropping of stone on one end. Near that outcropping was some type of tree that hung over the water's edge. As he reached the edge of the beach, he slowed down and angled near to the tree. While the waves were washing over the rocks to his left, the water was relatively calm beneath the tree. He allowed the skimmer to submerge and after about three feet, it was firmly on the bottom. Mathew signaled it to remain there.

As he walked onto the beach, he used his heat vision to scan ahead just in case there was anything lying in wait. He didn't detect anything that appeared to be a threat. He continued on into the forest, its growth mostly palms and ferns with lots of vines.

There were a few larger trees and even larger vines but none were familiar to him. It was becoming lighter as the sun continued to rise. The Hawk hovered nearby in cloaked mode ready to provide direction or assistance as needed.

"Give me a heading in the general direction of the stone altar," he instructed Glen.

"It's directly north of you." Glen replied.

"According to our sensors, there is movement about a hundred yards ahead of you in the same area. It appears to be a fairly large crowd."

Mathew continued to work his way forward. Soon, he found a well-used trail. He continued to scan the area ahead of him with his own heat sensor vision. Off to his right, he detected several small animals and what appeared to be a snake or serpent of some type on a limb above the small animals.

As he focused on the area, the snake appeared to drop off the limb onto the animals below. He heard a squeal and then several of the animals fled. All but one which was obviously now taken by the snake.

Mathew continued to move forward. He alternated his vision when there was a gap in the trees to long range then back to heat sensory.

Glen spoke. "According to our sensors, there appears to be a commotion within the crowd and some people are being forced along by others."

"Thanks," Mathew acknowledged.

He wondered what he was fixing to get into and he was sure that whatever was going on up ahead had something to do with the reason no one was out and about. As he moved forward, he could make out human chatter. It sounded like shouting combined with screaming and even crying. He sought to locate a position where he could see without being seen.

There was an outcropping of rocks to his left. He made to skirt it hoping it would provide some cover as he moved forward. He could hear pretty well now and most of what he was hearing was understandable which was helpful at the least.

The unmistakable smell of Sulphur or lava was in the air. As he made his way around the base of the rock outcropping, he began to see gaps in the foliage. In a few seconds, he reached a spot where he could look down on the crowd not far below and before him. He could plainly see people moving around the stone altar. They wore elaborate headdresses of feathers and there appeared to be some kind of bindings but what they were made of was not clear to him just yet.

Everyone's attention was on the larger man in the middle. Mathew labeled him as a priest. He appeared to be performing some form of ritual. He reached into a basket and pulled out some type of snake. He held it just behind its head and as it writhed in his hands he squeezed the head causing what appeared to be venom to squirt from the snake's mouth. He did this several times. Mathew noticed the venom was directed onto the altar.

Moments later he whipped out a knife from his side and shifting his hand, hacked off the snake's head. He tossed the snakes body towards the middle of the altar and Mathew realized it was open in the middle as the snake disappeared from sight. There was a short puff of smoke from the opening as if the snake had suddenly burst into flames and that was an indication there might be a lava pool directly below the altar.

Mathew realized there was a subtle drum beat in the background. From where it came, he could not yet determine. He noticed that the tempo was increasing. Then two men, obviously assistants to the priest, moved into the crowd. As Mathew watched, they seized a young woman and began to drag her towards the altar.

The crowd parted as if there was nothing else they could do. Mathew observed a young man off to the side but he was being held back by two men wearing the headdresses. The young woman screamed and fought but it did her no good as the two men held her firmly and forced her towards the altar.

Mathew had seen enough. It was now obvious to him that this woman was going to be the sacrifice. He knew it would take him perhaps too long to get down there to save her but the distance was not too far for him to intervene. As he looked on, the larger man climbed up onto the altar where he could receive the young woman and force her into the hole in the top of the altar where she would no doubt plunge to her death.

He knew his interfering was going to cause him trouble but that had not stopped him before nor would it stop him now. He needed something of a diversion to keep attention away from himself and he decided that the guards attending the young man who struggled to help the woman might be just what he needed.

He positioned himself and selecting one of his stars, reared back and flung it as hard as he could towards the guard on the young man's right. The star tore through the guards' throat. The young man felt the guard release his hold and began grappling with the other guard. In a moment with surprise being on his side, he thrust a knife into the other guard, then began pushing through the crowd in an effort to get to his woman.

The two assistants managed to force the girl onto the altar, one on each side of her as the Priest reached his arm around her chest. In his hand he held a large knife. He gestured to the sky with it.

It was at that moment the young man reached the base of the altar. His being there was now causing a distraction for the crowd and one of the two men holding the girl was forced to release her to tend to the young man.

Mathew chose this moment to pick his next target. He chose the other man holding the girl for the priest. His throw sent the star through the man's throat and as he was standing sideways, the star carried on and struck one of the posts behind the altar lodging deep into it.

Mathew had not noticed the bird sitting on it until the striking of the post dislodged the bird causing it to suddenly fly up. The man collapsed alongside the altar. He didn't get a chance to scream. He had nothing to scream with. The young man and the other were struggling. Mathew was trying to get closer as all eyes were on the struggle both on and beside the altar.

The girl slid down in front of the priest forcing him to release his hold on the knife as he struggled to get control of her. It was necessary for it to appear that he had control of her or his ceremony would be for nothing. Being larger, he quickly got a grip on her throat and managed to get his knife back. He was shouting to the sky or the gods, neither of which seemed interested, in Mathew's opinion.

The priests' assistant managed to club the young man down and was back onto the altar. He didn't know what happened to the other man only that he must help the priest finish the ceremony. He grabbed the woman's legs and jerked them out from under her, forcing her onto her back. Then he positioned himself on her legs and reaching forward took hold of her arms to pin them down.

The priest continued to wave his knife and scream to the skies as he moved to the side and in a position to stab the girl. Most likely in the heart, Mathew thought or even to remove it before he dumped the girl.

Mathew was now nearly to the back of the crowd. He still had a height advantage but once he got off the rocks would be at the same level as the crowd and would not have a direct line of sight on those on the altar. He chose this moment to let fly with the next star.

It took the other assistant in the back of the head. He fell forward and the girl shoved him off as she struggled to get off the Altar. The assistant slide past her into the hole and a flash of smoke was seen to issue from within the altar. The priest unsure what had happened with his assistant, took this moment to grasp the girl by the hair as he raised the knife over his head to strike.

Mathew didn't have time to use another weapon and chose to send a fire ball at the priest. It struck him high in the chest and he literally evaporated in an explosion of fire as his headdress burst into flames and he ceased to be. Mathew took a moment to remove his head gear allowing the cape to cover his head. He entered the crowd and pushed through them towards the front.

Mathew estimated there were about forty people in the crowd as he worked his way through. The crowd itself had now grown quiet following the priest bursting into flame and hadn't yet realized another force was at work among them. For the moment, that was working to Mathew's advantage.

The young man recovered and began helping the woman off the stone ledge before the altar. She was in shock and crying as he tried to comfort her. Another group of the priests' assistants suddenly appeared, unsure what to do and sought to hold the man and woman back until a decision could be made.

"They must have been responsible for the drums," Mathew thought, as they forced the couple back with their spears at the ready, Mathew entered the area using his sword to slice through the spears and force the men back.

The crowd now realized that something was up and someone new had arrived who had struck down the priest and his assistants. The gods had somehow intervened or at least that was what they were saying.

Mathew stood between the couple and the priests' assistants, as they rallied to charge him. "You had your chance," Mathew thought as he pointed at the men.

He splintered them all. No one but he knew what he had done and as the men fell dead, the crowd, which moments before was again full of chatter, now became deathly silent.

Mathew jumped up onto the altar and turned to face the crowd. No one dared to speak as he surveyed those that stood before him.

Many of them began to back away. Then he looked down on the two below him. The young man and woman stared up at him, neither able to speak at the moment.

Mathew spoke to the man. "The woman, she is yours?"

The man seemed unsure what to say. His mind telling him this god had spoken to him.

"Speak man," Mathew spoke louder. "Is the woman your chosen?"

"Yes, yes," he replied in a shaky voice. "She is my chosen."

"Then take her home and tend to her needs. Treat her well."

"Yes, yes I will," he replied and as fast as he could, he began to move her through the crowd and the way out.

There were many at the front of the crowd and as Mathew studied them, he chose the one he felt was the best to speak to, pointing at an old woman who appeared to be wise beyond her years judging by her gray hairs.

"You," he said, pointing and gesturing for her to come forward. "What do they call you?"

"The call me Old Mother," she boldly said as she limped forward.

"What do you do for these people?"

"I am their medicine woman."

"Who is their leader?" Mathew demanded.

"Our leader is dead," she replied. "She died of the sickness a few days ago."

"What sickness?" Mathew inquired. "Where did she get the sickness?"

"The high priest sent one of his birds to her. She was poisoned and died."

"What did you do with her?"

"We did nothing. The high priest said to touch her was to die. He sacrificed her body to the gods."

Pointing up to the birds on the stakes, he asked. "Are those the birds?"

"That is what is left of them, yes." Old Mother replied.

"What happened to the others?" He asked.

"There was a storm and many disappeared. Those are what are left."

Mathew could see four birds remaining on the posts.

"They must take orders from the priest," he thought. Then turning back to the villagers he spoke again.

"Where is your village?"

"Through that opening in the rock face over there." She pointed at the place across from where Mathew had entered from the sea.

"Send your people back to their village," Mathew told her. "Have them prepare a meal for everyone including me. When I am through here, I will come to your village and we will talk."

"It will be as you command," she stated.

She signaled to the crowd and a young woman came to her side. Mathew remembered that she was or appeared to be crippled.

"Wait!" he shouted. He pointed at the one called Old Mother. "Help her back to the village."

From where it came, he didn't know but suddenly a chair on rails was produced. Men gathered around and helped her in it and then proceeded to take her away."

Chapter 4 – Island Brutes

As the last of them went through the cliff face, Mathew turned towards the birds. He quickly splintered each one in its shoulder wing, watching as they fell to the ground. Then moving over to where they lay, he took from his pouch the bag and proceeded to stuff the four wounded squawking birds into it. Activating the gas cylinder, he watched as the bag rose up into the air.

"Birds on the way up," Mathew informed Glen who was holding his position not far away.

"We see them," Glen replied. "What about you, sir?"

"Take the birds back with you. Come back for me tomorrow. I need to tend to business here first."

"As you wish, sir," then moments later, "we have the birds."

"Good. Call me when you get back tomorrow."

Being busy, Mathew didn't see the young woman who came forward to tend to the woman they called Old Mother. She crept back through the cliff face and was watching from a distance. She was not able to hear what he was saying but she had observed him taking the birds then sending them into the sky. She thought he must be talking to the gods as there was no one with him.

She was scared but in awe of him. She was training to be the next medicine woman and was open minded to just about anything but this was certainly something she hadn't expected to encounter.

She watched as he walked around the altar.

"An evil place," she thought.

She didn't have much faith in the so called priest and his followers and she realized that today, because of this new man or god, or whatever he was, the priest and his followers were now dead and gone from their lives. Hopefully, things would get better around here. Then she remembered the others. Maybe he could do something about them too.

As she watched, he walked around the altar. Then with little effort, he severed the posts that held the skulls and were perches for the birds. Upending them, he shoved each of them into the hole in the altar. Afterwards, he walked again around the altar. He appeared to finger the altar. He wiped his hand on it and then studied what he found.

"Most likely blood," she thought. Then as she looked on, he began to push on one side at the top.

Sure enough, the stones began to slip towards the middle and the hole there. Soon, they were falling through the hole as he moved to each side and pushed.

"He must have tremendous strength," she thought, to be able to do that.

Moments later, there was nothing left that resembled the altar, only a pile of stones.

When he turned to leave, he spotted the girl. She went to run but he pointed at her and told her to wait. She stood, afraid and trembling as he approached her.

"What's your name, girl?" Mathew asked.

"Lindell," she replied.

"Are you a medicine woman, too?" He asked.

"I'm in training," she replied.

"Would you like to learn more?"

"Yes, please," she replied.

"Very good," Mathew said. "I will see to it."

He wasn't sure how he was going to work it out but he would figure out something.

"Let us go to the village," he said to Lindell.

"What about the temple grounds?" She asked. "What should I tell the others?"

"Nothing about the birds," Mathew said. "You may say the temple is no more and there will be no more sacrifices."

"That is good," Lindell replied. "Thank you."

They walked for ten minutes on a well-traveled path. As they approached the village, the path took them near to the sea and sure enough there were boats and some houses on stilts, just as seen in the scans.

He noted that some of the houses had decks near to the water and places to sit and he realized they were toilets and bath houses. At least they had some rudimentary facilities. He could see that several of the boats were smashed up onto the bank.

"Lindell, what happened to the boats?" He asked.

"The sea beasts smashed them," she replied. "They come every night in search of food. It is difficult to fish with them around. We have lost so many people to them."

"Can you see them in the daylight?" Mathew asked.

"On the other side of the island is a lagoon. They rest there during the day before they hunt."

"Okay," Mathew replied. "Perhaps, we can arrange for them to never leave the lagoon."

"It would be most wonderful, if you could arrange that," Lindell said with a giggle. "I think you can arrange a lot of things."

"We will see," Mathew said, all the time telling himself not to get in too deep.

Soon, they entered the edge of the village. Most of the village houses or huts, if you could call them that, were made from trees, mud and thatch. Located in the middle was a long house. The building materials were the same but it appeared to be sturdier.

It also appeared to be the location they were headed as villagers were going in and out with trays and bowls. Most were made of wood and some seemed to be made of leaves or fronds from the large palm trees or whatever they were. He hadn't seen anything that resembled a coconut so they were maybe of another species. Whatever was going on in there, he hoped it was something to eat.

There was a sign or plaque in the center of the yard before the long house. Mathew stopped to study it. On it was inscribed the words.

'Someday, our savior will come. On that day, we will be blessed with the presence of our Prince. God grant that each of us live to see that day.'

"Okay," thought Mathew. "So what do I tell them, when they ask my name? Is this the beginning or even better yet, the end of another prophecy or is it even about me?"

"The sign has been there for many years," Lindell said. "Many have suggested we tear it down but others have said no. The Prince will come."

"And what do you think, Lindell?"

She looked up at him and spoke. "I think he has come."

"Mathew didn't reply right away. He didn't want to be a god to these people or their savior but perhaps their Prince. At least till something better could be worked out. They did need some guidance and someone in his place to look after these people and guide them into the future.

As they approached the steps into the long house, he paused. Four women were entering the house. He was curious. The only activity he had observed thus far was those going into the long house.

"Surely," he thought, "there were others here too and where were the children. There were always children running about."

He hadn't noticed any animals aside from those in the forest. Then something else dawned on him. The women going in the long house were the same. They had obviously gone out the back and circled around to enter again.

He paused then backed away from the front of the long house. Wanting some room between whoever or whatever was in the building. He suddenly felt uncomfortable as if he was being stalked. Using his heat vision, he stared at the building. He could make out large outlines along the walls on both sides. Whatever was in there was larger than the villagers.

"Something wasn't right," he thought.

The woman, Lindell spoke.

"What's the matter? You can go in. They are waiting on you."

"Who are they?" Mathew spoke.

He drew his sword as he moved further back from the building. Whatever was in the long house was not the same villagers seen earlier. So where were the villagers?

Lindell began to cry as she spoke. "If you don't go in, they will kill all the others."

"Who are they?" Mathew demanded.

"They are the beasts who rule the island," she said. "They force us to feed them and when it is not enough, they eat us instead."

"I suppose they are planning on eating me too!" Mathew snarled. He was getting angry for allowing himself to be fooled.

"I'm sorry," Lindell stated, her voice breaking. "I did not realize until just now that they were here. They must have forced the people into the pen behind the village. If I had warned you, they would have attacked instantly and we would all die."

"You don't think they are warned now?"

"They are brutes. Not people. They are not that smart but soon they will figure it out."

"How long do you think we have before they figure I'm not coming in?" Mathew stated.

"Not long," Lindell replied. She appeared to be less frightened now.

"How many are there?" Mathew asked.

"All we have ever seen are eight," she said. "They came ashore one day and the killings started. Our best warriors tried to stop them but they were all killed. Then the beast indicated that they would let some of us live if we provided for them. They live in a cave on the other side of the island. We must deliver their food and if we don't, they come and take someone or something."

"And even with that, your priests were offering your people as sacrifices."

"They said it was punishment for our evil ways. No one here was evil except for the priests and those that served them but now they are all dead. You saw to that."

"Stay here," Mathew said, "or run away. It's your choice."

"What are you going to do?" She asked.

"Even up the odds," he replied as he walked along the side of the long house.

Staring at the wall of the house using his heat vision, he could make out the outlines of the eight beasts standing there with four against the wall nearest him. They appeared to be moving as if they were restless. He didn't see any metal which would have indicated weapons. Maybe they only used their hands or wooden clubs.

"Time to stir up this nest," he thought. He pulled several knives from his pouch. Taking a stance, he flung them as hard as he could towards the thatched walls of the house.

As he prepared to throw more knives, he observed two beasts falling forward away from the wall. It appeared the others were not sure what was happening as it was dark in the house. He wasted no time in flinging two more knives. There was a loud shriek then a snarl and instantly the house shook as the beasts made for the front door. Mathew only had time to note that another one had fallen and the other appeared to be wounded. He moved away from the house. He didn't see the woman. Perhaps she had run away as he suggested.

The remaining beasts exited the house and trotted into the yard. Mathew was hardly prepared for what he saw. They were humanoid in shape but not in size. Much similar to what he would call a Neanderthal man but more apelike. The injured one had blood running down its side where the knife had entered its back.

"Perhaps not a killing blow," Mathew thought.

The beasts now had him in their sights and began to approach him in a stalking march. They made grunting and smacking sounds as they approached and all of them had large canine teeth.

"Nothing intelligible about that," he thought.

He noted their extremely large brows and skulls might be a bit of a go for the splinters but he could try. He pointed at the one nearest to him, sending a shower of splinters towards its chest and head.

The beast reeled and roared but stopped its advance then slapped at its head.

"Damn," Mathew thought. "It's going to take a lot out of me to kill these things. At least there were only four left and one of those was wounded."

Moments later as he and the others looked on, the beast slumped over. Glancing at it as he prepared to meet the others, Mathew couldn't tell if it was a male or a female but he suspected that all of them were males.

He took a stance with his sword and positioned several stars for quick access for throwing. In the background, he heard noises as if from a crowd. Suddenly the villagers rounded the corner. The woman Lindell was at the front. She had a spear as did many of the villagers. It appeared they were ready to do battle.

"Was it with me or them?" Mathew wondered, but that was decided quickly as two of the beasts charged the crowd, scattering many before them but not before one of them had been wounded by the spears.

The villagers set upon it trying to finish it off while the others tried to hold the other beast at bay. As he watched from the corner of his eye, it snatched a spear from one of the men and using it like a club was able to knock several of the people down. The young woman ran at it to stab it but received a good blow that flung her across the yard.

Mathew engaged with one of the beasts. It tried to reach him to grapple with him but Mathew was having none of that. With his speed and agility, he quickly used the sword to his advantage making the beast pay for its efforts by inflicting serious wounds on its arms and legs and following that by stabbing it through the side.

The beast howled as it died on Mathew's sword. While he was engaged with that one, the wounded one made an effort to enter the fray but was too slow and Mathew was able to draw his sword free and spinning about impaled the beast through its eye socket.

Looking up, he saw the beast with the spear, since broken off was standing over the woman Lindell. The beast had been able to hold the others at bay with his strength. Now it reached down and took her by her arm. Mathew was not sure what he was going to do with her but he had seen enough to know it wasn't going to be good.

He directed a stream of splinters towards the beasts' rear and back. This got its attention as it dropped the woman to see what was attacking it from the rear. Mathew was now close enough to seize the moment and leaping up above the beast, he dropped down onto its shoulders leading with his sword alongside its neck and into the body below.

The beast made a blood curdling howl as it collapsed onto the ground. No fight left as it died from its wound. The villagers rushed in to stab the remaining life out of it with their spears. They finished off the other one and some were checking the ones Mathew killed, giving them more stabs just for good measure.

It took eight men to drag the three dead ones out of the long house. Women began carrying containers of water and bowls of sand inside to wash up the blood before it dried. Mathew watched as the old medicine woman tended to the young woman and was pleased to see others helping her to her feet. She was going to be okay. No one had spoken to him although many glanced his way as if to make sure he was still there.

He looked around. He was a little winded and thirsty. He was looking for some sign of fresh water. In the short distance behind the village he could see ridges and rock faces and what appeared to be a mist of water.

"Perhaps a stream or fall," he thought as he began to walk that way. No one got in his way as he continued through the village and soon exited on a path on the other side. He didn't get far before he came across a small rocky stream.

"How convenient," he thought as he moved over to a clear area where he could scoop up some water to drink.

He looked the stream over, not overly anxious for something to surprise him. Then checking his surroundings and the path behind him, he knelt and took water in his hand to drink. His other hand remained on his sword. Maybe he was being overly cautious but he knew, you had to be prepared at all times for the unexpected. Once his thirst was quenched, he felt much better though he was still hungry.

He heard someone or several someone's coming up the trail and stood to see who it might be. In a moment, the young woman, Lindell, appeared. She was limping, favoring her left leg.

"It didn't appear to be broken," Mathew thought, "most likely badly bruised."

"My Lord," she said. "The villagers are preparing a feast for you. They are sorry for what happened back there but so grateful for what you have done and your acts gave them the courage to act. Please come back with me and they will provide for you."

Mathew approached her. "Your leg," he said. "It is injured?"

"It will be okay after a while," she replied. "It only hurts a little where he struck me with the spear."

There was a large rock nearby. It had obviously been in use many years for its surface was smooth. It would work okay as a place to sit.

"Sit here," Mathew said, pointing at the rock. "Let me look at your leg."

"Oh no," she replied. "It is okay. The medicine woman has tended to it. I will be fine."

"Sit," Mathew said again. "I will fix it better."

The woman smiled and moved slowly over to the rock. Her leg was too sore for her to just push up onto the rock with it, so she was trying to use her hands.

"Oh," she said, startled as Mathew reached out and lifted her onto it. She looked down and said "thank you."

"I will touch your leg," Mathew said. "Tell me where it hurts."

That quickly became unnecessary as she winced when he touched her anywhere between her knee and thigh. Using his other hand to help conceal what he was doing, he injected her in several places between her upper thigh and knee. He didn't want to get too personal so he stopped and stepped back.

"You can get down. I think it should be better now."

She braced herself as she slid off the rock, expecting it to hurt as before. Her face quickly broke into a smile as she realized there was no more pain. The leg no longer hurt.

"What did you do?" She asked. "We don't have those kinds of skills."

"You will learn them one day," Mathew replied. "Now, if you have food, I am hungry."

Looking up at him, she said. "This way," and started down the trail."

The day was now evening and the sun would be down soon.

"Funny how time flies when one is having fun," Mathew thought.

He wanted a place to rest but he also wanted it to be safe. He hoped the birds he had sent up were what they needed for his Princess and her mother. Perhaps tomorrow would bring good news. He followed the woman towards the village. Now he could smell food. Whatever it was, he was looking forward to it.

Chapter 5 – Finding the Group

Trainer was monitoring internet traffic as he always did. Like the government agencies that did likewise, he looked for key words that signaled a conversation worth investigating. Recently, he picked up on emails that involved the key words Eagle One.

He was not sure but as it was the code name for the president, he didn't want to let it slid without some checking. He quickly determined the source was a young male working at the white house. A politician's intern whom he initially thought to disregard as just political chatter or boasting, until other remarks referring to 'The Group', which he knew was an anti-government movement.

There were requests for travel updates which got his full attention and he began checking out the sources of the emails as well as any phone or texts from those tied to it. It didn't take him long to figure out that there was a serious threat to the president and various other politicians and military figures.

By his estimation of time, something was going to happen somewhere in the very near future. He didn't waste any time informing those that needed to know about the threat. His first call was to the president. The two of them had a routine for weekly updates and so his call was not out of the ordinary except that today, it was a late evening call.

While a switchboard normally took the presidents calls so they could be screened, Trainer had no problem ringing directly into the president's bedroom. The president didn't normally take calls in there and so thought it kind of odd but he answered it anyway.

He always answered his calls by asking who was calling. He was surprised to hear Trainers voice. He knew it must be important for Trainer respected his privacy probably more than anyone else he knew.

"Mr. President. I'm very sorry to disturb you at this late hour but I have concerns which you need to be aware of."

"Yes, Trainer, go ahead. I'm all ears here."

Trainer went on to inform him that he had discovered a plot to kill him using weapons designed to take down airplanes or helicopters. It appeared that an intern within the capital was passing information on to a party of people who called themselves 'The Group.'

"Yes," the president replied. "I have heard of them. I believe there are two groups of them. One in Montana and one in Maine and you believe they pose a threat to me."

"Yes, Mr. President. I believe an imminent attempt on your life is going to be made in the next few days or weeks using a military weapon referred to as the stinger. I know you have a heavy travel itinerary over the next few weeks and if I am correct, somewhere along the way, someone is going to attempt to take your life and anyone near to you.

"Do you have any recommendations, Mr. Trainer?"

"Only one at the moment, Mr. President. Don't go out."

"You know I can't do that and I won't allow myself to be manipulated by these fringe groups. Spread the word among the various agencies that are supposed to be looking after me and we'll hope for the best, and Trainer."

"Yes, Mr. President."

"Thanks."

"Dealing with high profile people is hard work," Trainer thought.

Even as those thoughts were going through his computer brain, he was sending out what information he had to John Michael at the FBI office and various other agencies he thought should know including the secret service, who were responsible for providing security for the president.

Following that, he sent for his resident team at the base. In short order, they were mustered in the conference room. It was late night now but he sent a signal to Brad at Area 51 requesting he attend a video conference of high priority with any team members available at the moment.

At Area 51, Brad contacted Terry's team and they were soon arriving in the conference room. The new teams from Europe were still recovering from their surgeries and with them, all was going well. Shortly after Trainers message, both teams were in their respective conference rooms.

Trainer filled them in on the growing threat to their president as well as other politicians and military figures. The threat was coming from an anarchist group known as 'The Group'. At present there were two divisions of the same band of individuals. One was in Montana and the other was in Maine.

At this time, it appeared that one or more individuals from the Maine group were in close consultation with members of the Montana group regarding using military grade weapons to take out designated targets.

At least one of those targets, according to information received, was the President. The lesser targets consisted of other politicians and military figures.

"What type of weapons are we referring to?" Terry asked.

"I believe it to be the shoulder fired stinger missile. I don't know how many they have and at the moment, I don't know where exactly they plan on initiating their attacks."

"Do you have the locations of the headquarters for both groups?" Jade asked.

"Yes," Trainer replied. "I have the location for the Maine group and an unconfirmed location for the Montana group. The information will be provided for your use."

He continued.

"I picked up on this from the emails of a young male subject working as a political intern in the capital. He is sponsored by a congressman from Maine although I don't have any indication that the congressman himself has anything to do with this situation. I suspect the intern is an avid follower of the group and this is how he is supporting them."

"Is it possible we could arrange to get personal with this individual and perhaps learn something of great importance?" Terry asked.

"Very likely," Trainer replied. "He likes to hang out at a Hooters restaurant in D.C. and a few others like Fairfax, Virginia. He seems to think he's a ladies' man based on his email messages and chats with others online and likes to boast about how many Hooters girls he has been with although I don't think his so called conquests are limited to Hooters."

"Maybe we could get some information out of him by pretending to be one of the girls working at one of the restaurants," Lydia stated.

"I agree," Jade replied, "only let's not limit his target to one girl but give him multiple targets, just in case he has a friend with the same mindset as him."

"How far are you willing to go," Terry asked.

"Sorry, Terry," Jade replied, "but as far as it takes to get them talking. At the same time, we could perhaps provide some misdirection by letting him think we can provide something of value to them, like more weapons."

Trainer spoke up then.

"A good starter plan ladies and as for the men, I think a little reconnaissance on both ends of the country would be good as well."

"Your right," Terry admitted, "but who is going to back up the girls."

It was obvious to everyone on the conference that Terry wasn't too comfortable with Jade having a personal encounter with anyone other than himself.

Brad spoke up.

"I understand your concern, Terry and I have similar feelings but I think we are just going to have to let the girls handle that part of it and trust their best judgment. Francis can be their backup, making it a threesome if Trainer is okay with that and the rest of us can split up for the two Group bases of operation.

"Let's get the details sorted and get this operation going. We need to make sure nothing happens on our watch if we can prevent it," Trainer stated.

"Yes, Trainer," several of them replied at once.

Using the information on the board as to locations, it was decided that Cato, Van and Nick would attend the Maine Group and Terry, Martin and Aden would look in on the Montana Group.

It was a given that anyone not local was going to stick out like a sore thumb, so the decision was made that Van would stand off in a cloaked hawk, after letting Cato and Nick out near the Maine Groups bunker and Aden would do the same for Terry and Martin in Montana.

Just after midnight the following day, Aden dropped Terry and Martin off a few hundred yards from the location of the Montana Groups bunker. It was located about thirty two miles outside of Wolf Point, just off highway 2. Information showed it to be on an unlisted farm road that ended about a half mile off the highway with further vehicle travel via either four wheel drive or atv.

They located the bunker via the monitors on the hawk. There did not appear to be any human life signs in the area, so they chose a low spot on a nearby ridge with some brush for cover and a good line of sight. Before landing, they performed several side scans looking for sources of metal or any indication of sensors placed by the group.

They didn't find anything close but then this area had only a few trees and was fairly open. They sent Aden away to hover in a more remote area close enough for him to be able to return in seconds if and when they needed him.

The bunker area in Maine had been more difficult to locate. There had been a good hard effort to delete from any data base, the location of the Groups bunker in Maine, indicating they had a lot of support both on the ground and some ways away.

Needless to say, if the information once existed, Trainer was going to be able to find it and find it he did.

The bunker was not far from the Bethel, Maine airport. The adjacent side road that connected to an airport service road and further access to two connecting roads. The area looked like a mining area but showed little use. They had gps coordinates to help them locate the bunker which was in a clearing near a wooded area.

They did an extensive scan of the area looking for signs of traps or any indication of security devices. Using a power emitter scan they detected a power cable that ran alongside the road and appeared to be a source of electrical service for the bunker.

Someone obviously had money to be able to afford something that far reaching as well as underground. Metal scans indicated an adjacent underground structure that appeared to house a generator and there also appeared to be a ground controlled lift that opened up from the ground.

Possibly for a solar panel array as it had no real depth to it but cables ran from it to the bunker. A side scan showed them small metallic signals which they decided were either for remote cameras or a remote weapons system. They would check into that before they made themselves comfortable.

Van dropped them off in a small wooded clearing a short distance away. It would provide enough cover to prevent them from being detected by someone less skilled than they were. Then he lifted up and took a cloaked position a half mile away in the most rugged spot they could locate for the area. He was only seconds away if needed.

Trainer was monitoring all areas where he thought he might get a lead on the two groups but in the last few hours there had been no activity. Not online nor via telephone. He was also concerned that they might show up where he had no assets.

Without more information, they were vulnerable. He continued waiting and also expanding his search criteria in case they had dumped their previous phones and were using pay as you go or what some called burner phones.

Chapter 6 – Good Medicine

Logan was waiting in the Phoenix control room for the test results from the bird he captured. He had been there most of the day as his foray on the other continent had gone well and now he only had to wait. Only an hour earlier, the pilot from Prince Mathews hawk arrived with four birds in a bag. They were immediately taken to the vessels laboratory for testing.

When he questioned the pilot as to where Prince Mathew was, the pilot stated the Prince had encountered several situations on the island and instructed the pilot to come back the following day. The pilot did know there had been some type of altercation or fight at a location that looked much like a sacrificial site. That was the location where human skulls were mounted on poles. That was all the information he had.

Logan thought long and hard about going back with the pilot, then decided that Prince Mathew was more than capable of taking care of himself and he wanted to be near his queen if a serum was forthcoming.

As he stood looking out the Phoenix's blast windows he realized a med tech had entered the room. He looked at the Commander who stood across from him, then at the med tech.

The med tech did not hesitate but spoke straightforward.

"I'm sorry, my Lord," he said, "but your bird has no traces of the virus. We are examining the birds sent by the prince and should know the results in a few hours."

He then turned and left the bridge.

"If the other birds are infected, they will find it," Commander Borne stated.

"If they are not, then I think we will have to get more aggressive in our search and damn the consequences."

"Yes," Logan replied. "And that is exactly what we will do but for now, we will give it a little longer."

#

Mathew arrived near the village center with the young woman, Lindell. The smell of food was strong near to the long house and there were lots of people milling about. It appeared that some wanted to approach him but were either scared or did not know what to say.

That was soon sorted out when four men came out the long house with the old woman. They still carried her on the chair on rails. Others followed her out until there was a large crowd gathered before and around him but they still did not crowd him.

Mathew was expecting the woman to speak. He noticed drag marks in the sand around the area indicating that the villagers had finally managed to drag all the dead beasts away. He wondered what they had done with them but owing to the direction the marks made, he figured they had ended up in the sea.

The woman stood. Positioning herself so as to stand as straight as she could, she spoke to Mathew.

"The people have asked me to speak on their behalf. They wish to know to whom they owe their salvation, for you have certainly given them back their village and their lives."

Mathew thought for a moment, then decided that the truth was the best way forward.

"I am Prince Mathew," he said.

Immediately there was a hush where before there was a murmur. The old woman made as to get down on her knees. The crowd had already done so as had the young woman beside him.

"Stop," Mathew demanded, pointing at the old woman. "Do not bow to me."

She was so startled, she almost lost her balance.

"Please have everyone to stand up," he said in a loud voice."

Almost as one, they began to rise.

"You do not bow to me. You do not bow to anyone. Show your respect if you wish by nodding your head when you meet me but know this. I am no better than you, just another man."

He then continued.

"What I did today, had you been able, you would have done yourself. I hope that in the future you will be more diligent and not allow yourselves to be enslaved to another. Now, would someone tell me when we are going to eat? All this work has made me hungry."

The crowd as one, broke out into laughter. One man approached him, reaching out his hand towards Mathews shoulder. Mathew allowed him to rest it there then placed his hand on that man's shoulder. The man turned away with a big smile on his face, shouting to several others to help him get the food.

As the man walked away, it suddenly dawned on Mathew that the only young man he had seen so far was the one that had fought for the girl the Priest had attempted to sacrifice.

"Had all the young men been killed," he wondered.

The men he was seeing here were well up in their years. Still able in some ways but maybe not so much in others.

Mathew walked over to the one called Old Mother. She had managed to sit back in the chair and the men stood ready to do her bidding. She looked up at Mathew and spoke.

"For too long we have waited for you to come. I wish that I might have been younger that I could thank you properly. No, matter, now you are here and everything will be much better. I am sure you will see to that."

Mathew chose his words carefully for he did not want to upset the old woman or the villagers.

"Old Mother, I have been a long time getting here and for that I am sorry. Now, I must tell you that I cannot stay, but." he held his hand up as if to silence her for her face instantly fell in concern and worry.

"I will not desert you. I will send someone in my place who is kind and good and will see to it that you will move forward in many more ways than you can imagine and I will return to make sure you are making the progress I will be expecting."

"You promise," Old Mother asked.

"I promise," Mathew replied, "now how about something to eat."

The woman laughed and said to another, "A typical male, always thinking of their stomach."

She instructed the men to take her inside. Mathew followed. Inside were lights in bowls. Oil lights, he observed, probably from some of the trees or even possibly from fish. He would ask later.

The woman indicated he should sit near to her. Mathew directed the young woman to sit beside him as well. There were bowls of food on the table.

Much of it appeared to be vegetables of some kind and a lot of pounded foods which likely came from something like a tuber. There was fish aplenty but he did not see any kind of red meat or pork.

Everyone was served but no one took a bite. The young woman spoke to him.

"They are waiting on you my lord."

Mathew stood and spoke. "Before we eat, I will thank our god for the food."

He bowed his head and offered a short prayer. When he looked up, many also had their heads bowed and those looking on had tears running down their faces."

The young woman spoke again.

"The priests said our god had left us and we were not to pray to him anymore. You have brought our god back to us."

"Let us eat," Mathew said.

The room erupted in laughter as did the conversation and finally Mathew was able to eat. Later, Mathew looked at the young woman then posed a question.

"Where are the children and the animals?"

"The few children left, if they have survived, are on the island to our north. We tried to send them there with a few adults when the beasts arrived for we knew they would eat them as they have done with so many of us. We sent the remaining dogs with them as well. We don't know how many made it because of the giant sea beasts."

"Tomorrow, we will see about this," Mathew said.

"But what of the sea beasts and how will you get there?" She asked.

"You have your boats and I have mine," Mathew replied. "Tomorrow, we will see."

As he was finishing up his second helping of fish and some vegetables, he noticed that the old woman was favoring her hands. He could see that they appeared very arthritic and were obviously causing her some pain. He reached across and placed his right hand on her left hand. She glanced at him as he spoke.

"Let me see your hand."

He gently ran his fingers over the joints of her hands. He could feel her tremble as he carefully gave her the little injections. So quickly that she could not see or feel anything.

"Now the other one," he said.

She reached across her body with the other hand so he could reach it. He did the same with that one then remembering that she had bad knees too, he instructed her to have the men move her away from the table so he could see her knees.

The men were quickly there and in a few minutes, he had touched them as well. As they went to move her back to the table, he told them to wait a few moments.

He sat there for less than a minute then looking at the old woman, instructed her to stand up. She looked at him a bit oddly as if to say why do you want me to suffer but then she placed her hands on the chair arms to help lift herself up.

She quickly noticed that she could grip the chair arms and it didn't hurt. She raised her hands up. Clenching and unclenching them. She moved her legs a bit then placing her feet firmly beneath her, she stood up.

"Move the chair," she told the men.

Two rushed forward and pulled it back. The woman then stepped away from the table and whirled around. Everyone was astounded including her.

"Oh my lord, thank you, thank you," she said. "You have given me a second life. How can I ever repay you?"

"You will require more treatments in the future as it only lasts so long but you don't need to thank me. It is only good medicine."

"This is medicine. Oh how grand it is. Please, can you teach me how to do this for my people?"

"No, I cannot," Mathew replied. "Not this particular medicine but the man or woman I send in my place will be able to treat you just as I have and I have promised this young woman," and he indicated Lindell, "that she too will be able to learn good medicine."

Soon after, when all the questions had stopped for a while, Mathew questioned the young woman as to where all the young men were.

"They are all dead but one, sir. The only ones remaining that were not killed by the beasts were in league with the evil priest. They took whomever they wanted when they wanted but for some reason, very few children have been borne.

Most of the women here are too old and there are only a few young women, myself included. There are some young girls on the island or at least we are hoping there are."

Mathew thought about it. This village was doomed to die if those young girls were not alive on the island but they would need mates soon as well. It was a problem he would have to work on.

"I would like to rest now," Mathew told the young woman. "Do you have a place I can lie down for a while?"

"Yes," she replied. "The villagers have cleaned out the former hut of the evil priest. There is nothing left there to remind us of him or his followers. The only things there now are the oil lamps and clean mats for sleeping."

"Please show me the way," Mathew replied, "but first I must tend to my toilet needs. I believe that is down by the sea, yes?"

"You are right and very observant," she said with a laugh. "Come, I will show you."

She led the way down to the sea. The little stands on stilts were not houses but stalls for the people to tend to their toilet needs. He had noticed earlier that there were sea sponges by the stream and he guessed that is where they washed themselves and their meager clothing. What he had seen so far was pretty ragged.

When they were finished, she led the way back to the village and up to a hut a bit away from the others. It appeared the former priest required some privacy from the villagers.

"This is it, my Lord," she said. "It is not much but it is the best we can do."

"It will be fine, thank you," Mathew said as he entered.

For the moment he was on his guard but he found nothing inside that appeared to be a threat and began to relax.

"Do you require anything else?" She asked.

"No, I'm fine," he replied. "Thank you for asking."

She stepped back and let the cover fall across the doorway, then left him there.

Mathew removed his cape and sat on the mat for a moment then got up and moved it. He wanted to be able to see if anyone entered the doorway. Before he sat back down, he walked around the hutch checking the thatch walls to see if there were any places a person or animal could enter. Surprisingly, he found none.

He placed his weapons where he wanted them, then removed his armor down to his shorts and rolled it up for a pillow. He extinguished the two lamps then using his cape for cover, he lay back down.

He lay there for a while, his mind wandering and also hoping that the birds he sent up this morning would provide his Princess and the Queen with the anti-viral serum they needed. For some reason, he was confident they were the right birds based on what the islanders had told him earlier. Now, it was just a waiting game.

As he was about to drift off to sleep, he detected movement at the doorway. He was not surprised as he had halfway expected it. Sure enough, it was Lindell. She cleared her throat as if to let him know she was inside.

"Good girl," he thought as he spoke. "I see you, Lindell. It is late. Shouldn't you be in bed?"

"Yes, but old mother said I was to sleep in your bed. That it was time and I must not waste it. She also said I must rub you with the soothing oil as you must be stressed from the battle you waged on our behalf earlier."

Without another word, she moved over to where he was lying. Kneeling down, she asked him to turn over, which he did.

Then she began applying small amounts of the oil onto his back and shoulders. She began to massage the oil into his skin. She was very thorough and it was all Mathew could do to stay awake. Soon, she was down to his waist and encountered his shorts.

"What is this," she asked. "Please remove it."

Mathew did as instructed and she continued to massage his lower back and hips. Soon she had worked all the way down to his feet. Mathew wasn't sleepy now.

"Turn over," she requested. He did.

She began rubbing his chest and shoulders. She moved across his body and sat on his stomach as she leaned forward to massage his chest. Then she slowly slid down his waist as she progressed lower.

Very soon, Mathew knew, she was going to reach his nether region and there wouldn't be any turning back and then it was so. She slid lower and feeling his manhood beneath her, lifted herself up and let him slide right in.

What followed next was neither new to Mathew or beyond the young woman's understanding. After a few minutes, both were resting side by side. Mathew wasn't tired but he felt himself drifting off to sleep. It was reassuring to hear her heavy breathing as well.

A few hours later, Mathew woke, realizing that the young woman was touching him as if to see if she could make him ready again. It didn't take long but this time, he guided her over onto her back and took the top position. Soon after, she was past the point of no return as he was and they lay together again.

"This time, I hope she stays asleep," he thought as he drifted off to sleep.

He awoke at about the time the sun was rising up out of the sea or so it seemed. Lindell was still sleeping as he moved away and began to dress. With the cape around his shoulders, he stepped outside to the fresh morning sea air.

Then he made his way down to the sea and tended to his toilet needs. He felt refreshed after sleeping and wondered how long it would be before the Hawk was back. That thought was barely out of his mind when his communicator spoke.

"Prince Mathew. Are you there, sir?"

"Yes," Mathew replied. "I have a mission for you before we go."

He went on to explain about the pool on the other side of the island and the giant fish that might be in it. They were to be destroyed, if they were there. Then he was to overfly the island to the north and look for signs of life. There were supposed to be villagers on the island consisting of mostly kids and some animals."

"On my way," Glen replied as he swung the Hawk around and departed.

Mathew walked over to that part of the beach he had arrived on earlier. He signaled the skimmer and it began to surface. Mathew let it settle back down and he turned and went back towards the village. He checked in on Lindell and found she was no longer in the hut.

He continued over to the long house but didn't find anyone there. Hearing noises, he saw several people coming from the direction of the stream. Their hair was wet and they wore something like a towel around their waists.

"Must be taking a bath," he thought. "Not a bad idea."

He headed off that way knowing it would be nice to get some sand and dirt off his body.

Chapter 7 – Island Survivors

Most of the villagers were in the stream washing off. It did not seem to matter whether they were male or female. They were unclothed and washing off with numerous people helping each other. Even the old woman was there, laughing and splashing with the others.

They stopped for a moment when they observed Mathew approaching but resumed their chatter and laughter when they saw him removing his cape and clothing.

"Nothing beats a good bath in the morning," the old woman said, then added, "well some things do, but that's for the young ones."

"Woman," Lindell muttered. "Behave."

"Ha," the old woman said. "Who are you to talk, our pregnant one."

"How do you know," Lindell said. "Besides, it is too soon."

"How many times did you do it," the woman asked.

"Twice, old Mother, only twice."

"Then hopefully it was enough and you are pregnant." With that she waded out of the pool and headed back to the village. Most of the others had already departed.

Mathew stayed out of the conversation. He was nearly finished with his bath and everyone had departed except for him and Lindell. She came over and reached out to touch him.

"Would you take me one more time?" she asked.

"It is important for me and I want to be sure I'm carrying your seed."

Mathew didn't say anything. He led her to the sand at the water's edge and laying down with her they took up where they had left off earlier. Soon after they were both spent and he rose to wash the sand off. She followed him and helped him rinse off and he helped her. Then they left the water and he began dressing as she found a piece like a towel to wrap with.

At that moment, Glen called him.

"My lord, the pool is soaked in the blood of eight of the giant fish. Already there is a feeding frenzy from the smaller fish. I flew over the north island. There near the beach was a group of young children and they look as if they are not well. Perhaps it is from lack of food as there is not much on that island. It is about a mile from the one you are on now, sir."

"Very well, Glen, it appears we need to perform a rescue mission. Please return to the Phoenix and bring back a shuttle. We will need food supplies, some basic medical supplies, equipment and a generator.

"Also, we are going to need a med tech to stay here until we make other arrangements. Please have that one bring a medical trainer. The med tech will be the governor and doctor. I will remain until you return. Now, more importantly, what is the situation with the birds and the anti-viral medicine?"

"The four birds were all carriers. The ship is synthesizing the anti-viral serum as we speak. It should be ready by this evening."

"Good. I can hope to be back on the Phoenix in time to wake the princess."

"We will see to it, sir."

Glen departed. Mathew turned to see Lindell staring at him. She overheard him talking to Glen but to her it was as if he was talking to the gods.

"I was speaking to my ship," Mathew informed her. "It appears your children are alive on the north island but they are not well. I suspect there has been a food shortage. I have requested another ship with food, medical supplies and a governor to help look after you."

"Will it take many days," she asked.

"Only a few hours," Mathew replied. "Come, let's return to the village."

As they walked, Lindell said nothing for a few minutes then she spoke.

"Only a few hours. How is that possible, my Lord? Boats do not move that fast."

"It is a special boat, Lindell. Wait a little while and you will see. Now come, for I have questions for the old mother."

When they reached the village center, several of the men and women were gathered near the front steps of the long house. The old woman was there only she was no longer held back by her disabilities and she wasn't wasting time sitting around. She was directing people to do various things around that had apparently been left lacking in the past.

"She will work well with the new governor," Mathew thought.

Old Mother observed Prince Mathew and Lindell approaching. Her face lightened in a smile.

"It was good," she thought. "He granddaughter now carried the seed of the Prince. At least there would be one new child for their village. Who knew, perhaps there would be other benefits as well."

"I have a question for you, Old Mother," Mathew said as he kneeled down near to her. "Please forgive me but I do not know your name."

She laughed. "Old Mother will do just fine," she said. "It is what I am and it fits me well. Now, my Prince, what is your question?"

"How did your people get here? There are so few of you and you could not have originated here, I think."

"Yes, you are right. The story has been handed down for years. From my mother and her mother and so on. I was told that many years ago, our people were on a giant ship that wrecked nearby. My people escaped on what they called a life boat. I do not know what that means only that it held many people and the animals they call Houns."

Now he understood how they got there. The Zetan ship that crashed in the sea had managed to launch a lifeboat. Maybe more than one. So, the Houns on Bara or his part of Bara had reached their continent without the humans. Some reached this island and he suspected that the ones on the desert continent might be the other survivors."

"What of the Houns?" He asked. "Are they still alive?"

"Yes, a few. They are with the children. They are the last litter and one is quite old. She is not well, I think."

"Good," Mathew replied. "I must speak with them."

"Speak with the Houns. Don't be silly. They do not talk to us."

"Actually, they do but you have obviously lost the ability over time. No worry, for some of you, it will come back." He stood, looked around at those gathered near and spoke again.

"If you would all humor me, please make a space for my ship. It will come soon, I believe."

"You mean it's coming here, on land. How can that be? There is no water here."

"Old mother, I did not say it was a water ship."

About then, Glen spoke to him.

"We are here, Prince Mathew. Where should I set down?"

"Take a mark on my position, Glen and set in the middle of the village."

"As you wish, sir."

The villagers could see him speaking to someone but there was no one there. Then suddenly in the sky above them, a craft like nothing they could imagine or had ever seen before, suddenly appeared.

"Please stay where you are," Mathew commanded.

"The ship will land in the middle of the yard," and he indicated the area before them.

The old woman spoke. "It's an air ship."

"Yes," Mathew replied. "It's an air ship."

In a few moments, the shuttle landed. Almost before the dust settled, the rear door was opening and out marched a group of marines. Very quickly, they began unloading the cargo within. Several men moved a generator out. It was on wheels and was easily maneuverable until they got it out into the sand where it began to be a bit more difficult.

Mathew instructed the villagers who had till then stood back, staring at the ship and the marines to help move the generator over near to the long house.

At first a bit reluctantly then with a bark from the old woman, they moved in to help.

An aide approached Mathew.

"I am Lauren," she said. "You requested a governor and a med tech. I am at your service, sir."

"Welcome, Lauren. Please let me introduce you to your new assistant and the old mother of the village."

He led her over to where Lindell and old mother were standing.

"Old mother, Lindell. Please allow me to introduce your new governor and doctor. This is Lauren. She will be helping you, old mother, with governing these people until we can arrange to move you. And you, Lindell, will be her assistant. She will be teaching you how to be a doctor."

Old mother was obviously pleased and moved forward to embrace Lauren. Lindell stood, mouth open. Not sure what to say.

Lauren took the lead. "Lindell, I understand you want to be a doctor. Good, please come with me and we will start preparing for our first patients."

The marines had been busy as they talked. They selected a site nearby and erected a tent like structure which would house the medical equipment and could be used as a triage center for the patients. They brought along a food process unit which, when questioned, Mathew had them place in the long house to limit contamination from the sand and weather. Lines were run from the generator to power the med unit and the food processor.

The shuttle was now empty. Mathew looked around and seeing Lindell and Lauren were standing nearby talking, requested they accompany him to the island to bring the children back. He Left two marines to continue arranging the stores and with Glen piloting the shuttle, they quickly departed.

Lindell was too caught up in the moment to realize that now she was on a shuttle flying through the air. She was sitting on one of the jump seats.

"It is too much too soon," she thought. "So much happening so fast," she said to Lauren as they approached the island."

"Don't worry dear, you will get used to it. Before long, it will be as if you had been doing this all your life."

As they approached the island, the children spotted them. They were pointing up into the air as the shuttle came in to land just a few yards from where they were gathered.

"Perhaps, you should go out first," Mathew said to Lindell.

The children were in a group and standing back unsure what to do. Most of them were thin and sickly and really too tired to run. Each of them recognized Lindell when she walked off the ramp and those that could, cried out and ran to her. She reassured them that everything was okay and she had come to take them home.

Mathew walked off the shuttle. Near to the children sitting on the sand were three Houns. He did not see the adults that were supposed to have accompanied the children. As he approached the Houns, he could see that two of them looked at him with their big brown watery eyes. One was lying on the sand. It was obviously too weak to move.

Mathew had not tried to speak to them just yet and they likely did not think to try to speak to him. He knelt down beside the weak one. He saw she was a female. As he slid his hands beneath her to lift her up, he mind spoke her.

"Come with me, little one. You are safe now."

Instantly, as if given an injection of life, she raised her head and looked into his eyes.

"Who are you?" She spoke him."

"Prince Mathew," he replied.

"Yes, you would be," she replied. With a sigh, she laid her head on his arm then spoke him again. "What took you so long?"

Mathew laughed as the other two Houns began flooding him with talk. Soon, he knew all there was to know about these three Houns. They all boarded the shuttle.

The children told them the adults had gone out fishing some days back and the giant fish had wrecked their boat and no one survived. They finished all the food a few days back.

Moments later, the shuttle landed in the clearing and they began unloading their cargo of children and Houns. Mathew carried the weak one into the triage center.

"She is very weak," he said to Lauren as he placed her on an examination table.

"I will tend to her," Lauren replied.

Lindell was helping gather up the children too weak to walk and they were moving them into the triage center. Lauren instructed her to have the ones that could sit put together on a low lying cot while they looked after the weaker ones first. She then requested specific food items which two of the marines hurried off to secure.

It appeared to Mathew that things were under control. Glen informed him that a Hawk was standing by to pick him up and return him to the Phoenix. He went over to the old mother and told her he had to go now but would return later.

She thanked him for everything he had done and looked forward to his return. Mathew told her that in the near future, he would be moving them to another location near to others who had come from the same ship many years before. As he was about to depart to the beach to retrieve the skimmer, Lauren came out and spoke with him regarding the weak Houn.

"She needs better treatment than I can provide," she said. "Can you take her back to the Phoenix with you? I have put her into a sleep as she was in so much pain."

"Certainly," Mathew replied. "Give me a few minutes and I will come collect her."

He looked over at Lindell but she was involved with the children, so he left and hurried down to the beach. Once he had signaled the skimmer and taken control of it, he sent it up to the Hawk visible just a few hundred feet up. Brady was at the controls and had the ramp open for him.

"Take us down as near to the shuttle as you can," Mathew instructed. "We have a patient to take back with us."

Brady set the Hawk about sixty feet from the triage center. Mathew left by the ramp. More wide eyes stared as he went into the triage center. There he scooped up the Houn and left the triage center with her.

The other two Houns wanted to know if she was going to be okay. Mathew spoke them, saying he could only hope so and would let them know as soon as he could then he boarded the Hawk.

"Take us home, Brady. To the Phoenix."

In a half hour, Mathew was on the Phoenix Bridge talking to Logan and Commander Borne. The med techs had only just administered the anti-viral serum to the two women and were monitoring the medicines progress.

The Houn was moved to the surgery center. The specialist doctors there were already running diagnostics on her. Logan asked him how things had gone on the island. Mathew began relating the situation there and what had happened once he was on the island.

Eventually as they talked, he got to the part where he had found the plaque in the yard and how the people had reacted when he told them who he was. He also related how the people had arrived on the island and were likely Zetans just as the ones from the white continent were.

Logan was silent for a moment, then he spoke.

"I believe Prince Mathew has another pressing mission waiting for him and it is, I think, only something he can do."

He went on to tell him how they had secured the one bird from the nests and after causing a ruckus, they moved around looking for other signs. They didn't find any at that location but they did observe humans on the ground.

They were at a statue placing wreathes when they were set upon by large hulking ape like beasts. Perhaps similar to those Mathew had encountered on the island. They all managed to get back to a gated fort or outpost. It was pretty obvious to Logan that those beasts could probably overrun the fort at any time. They simply were not well enough organized but it was only a matter of time.

"So you think we need to intervene," Mathew said.

"Not we, Mathew. You. I left out one part. The statue is almost an exact likeness of you and your Houn, Shadow. Like these people you just found and the ones on the white continent, they are waiting on

Prince Mathew and I think it is urgent that you get there while they are still alive to greet you."

"Very well then," Mathew replied. "As soon as I have greeted the princess, I will see to it."

As the day progressed, the med techs confirmed that the anti-viral serum was working and the women could be brought out of the stasis chamber. Another day or so in the hospital ward would be sufficient for them.

Mathew was standing beside the stasis unit when it was opened for Princess Alexis while Logan stood beside Queen Marie. Both men wanted to be one of the first sights their women saw when they wakened. It was only a few moments later when those beautiful eyes opened for Mathew. He leaned over and kissed her on her forehead.

"Hello Princess," he said. She smiled back at him. He had a cloth and he wiped her eyes and mouth. The med tech told him she would need to do that when Alexis awoke and Mathew told her he would be there and would do it. He then offered her the end of a straw with which to sip some water. After she had swallowed some of the water, her mouth was moist enough for her to speak.

"Hello my prince," she said. "You said you would be here and you are."

"I wouldn't be anywhere else, dear. And just so you don't have to ask. You and our son are doing just fine."

"Thank you," she replied. "That was going to be my next question along with one other.

"What is the other?" he asked.

"Who is old mother and Lindell?" she asked.

"Now where did you come up with that," Mathew asked.

"I'm not sure," she said. "It was as if they were in my dreams. Them and many others whom you killed. That is what I dreamed. It seemed so real though."

"Well dear. Perhaps your mind and mine are so in tune that you are living what is going on with me either during or after it happens because there was an old mother and her granddaughter named Lindell and I did fight and slay some beasts and false priests and free a village from enslavement to all of them."

"Okay," she said, "and is there anything else you might want to tell me."

Mathew looked down at her and spoke.

"I think, my dear that you already know what happened and I think you also know that you are the love of my life and nothing will change that."

"Good answer my prince. Yes, I know that. Now, give me a kiss and then help me out of this thing. I need to try to stand. I feel weak and I'm very hungry."

"Yes dear," he replied. He signaled a med tech who was standing nearby as there were things to disconnect before she could come out of the stasis chamber.

The med tech quickly made the needed adjustments, one of which got a short, "Oh," from Alexis. Then they both helped her out of the chamber.

"You need to sit for a moment, the tech said. Then we'll move you to the hospital."

"Is that necessary?" Alexis asked. "Can I not go home?"

"Sorry dear but you must be monitored for at least another day or so. It is for you and our sons own good."

"Okay but let's not make it any longer than necessary."

Chapter 8 – The Maine Group

Cato and Nick spent two days watching the group bunker in Maine. At no time was there ever any indication that anyone was there or that anyone was approaching. As the third day started, they contacted Van to let him know they were going to do some investigating around the bunker and see if they could get inside it. Van replied that he would keep a watch for them.

Earlier, they located several security cameras, each of them battery operated which they figured out were actually motion activated game cameras normally used by hunters to determine what the local wildlife were doing at any given time of the day.

At one point, they observed the bunkers solar array open up during a period of sunshine. It was not a surprise as earlier scans indicated that something shallow was in that location. It only confirmed their suspicions.

They still exercised caution with Cato using his superb visual skills to check out their route to the bunker. The entrance was fairly non-descript with some scrub to help camouflage it and its doorway area only slightly elevated, probably to help keep out runoff from rain or snow.

There was a cover that had to be lifted to access the entrance steps. Using a small scan stick, they lifted up the cover just enough to insert it to see if there were any triggers attached to the doorway. Sure enough, there was a wire around a hook. The wire ran away to the right side of the door and had they lifted it up, it would have triggered something.

Carefully, they located the wire and followed it about a yard from the door. Inside a small concrete square box covered with limbs and leaves they found where it was hooked to another catch.

Cato didn't care to source out the other end of the hook but released their end so they could access the bunker. If they had time later, they would see what the trigger was connected to. They lifted the cover, making sure there wasn't another booby trap as they did. Inside, they found where steps led down into the bunker up to a door.

Using a light, Cato led the way. On the way down, he found several small compression devices on the steps that without a light one might not have seen until it was too late. Each of them was similar to an animal trap with spikes designed to inflict damage on the unsuspecting intruder. If encountered they would have no doubt given someone reason to abandon his search.

Upon reaching the door, they found a push button combination lock. Cato expected something similar and brought along a device he attached to the door. He began pushing buttons and watching the digital monitor. There were nine buttons on the lock. After he punched all nine from top to bottom, he repeated it in reverse order.

The monitor gave him three numbers. It didn't say in what order to punch them, only that those were the numbers that properly sequenced would open the door.

He began with one combination. The door didn't open. He tried a second and still no luck. On his third attempt, it came open.

"About right," he said to Nick. "Numbers one two and three."

Carefully and again, he used the scan stick only opening the door ever so slightly. Sure enough, there was a trip wire at the inside top of the door. You could just barely get your hand in to unhook it.

Slowly he opened the door, keeping a grip on the knob in case he needed to jerk it shut. There didn't appear to be any more traps. The one he had just unhooked was connected to a spray device. Upon checking, he saw it was pepper spray.

"Whatever works," he thought, as he messaged Van they were inside.

"You're still all clear up here," Van replied.

They opted to not turn on any light switches just in case it triggered something else. Moving quickly over to the rooms center table, a rather large and long one, they found numerous maps and writings on it. Nick had a small camera and began taking photos of everything.

Unlike Cato, he didn't have the ability to record what he saw. In a few seconds, he had covered everything on the table. He then proceeded to photo the surrounding room while Cato explored the room's contents.

In a closet, he found a large stockpile of military MRE's. Studying a wall area that seemed oddly vacant, he looked for and found a release lever poorly camouflaged that when engaged released several plywood doors along the wall.

Opening the first one, he found a wall mounted weapons rack. On it were several different hand weapons ranging from pistols to short barreled shotguns. There were boxes of ammo stacked at the bottom.

Within the second door were shotguns and rifles. Again boxes of ammo were stacked at the bottom. Within the third door were the heavier weapons. Several Uzi's and cheaper versions of the same and several high caliber sniper rifles.

"A gun collectors dream," Nick thought.

At a glance, they hadn't seen anything to give them any information, so they thought it time to leave. Cato planted a few bugs in the room. With any luck, if they were close enough to receive them, they might collect some data.

They closed up the doors to the gun cabinets and checked around to make sure they hadn't disturbed anything. Cato's sharp eyes detected a blinking red light revealing another game camera across the room.

He quickly moved to it and assessing its position unsnapped the front cover and removed the camera disc. After closing it, he joined Nick at the door and they began their exit.

Cato re-attached the wire hook and they made their way back up the steps avoiding the spike traps.

Re-connecting the wire hook to the entrance cover that was nearby, Nick began to source out where the trip wire from the concrete box went. He found it was attached to a lightly covered battery operated siren alarm obviously meant to scare someone away.

That was good. At least they were giving the intruders the option to leave.

As they cautiously made their way across the woods and back to their vantage point, Van spoke to them.

"Several vehicles just turned off the main road. Possibly they are headed this way."

"Perfect timing," Nick replied. "Maybe now, we can learn something."

They continued on to their lookout point and made themselves comfortable. It was over five minutes before the first of four vehicles showed up. All of them were trucks except for one midsized car. It was a popular four wheel drive model.

As the men began to get out of the trucks, Nick and Cato could see it was a mix of different types of people. The first out was obviously a farmer or someone who worked with his hands. A large hulking individual wearing dirty stained bib overalls. He appeared to be chewing tobacco as he continually spit once he got out of the truck.

The man with him was of similar design with jeans and old boots. The second trucks occupants were completely different. Belts and shirts with ink pens in their pockets. The merchant type, was how the team would describe them.

The next truck was altogether different. They wore suits although none wore a tie. Polished dress shoes indicating they were of higher ilk than the business men. Either they were politicians, lawyers or possibly even bankers. Cato was snapping their pictures individually via his weapons scope and forwarding them to Van who was forwarding them to Trainer.

After all the others were out, the Subaru opened up. To both men's surprise, there were too young men and two women they knew well. Lydia and Jade. They were laughing and acting as if they were the best of friends.

They're actions were apparently not too pleasing to some of the men. The big man in the bibs shouted back at one of the men to cut out his shit and come on in the bunker. The laughter quickly stopped as they moved up towards the bunker.

"Van, are you getting this."

"Sorry guys, I only learned a few minutes ago via Trainer that the girls were enroute with two male suspects they joined back in Washington yesterday. Seems the girls convinced them they are the anarchist type and of course the men couldn't wait to show them off."

"Okay, thanks I guess," Nick replied. "Are you picking up anything on the recorders?"

"Only now. They're just getting into the bunker. Give me a few seconds and I will pass the feed on to both of you."

Shortly afterwards, the feed came through. It was just normal chatter so far. Nothing of real importance. It was pretty obvious that some of the men were not too pleased with the girls being there if one followed the line of questioning occasionally directed at them.

The big man was not the leader but was obviously one of the more outspoken. He must have opened up the gun cabinets as the girls walked up behind him. You could hear Jade making remarks about the guns.

Guessing she was looking at the pistols, they heard her say "Toys," then "Toys," then "Now some real guns."

The big man was heard to say. "You know anything about this one?"

It appeared he tossed the gun to Lydia. They could only imagine what she was doing with it as they heard slapping sounds then clicks.

Lydia caught the gun by the stock. Slapped it into her other hand. Released the clip, checked the bolt and tossed it back to the man."

"It's dirty," she said. "You need to take better care of your toys."

Obviously, he was a little impressed as he replied. "Yes, your right. It is a little dirty but we will be fixing that soon enough."

Nick could hear the sound of chairs being pulled away from the table. It appeared the group was setting down. Another man spoke to some of the men there then addressed the two women.

"Ladies, we have serious business to discuss. If you're not into it, I suggest you go outside. Anything you hear from this point on makes you one of us and there is no turning back. Is that understood?"

Jade spoke up. "Our friends here said they were part of something that would make a difference to our country. Make changes for the better. Right now, we have nothing but shit for a government, so if you're serious about real changes then we are in. If this is just bullshit talk, then we couldn't care less, because what you say won't amount to a hill of beans. Anyway, it's your show so get on with it."

One of the men said "Damn. She don't mince any words does she."

Another man spoke up. "You're welcome to stay but remember you were warned. What is said here does not leave this room. Understood."

"Understood," Jade could be heard to say.

One of the men had left the bunker a few minutes earlier. He now returned. Cato and Nick observed a man exit the bunker and now he was going to the game cameras and retrieving the camera discs. They were glad to see he only checked those they found earlier. They replaced the discs when they came back out. He went back into the bunker with them.

They heard him doing something, then he said "Shit. Who loaded this camera?"

He was obviously referring to the game camera in the bunker. "There's no disc in it," he stated.

Another man spoke up. "I'm pretty sure there was one in it when I set it up."

"Well there's not one now."

"Okay, Barney. Check the outside cameras discs and see if we've had any visitors. Even if there is nothing in this one, they should tell us if someone has been messing around."

"Doing that right now," Barney replied.

"Okay, people. Let's talk, another man spoke up. "Now that Montana has the stinger missiles, when can we expect some action from them?"

"Well, I imagine as soon as the friend of our young friend here gives us the latest travel itinerary, we will be able to help them with a plan. We need to do something soon and by soon, I mean this week, if possible. The longer we wait, the more progress they make and the closer we all are to being destroyed by these so called aliens.

"What have we learned regarding this military general who is obviously a tool for the aliens."

"Only that his name is Bradley Neagle. Other than that, it would appear he's a career officer who somewhere along the way was changed by the aliens. No one in their right mind would willingly do their bidding if they weren't forced to.

It was about now that Trainer spoke to the team. "It appears that the government has finally gotten involved. A swat team is coming into town and will be headed your way shortly.

Lydia spoke. "Any place to pee in here, or do we need to go outside?"

"Can't it wait?"

"You got a bucket?"

"Go outside but hurry back."

"May as well flush mine too," Jade said.

"I may as well," said the young man who brought them there.

The three of them made it outside as the others talked.

"Oh look," Jade remarked when they stepped outside. "A tree," and she started over towards it.

"Can't you just squat behind the car door?" the man said as he was unzipping his fly.

"Don't you have a sense of adventure?" Lydia remarked as she walked alongside Jade.

They went past the first tree and appeared to be squatting behind the two nearest.

"Come back in when you're finished," the man said and went back into the bunker.

As soon as he was out of sight, Van told the girls which way they were and both women broke into a run in their direction.

In the bunker, the men could now be heard talking about the president's schedule. The man with the schedule spoke of Denver as being the best location for taking out the plane.

"Yes, that is exactly what I told the Montana group was the most likely spot. So his travel plans have stayed the same since our last meeting."

"Yes, they have, so now we only need to see how much assistance we can offer."

Another man spoke. "I would think supplying the stingers for now would be enough until we can source some more."

"I already have a source," another man spoke up. "The same one we got the last ones from."

Outside, the swat team was on the ground. They were approaching the door to the bunker. As they checked the entrance, the men inside had no idea what was about to happen. Suddenly, the bunker door was opened and several tear gas canisters were tossed inside.

"Son of a bitch" was heard from within the room.

Then there was a concerted rush towards the door by the men inside except for two of them. They knew right where to find their gas masks and donned them. They knew where to find the bullet proof vests and each put one on. They also knew which guns were loaded and chose two semi-automatic weapons.

Outside, the swat team was instructing the men coming out the door to walk forward. They didn't know how many were inside the bunker and didn't want to risk a fire fight in close quarters if it could be avoided. Once the men were about half way between the bunker and the vehicles, they were instructed to get down on their knees. The bunker entranceway was still cloudy from the tear gas.

Suddenly, two men rushed out of the bunker exit. As soon as they cleared the entry door, they opened fire on the first targets they saw. The men who had been in the bunker with them were their first targets.

Barney fired from the left cutting them down and the big man fired from the right. Then they began firing on the swat team. The swat team was aiming high and the two men's bullet proof vests were protecting them.

Among the shots, one was made and Barney felt his left leg cut out from under him as Nick shot him just below his left knee. Even wounded, he continued to fire upon the swat team.

The big man was trying to make his way to his truck. The swat team took cover behind the other vehicles having no idea how many people they were up against.

As Barney continued to fire away in the direction of the swat team, trying to give the big man a chance to get away, there was another shot and Barney folded over as the shot took him in the back of the head. Cato took that one.

"Take out the truck", Cato instructed Nick.

"On it," Nick replied.

As the big man went to get into the truck he saw both tires on his side start to deflate as shots hit them. He knew the shots were coming from behind him but had no idea where. He was attempting to start his truck when he heard grinding sounds and the truck died. He knew whoever was shooting at the truck had taken out the engine. He jumped out, his automatic weapon reloaded and started around the back of his truck headed for another.

Two shots rang out behind him. Both sticking a leg. Suddenly he had nothing to stand on as his legs shattered below the knees. As he knelt on the ground he attempted to place the muzzle of the gun in his mouth. Another shot rang out from behind him smashing the gun from his hand and taking two fingers with it. He screamed in agony and frustration as he fell forward, knowing he was caught.

Almost as soon as it started, it was over. What seemed to some of them a lifetime was over in a little more than a minute? The swat team was moving forward. They quickly surrounded the big man, checking him for weapons, while several attempted to stem the flow of blood from his wounds and others tended to their fellow members, several of which had been wounded in the exchange of gunfire.

Other members of the team were checking the other members of the group, finding all of them had received multiple gun shots in the upper torsos and none had survived. Sirens could be heard in the distance as local assistance was now on the way.

While the swat team was working on their site, the other team made tracks through the woods to a location where they could be picked up. The Hawk was only equipped for four seated but they all managed to get in and Van departed the area headed back to their base.

"Good work, team," they heard over their headsets from Trainer. "Full debrief when you get back to the base."

"Yes, sir," Van replied as he piloted them towards the base making sure they were not being targeted by some government radar along the way.

Chapter 9 – Valley of the Beasts

Once the princess was situated in the ships hospital ward, Mathew told her he had a short mission to undertake but should be back in a few days.

"Yes dear, I understand," Alexis replied. "Please try not to be gone too long."

"I'll try," he said and gave her a kiss before he walked out the door. He went to the adjacent room where Logan and Queen Marie were lodged.

"Pardon the interruption," he said as he walked in.

"Hello Mathew," Marie said. "I hope all is well with you my young son."

She didn't acknowledge him as a son in law but rather referred to him on occasion as her son.

Logan has informed me of much of what occurred on the recent trips both of you took. He has also informed me of the urgency he believes is necessary if we are to save the group of survivors on the other continent.

"Yes my queen and I am ready to depart. I just wanted to check in with Logan. I wanted to take the same pilot he used. I believe it was Brady. He will know exactly where I need to go and one more marine for fire support if needed and I would like a shuttle handy as I suspect we will need to bring them out before it is all over."

While they were standing there, Commander Borne came to the doorway.

"Gentlemen, could I see both of you on the bridge as soon as you have a moment?"

They looked at each other, wondering what was going on that required their attention already. They proceeded to the bridge.

The commander wasted little time getting to the subject of the situation.

"We have received a distress call forwarded from the Tomarlins for two planets. One is Waardin and the other is Finnean. The gist of the message is that the Pache are inflicting severe losses on Waardin with the new war planes and the Finnean have suffered terrible loses and are unable to reach much needed feeding grounds held by the

Pache. They know what we did on behalf of the Tomarlins and are requesting our help. It is deemed most urgent.

Logan looked at Mathew. "As soon as you get back, we should go," he said. "I will make preparations as will Commander Borne. By then, the women should be safely back in the palace."

"I only have to pick up Shadow and I will be gone." Mathew stated.

"Safe journey," Logan said as Mathew walked from the bridge and down to the flight bay. Brady already knew he was coming and a shuttle was standing by as well.

"Mathew sent a message to Shadow, requesting her location and that she be ready to travel with him."

"I will meet you above the palace," she replied.

It was already late evening, so it was going to be dark when they arrived. They landed above the palace and Shadow boarded the Hawk with Mathew, the pilot and the marine co-pilot. They were soon in flight towards the desert continent and a short while later, as they hadn't hurried, they arrived in cloaked mode over the valley above the statue.

Mathew had Brady move over near to the fort. He could see campfires within the stockade. Using heat sensors, they tried to determine how many people were inside the stockade. By their count, it appeared to be between fifty and sixty. Additionally, there were smaller heat signals removed from the humans. Possible animal signatures Shadow suggested might be Houns.

#

Within the compound, most of the men and a few women gathered to talk about the last few days and how aggressive the beasts were becoming. They had been stockpiling arrows for their bows but as the oldest man stated. If there were enough of the beasts, then once they got over the walls, it would be the end for all of them.

Another man said he expected they would wake up one morning soon to find at least a hundred of the beasts massed outside their fort. They would have to kill a lot of them with their arrows to have the slightest chance of winning the first round. After that, it depended on how many survived to fight the next round.

Brady moved the Hawk away from the stockade and they began checking the area between the fort and dry plains that led to the brushy growth bordering the wooded area just past the statue. As they approached the statue, not visible due to the darkness, they could detect heat signatures in the area that led well past the statue into the woods.

By all indications, there were hundreds of the beasts if that was what was actually down there. They appeared to be massing as if there was a plan they were following or that was the impression Mathew got. For sure, they were not sleeping and it was well past midnight now.

Just before daylight, they detected a pattern of movement in the direction of the fort from the woods. In single file, the beasts were moving towards the fort. They stopped a few hundred feet before it and began to spread out.

The fort was butted up to the cliff face and there was no access above it. The overhang many feet above prevented anything from landing within the stockade.

Mathew could tell from the sensors that well over a hundred of the beasts were massed on the plains in front of the fort. He instructed Brady to let him and Shadow out near to the statue.

Brady was to take a position that would allow him to interfere if the beasts began to breach the fort. Mathew hoped to deter them from that by taking them on from the rear. He had a full complement of hand weapons and a bow and arrow set with exploding barbed heads. There were a few regular arrows ideal for long shots.

Shadow asked if there was a saddle she could carry?

"Now that you mention it, there is and it will be ideal for carrying grenades and extra arrows," Mathew replied.

"Good," Shadow replied. "I would certainly like to be able to help."

Brady set the Hawk down behind the statue. Mathew and Shadow exited and Brady took off, moving near enough to the fort that he could assist when he was needed.

It was just breaking light and a few minutes' walk from the fort but Mathew wanted it to be light so he and Shadow could be seen. He wore his armor and the cape which he had come to be very fond of. The statue, he could make out, showed the man wearing the cape and standing beside the Houn. The Houn was on his left side. That was how they would approach. In the distance he heard the blare of a horn. Most likely it was the fort alerting everyone to the danger outside.

He knew they had guard towers so they would be able to see him approaching if they were looking. It was light enough and he decided it was time to go. He checked his rear towards the woods and saw no sign of the beasts so hopefully they would remain in front of him as he and Shadow began to close the gap between them.

"If I hadn't come today," he thought, "it would have been too late for those in the fort. Who arranges these situations? Why does everything center on Prince Mathew?"

In the fort, the sentries spotted the beasts lined up before the fort. It was looking like this was going to be the day they died, or so many of them thought. They're leader, an aged man who as he often said, had long outlived his usefulness, went to the tower to see what the others saw. His name was Jason.

Many years ago, he helped build the statue. He heard the rumors or prophecies as many called it. Pulling on his memory of how such an individual would look, he helped design and build it. The statue gave all of them hope for many years but now it looked as if their hope was all used up.

As he looked across the ground before him and way out past the beasts lined up before them, thinking perhaps to gaze on the statue one last time, he thought for a moment he saw movement just this side of the statue. Something other than the beasts.

Jason's eyesight was not good but he was not blind. He stood for a moment then shouted for someone to bring him the glasses. A young woman, his granddaughter, came up the ladder a moment later and handed them to him.

"What do you see papa?" she asked.

Jason stared through the glasses. "Surely I'm not losing my mind, not today of all days." He thought.

"Here," he said to the girl named Shania, handing her the glasses. "Tell me what you see."

Shania looked to the statue. "Oh God," she exclaimed. "It's him, it's him Papa."

The man nearest to them exclaimed. "What do you see, girl?"

"I see the Prince," she said. "It must be the Prince. Prince Mathew."

"It's not possible, let me look," he said as he took the glasses from the girl. After a moment, the man murmured. "It's not possible, it must be a mirage."

"Wait, you will see," Shania exclaimed. "It's a man and a Houn. Just as foretold, you will see."

It was at that moment that the beasts began beating their clubs on the ground. Almost in unison, they beat them on the ground. There appeared to be one larger than the others who stood off to the side.

It appeared they had a leader. One perhaps a little smarter or stronger than the others and he was apparently the driving force behind today's massing of the beasts to attack the fort.

In the fort, the word spread quickly although many refused to believe it. The Prince was coming. He had been spotted behind the ranks of the beasts.

Another man stated, "He is only one man. How can he go up against more than a hundred of them?"

Jason spoke up. "Ready the arrows and spears. When it starts and if they turn towards him, we must attack from the rear. Stand ready," he ordered. "Today, we either live or die."

Mathew could see the beasts were building up their courage to charge the fort. He also observed that there was one larger beast off to the side urging them on.

"So they have a leader," he thought.

He was now halfway across the span between the statue and the fort. Still the beasts had not spotted him. Shadow kept a sharp eye behind them but so did Brady in the Hawk. The shuttle was further back and could provide fire power if needed.

The larger of the beasts struck the ground and made several steps forward. The others followed his lead. Slowly, they began closing the gap until they were only a hundred feet from the fort. The noise they were making was deafening. Mathew was only a hundred and fifty feet behind the beasts. Close enough for now, he decided. Time to start lowering the odds.

Taking up his bow and adjusting his quiver for easy access he pulled back and began launching his arrows. He had three in the air before the first one struck. He had chosen those near the back. He continued to fire his arrows. As they struck the target, the arrowhead burst sending out metal slivers that cut and sliced into the target. It was almost instant death to the beasts that were struck. They dropped where they stood. By the time he had slain ten of the beasts, one noticed another falling beside him. Turning around he started to make a cry when the arrow struck him in the chest. He died without making a sound.

Nothing good can go on forever. The larger of the beasts realized something was occurring across the line. He saw the dead lying on the ground and wondered why as they had not yet engaged with the fort. Then, as more of the beasts continued to fall, he saw the one behind them.

His mind wondered from where it had come. How could it be there behind them? Everyone was in the fort. They were always in the fort when he and his fellows were out and why did this one look like the one in the stone behind them. Perhaps, it had hatched like the big birds.

As he looked on, more of his fellows continued to fall as the arrows pierced their bodies. He roared and pointed at the man behind them. As one, they turned. All could witness the death of many of their fellows and see the cause of it. He smashed his club into the ground and began advancing on the man behind him.

At the fort, those watching were amazed at how many of the beast were being killed by the man behind them. Knowing it was time to act, Jason ordered the archers to fire at the back of the beasts while they were still in range. A volley of arrows flew from the fort, striking as many as ten of them. A few fell dead but many more were wounded. The beasts roared in rage. Some turned back and began their slow trot towards the fort. Their leader forgotten. It was for them, the reason they were here today and that was to kill and eat those in the fort.

Mathew saw the beasts were now on to him. He paused only long enough to take a few grenades and more arrows from the saddle Shadow carried. He placed the grenades in his pockets. As the beasts began to get closer, some within fifty feet, Mathew continued to fire his arrows as fast as he could. By his estimate, there were only forty or fifty left.

"Not so bad odds," he thought as a club flew by his head. "Damn, that would hurt like hell if it hit you."

As more clubs came flying by, he spoke Shadow.

"Watch out for the clubs, Shadow,"

"Look out for yourself, Prince. I will be fine," she replied.

Another club came bouncing by and Shadow had to jump aside. Two more came flying in and one caught her a glancing blow on her side. She yelped in pain.

Mathew took this moment to fling two of the hand grenades. The ensuing explosion sent six of the beasts flying through the air. Mathew fired off a few more arrows then taking his sword in hand, began to engage the beasts.

He literally flew through the air as he stabbed and sliced his opponents. Never still, always moving. One moment he was striking with his sword, then the next flinging a star at the throat of another. As he moved among the beasts he was mindful of where Shadow was. A sudden yelp drew his attention to her. A flying club struck her leg and she was on her side.

She spoke him. "Watch your back."

Mathew turned from his distraction to find the large beast smashing his club down at him. He side stepped and flicked his sword at the beast's arm. The beast roared and jumped back. Mathew glanced over towards Shadow and saw she was between two of the beasts and they had her in their sights. He flung a star at the nearest one and sent splinters towards the other.

Turning back to the large beast, he realized he had left it too late. He only had time to hold out his sword before the club smashed it from his hands. He stumbled back and came up facing the beast.

He could see the murderous red eyes were focused on him. Checking on Shadow, he saw she was up and the two beasts were down. He observed that the people in the fort had come out and were engaged with the beasts and taking a toll on them.

Several of the beasts decided it was time to flee and were loping off towards the woods. The remaining ones in battle with the people at the fort were too much raged to give in now and were systematically being killed as the people had spears and bows to their advantage. A few people were down from thrown clubs but not many.

As Mathew faced the large beast down, he knew this one was the key for many years to come and could not be allowed to live. As they changed their stances the beast suddenly reverted to its animal instincts and leapt towards Mathew, his fangs bared.

As the beast was so close as to be nearly on top of him, Mathew went with the beast's charge allowing him to make contact with his upper body but rolling backwards so the beasts momentum carried him over and past him. Mathew rolled over and came up in a fighting stance. The beasts charge carried him ten feet past Mathew. Raising his head, the beast roared his challenge.

As he faced Mathew and prepared to charge again, Mathew took the opportunity to throw a knife. As he anticipated, the beasts open mouth was a perfect target for the knife and it entered his mouth, piercing his jugular vein. The roar ended in a gurgle and the beast collapsed where he stood. His short reign of terror over.

Mathew surveyed the site around him. The only standing beasts were those headed towards the woods. Scattered all around and behind him were the dead ones. Shadow was limping towards him and he moved towards her.

"Are you alright," he spoke her as he retrieved his sword.

"I'll be okay," she sent back. "Perhaps a little sore but okay. I think we need to finish our job, now."

"You mean killing more beasts."

"No. Looking to the ones who've been waiting on us."

"That sounds better than the former, so what say we carry our crippled selves towards the fort."

"You mean we can't get them to carry us," Shadow replied with a chuckle.

"Come along," Mathew replied, walking towards the fort."

As they slowly made their way towards the open gate, making sure the beasts along the way were truly dead, the people in the fort were slowly trickling out. Soon there was a crowd of over fifty people and what appeared to be three Houns.

"Can you talk to them?" Mathew asked.

"I think they are too dumbfounded to realize we are here," Shadow replied.

They continued towards the fort. People could be seen bringing what appeared to be water bags to the men outside. A few of them were sitting on the ground nursing wounds and bruises but no one appeared seriously hurt, or so Mathew hoped.

He stopped when he was about ten feet from an older man who stood holding a staff. Mathew thought he must be the leader of this small group of people. He noticed the man was licking his lips as if to wonder what to say. At that moment a young woman ran up to stand at his side.

Mathew beat him to it by speaking first.

"Greetings, friend. To whom do I have the honor of speaking?"

The man seemed at a loss for words.

The young woman spoke to him. "Tell him papa."

Mathew smiled at the woman then spoke to her. "What might your name be, young lady?"

This brought a smile and she replied, "My name is Shania after my grandmother."

"Well I'm pleased to meet you, Shania who is named after her grandmother."

The older man laughed then spoke. "I'm Jason. Her grandfather. Whom might you be, sir?"

Mathew smiled, then spoke. "Prince Mathew, at your service. Please accept my apologies for taking so long to get here."

"See, I told you so," Shania said to her grandfather.

There was a murmur within the crowd. Jason understood and asked. "Are we to bow to you, Sire?"

"Jason, my friend, I would hope not. We are all the same here and I would only hope to ask you to share some water with me if you have it."

"Here," Shania spoke up, handing her grandfather a water bottle. Jason offered it to Mathew.

"You first," Mathew said, "I'm sure you're as thirsty as I am."

Jason tilted the bag back and allowed a stream to enter his mouth. After a moment he stopped and handed the bag to Mathew. Mathew did the same, then returned the bag to Shania.

"Thank you, it was very wet."

"Yes," Jason said. "I remember when water was both wet and cold."

"Keep that happy thought," Mathew said, "for soon you will have both."

At that moment, Brady broke in. "Prince Mathew. It appears many of the beasts have decided they have not yet lost the fight."

"Very well, Brady. Give them a fight they will never forget."

"My pleasure sir," he replied and as Mathew turned to look behind them, the rest of the crowd could see the approaching beasts."

Jason heard Mathew speaking to someone who wasn't there. He lost that thought momentarily when he looked to where Mathew was looking and saw a large number of beasts approaching.

At that moment, Brady chose to uncloak the hawk. It was just off to the side of the fort and moving towards the beasts. As the people gasped in astonishment at what they were witnessing, the Hawk opened fire on the beasts. No one in the crowd had ever seen such firepower and hopefully never would again.

For the beasts, it was the beginning of the end as the photon cannon wiped them out in seconds. Where there had been life moments before, now there was none. The Hawk continued on over the forest sending beam after beam into the woods after the beasts fleeing there.

"Come," Mathew said to Jason. "We must talk."

"That's your ship?" Jason asked.

"One of them," Mathew replied. "There is another standing by when needed. What say we go into your fort and see what you have, what you don't have and what you need? I believe we can provide for all of it and a new home if you are willing."

They went into the fort. No one even thought about closing the gates as they went into the biggest room they had to talk. It was not a problem though as Brady returned and took a position in front of it.

Mathew soon learned all the survivors could tell him. Their ancestors survived a crash on the planet and made it here in a lifeboat. There were about a hundred originally but over the years, a low birthrate, sickness and death at the hands of the beasts wore them down. Now there were only sixty souls left and three Houns.

Jason even spoke of when they had tricked some of the beasts into entering the old lifeboat and shoved it out into the sea with them in it. They never knew what happened to them but they hoped the boat sank somewhere. Mathew realized that explained how the beasts got to the island.

"Where are your Houns? Mathew asked, realizing that Shadow was not with him."

"Shadow," he sent to her.

"It is okay," she replied. "I'm with my friends who have suddenly found their inner voices again."

"Okay, just checking on you."

He spoke to Jason.

"It appears my Houn is in conversation with yours and they have found their voices."

"You can talk to them," Jason asked?

"Yes, to the Houns, the Baar and many others."

"We we're once able to do so but have lost the ability over the years."

"It is okay. Over time your people will get it back. Speaking of getting it back, you might be pleased to know that there are other survivors not far from here."

"From our ship?"

"From yours and one other."

"The stories say the other ship shot ours down and we retaliated."

"The stories are partly true. The computer controlling the other ship went mad and went on a rampage firing on your ancestor's ship, then after it crashed, it began to systematically kill off the survivors."

"So, what do we do now?"

Mathew thought for a moment then decided to give the credit to his queen.

"My queen, Queen Marie will arrange transport for you and your people to the valley where the other survivors are locating. There are others to come from an island. They were on your ship as well. Hopefully, now that we know from where you came, we can eventually arrange your return."

"We have not yet made contact with your people in the Zeta system. It's just outside where we are exploring but we would hope to have a peaceful meeting in the near future."

"How can we repay you," Jason asked.

"For the time being," Mathew stated, "Let's just concentrate on being good neighbors."

It was now afternoon and Mathew was getting hungry. "What do you have for food stores here? m" he asked. He had worked up an appetite.

"Supplies are pretty scarce. We have some tubers we grow within the compound and in various locations outside. About the only thing the beasts didn't find and eat or tear up. A few other vegetables and some rodents we attract and kill."

"You can't survive long on that," Mathew said.

"As you can see from today, we didn't expect to. We knew this day was coming sooner rather than later. If you hadn't shown up today, I think we would have all been dead by now."

"Glad I didn't wait any longer," Mathew said to no one in particular. He knew there were some food stores on the shuttle and he called for it.

"Just set down in front of the gate," he said then turning to Jason he told him to bring some help to unload the food stores on the shuttle.

As they approached the gate to the fort, the shuttle was landing. Moments later the aft gate opened and the marine pilot stepped out.

"We only need some food stuff," Mathew said. "At least for now but tomorrow we will start transporting the people here to the valley."

Today, when he returned home, he would have engineers start arranging for housing of the people here alongside the other Zetans on the plain near the city. For temporary housing, they would put up a tent city with all the amenities of a regular home. It was going to be either equal to or better than what they had now but would definitely get better with time.

They began breaking open the cartoons of food stuff and soon Mathew was sharing a meal, everyone said was the best they had eaten in a long time.

"There's plenty here and much more where this came from," Mathew told Jason and those sitting near.

Afterwards, he spoke to Jason telling him he was returning to his home across the ocean and would be sending for them in a few days' time as they made housing preparations for them to be housed near to the other Zetans. The shuttle will remain here until the hawk returns to stand guard duty. Unload all the food stuffs before the shuttle leaves.

"I suggest you start preparing to leave here with the planned intention of not returning any time soon if ever."

"On behalf of all the people here, we are forever indebted to you, Prince Mathew. Please convey our thanks to your queen."

"I will," he replied then he turned and walked out the gate. He gave instructions to the marine with the shuttle to maintain a watch just in case the beasts had not suffered enough for one day. The hawk was standing by and Mathew entered it, instructing Brady to take him back to the Phoenix.

Chapter 10 – Plans for War

An hour later, he was once again on the bridge where Logan and Commander Borne were going over battle plans for the retaking of Waardin and Finnean. Logan glanced down at his armor as he had only shed the cape.

"Been busy, have you."

Mathew glanced down. His legs and boots were covered in what was obviously the dried blood of many of the beasts he had slain today.

"Oops," Mathew said and promptly walked off to get a shower and some clean gear.

When he returned, Logan grinned and remarked. "You smell better too."

"Thanks friend," Mathew replied slapping Logan on the shoulder as he joined them. "How are the women? Are they behaving themselves?" he asked.

"Maybe you should go check up on them," Logan said light heartedly. "I will be glad when we can get them back to the palace and I'm sure Commander Borne will too,"

"They're not that bad," Commander Borne said.

"Who's not that bad?" echoed from two voices across the room.

Both women stood in the bridge doorway.

"It's a good thing we showed up." Queen Marie stated with a smile. "We wouldn't want any false rumors circulating about us now would we."

Mathew was quickly by their sides, saying as he got near. "Hello, ladies. Please join us at the table. Then both of you can speak for yourselves."

Marie and Alexis found themselves fully involved in the battle plans. Marie had numerous questions but most of them were to satisfy herself that her men were not going to be over exposing themselves to danger.

Logan and Mathew both determined that it was going to be necessary to conduct battle on two fronts. Fortunately for them, on

Finnean, the Pache only had ground troops and a few ground vehicles at their disposal to try and force the Finns into subjection.

#

The Finns were an aquatic borne people. They could not survive long out of the water but much of their food grew on the beaches and shores. The planet was half water and the rest almost all desert and barren mountains. No one lived on the land.

Most of the Finns diet consisted of a combination of seaweeds, moss and shell fish While they could eat anything in the sea, they had their preferences and preferred to live in harmony with most of the sea life they shared the seas with.

According to information provided by the Tomarlins, when the Pache landed on the planet, they did a quick survey and determined where most of the Finns could be found. They initially tried to enter into an agreement whereas the Finns supplied them with fish from the sea in exchange for the foods they needed from the shores. When the Finns learned that most of the seafood went towards supporting the war effort on Waardin, they began to slowly shut off the supply.

They went unopposed for a few months then suddenly the Pache took a hard line on them. There was a small salt water lake that supplied them with most of their moss and shell fish. It provided easy access for them and at times the supply was overly abundant.

The Pache waited until the lake was nearly full of adult male Finns harvesting the food and came in, blocking off their access back into the sea. They posted guards and shot anyone who tried to escape.

The water was shallow at the entrance and Finn bodies floated everywhere, attracting the sharkfin and other carnivorous sea life. The water was shallow between the lake and the sea so the Finns could not just swim out. Then the Pache put up a fence across the gap to help keep the men hostage.

Soon after, the Pache began a systematic attempt to completely exterminate the Finns. They left the men in the lake but posted guards along the shores with instructions to shoot anything they saw. The toll began to mount with young males and females floating up onto the beaches all along the coasts. As the numbers declined, so too did the shooters.

At the lake, the men consumed much of their harvest and were growing weak and tired of being penned up. One night they attempted an escape.

Later, it became obvious the Pache had planned for this. As the men began to cross the short section of land on each end of the fence, they triggered land mines and the guards on duty opened fire with heavy weapons slaughtering most of the men before they could escape back into the deeper water of the lake.

A few, perhaps a dozen did make it to the sea but the damage was done. Over the next few days, the guards killed the remaining Finns in the lake, freeing them of needing to guard them. They posted a few men to keep them out of the lake and block access to the food they needed.

The Finnean population before the Pache came was near to a hundred thousand. With the continued slaughter, it was now just over a hundred with most of those being females.

Mathew was curious as to how the Tomarlin had learned all of this from the Finns. It turned out that years before, in an isolated cove near where the desert reached the sea, they gifted the Finns with a communications platform similar to the one they gave Logan. The Waardins delivered and installed it.

They Finns only had to leave the water by a few yards to access it and pass the message on to the Waardins as their planet was closer and the Waardins relayed the message to the Tomarlins.

Now, the Finns and Waardins, all informed of what had happened on Tomar, were pleading for help to stop the slaughter on their planets.

With Logan taking the lead in the planning, it was decided that Mathew would take on the Pache on Finnean and Logan would take on the Pache on Waardin. Logan would enter the planet's atmosphere in a formation of hawks. They would approach all the known locations and landing fields housing the Pache war planes. The locations had already been provided to the Tomarlins by the Waardins.

The Phoenix would take up an orbit whereby it could provide fire support, taking out military depots and any other assets deemed target worthy. Once they had inflicted as much damage as was possible, as many marines as could be spared, would start a ground operation in an effort to subdue the remaining Pache.

It was hoped that within a week or ten days, the operation would be over and the planet back under the control of the Waardins.

The nature of the treatment of the Waardins at the hands of the Pache meant that no quarter would be given. If they offered the slightest resistance, they would be destroyed just as they were trying to destroy the Waardins.

As per their plan, Mathew's squad would land as near to the communications platform as was deemed safe. They had the location and once there he would attempt to make contact with the Finns. He was prepared to enter the water and locate them if necessary.

With so few remaining, they were not sure what they would find. It was likely that since the request for help was now a month old that many more Finns had died. Five hawks would accompany him down to the planet. They would come in at night in cloaked mode, then while Mathew was making contact with the Finns, the Hawks would begin night missions, locating the Pache outposts and taking them out one at a time using marines on foot.

Of course they could use the hawk heavy weapons but if they wanted to maintain an element of surprise for a while, the stealth attacks might work to their advantage until the Pache realized something was up."

"An excellent idea, Logan and one we will initiate as soon as we arrive," Mathew stated.

Alexis spoke up. "So when do you leave."

"Tomorrow once we get you ladies home," Mathew replied.

"How goes the treatment of the others in the hospitals, now that you have the virus antidote," Queen Marie asked.

"Those not too far advanced will make a complete recovery," Logan said.

"How many did we lose," Alexis asked.

"Too many, I'm afraid," Logan stated. "Too many people and too many friends."

"Oh," Marie said, her voice making it obvious she was not sure she wanted to know who those friends were. "You must tell me, Logan."

"Maxim's wife and children were the first to die. Many from Seaview died. Had he not been in Seaport, he would have probably perished as well. Several of the Zetan men as well, including the husband of the one called Kieran. Carlos was his name. He helped Mathew shut down the ships computer. In our house, we lost one."

"Who was that?" Alexis wanted to know.

"The young woman Tina was training. Mindy.

Mathew pulled her next to him as she began to sob.

"Luckily, we were able to save Tina and Randall and many others," Logan stated.

"Yes," Marie said, "I suppose it could have been much worse. At least it is over now."

"What will we do with Maxim?" Marie asked.

"He will need someone," Mathew stated. "I think I know who that someone will be when the time is right."

"I won't ask who. We will leave that to you when the time is right," Marie replied.

"Come daughter, join me in my room. We have much to discuss regarding this and other things."

"Yes mother," Alexis replied, then gave Mathew a kiss on the cheek as she walked past him.

Chapter 11 – The Montana Group

Brad and General Neagle drove out the main entrance to the big dig area. Both wanted a break from the constant comings and goings that were taking up so much of their time. Some weeks back, they began taking an evening off and going into Salt Lake City for a meal and some shopping.

While they could get most anything they needed on the base, some items were better suited when done personally. For Brad, those things were socks, underwear and a spice called slap your mama. General Neagle wanted a certain brand of tea not available on the base, so it became a Thursday routine.

Trainer had yet to speak to either man regarding the threats made on General Neagles life. He was certain that several persons within the base compound were passing on the movements of both men. He chose now to speak to both of them regarding the danger to Neagle and Brad.

"Brad?"

"Yes Trainer," Brad replied. The voice came over the truck speakers.

"We have problems both of you need to be aware of."

"What kind of problems?" General Neagle asked.

"Death threats directed against both of you."

"From who and why?" Neagle asked.

"Right wing anarchist groups have decided you, your president and many others are now under the influence of aliens and their remedy is to arrange your deaths."

"How serious are the threats?" Brad asked.

"Very serious, I am afraid. We have already had an encounter with a group in Maine who supplied the group in Montana with stinger missiles meant for the president's plane. Only one man in that group survived."

"And this other group is headquartered in Montana?"

"That's correct and we did locate what we thought was their base camp but it turned out to be deserted. We don't know how many there are and how far spread out their members are."

"So, they could be around just about any corner and we wouldn't know it." Brad stated.

"That sums it up, I'm afraid. We will be providing some security for the both of you but you both need to be on your toes. This group is not heavy into internet or telephone communications making it a bit difficult to keep tabs on them."

#

At the base, a cell phone call was made. The call was answered.

"They are leaving the base now."

"Thank you," was the reply and the phone hung up. There was not enough dialogue or communications time for Trainer to pick up on it.

Trainer was not leaving things to chance. He assigned a hawk fighter to shadow the two men. It remained in cloaked mode, so it wasn't visible. Brad knew it was there, based on the instrument panel in the truck. He didn't say anything to General Neagle, but it was reassuring to know that Trainer had their back.

Brad and Neagle made small talk as they drove towards Salt Lake City. It wasn't because they had little to say but rather that Trainers message had given them unwanted worries and now they were more focused on their surroundings and anything that seemed out of place. At one point, Brad asked Neagle if he wanted to go back to the base. Neagles reply was that he did not want to give in to those making the threats. They would have to be more vigilant. Brad agreed and they continued on towards the city.

It was a two and a half hour drive if they went all the way into the city but they usually found what they wanted in West Valley City which was ten miles south of Salt Lake.

They passed through the small town of Dugway and proceeded towards the turn off where Stark road met Skull Valley road. They were about 3 miles out of Dugway when they saw six vehicles with flashing lights in the curve ahead.

Both noted none were police vehicles, just ordinary cars and trucks with flashing lights stuck to their tops.

"In the glove box, you'll find two nine millimeter pistols, if you need them," Brad stated.

"Good to know," Neagle replied.

The vehicles were blocking the road. Ten men, some young and some much older, moved out from behind the vehicles as they drew closer. Each man carried a rifle, shotgun or pistol. Brad stopped twenty yards short of where the group was standing. Right away one of the men in the group stepped forward with a bullhorn and began to shout for them to get out of the vehicle. The men around him brought their guns to bear on Brad's truck.

"Is this truck as tough as you say it is," Neagle asked.

"It's beyond tough, General," Brad stated. "As long as we stay inside her, we are in no real danger. Our friends out there, though. Well, they have no idea just how much danger they are in."

As he spoke, he touched a few buttons on the dash and a targeting monitor appeared. Red and green lights glowed and a voice spoke. "Targeting system activated. Awaiting voice commands."

"That sounds a bit hi-tech," Neagle muttered.

"It is," Brad said. "Now follow my lead, please. Computer, accept voice commands from General Neagle."

"Please speak, General Neagle," the computer stated.

Neagle glanced at Brad then spoke. "General Neagle."

"Voice inflection accepted," the computer stated.

"What does that mean?" Neagle said to no one in particular.

"It means the computer will take orders from you. Just say what you want to do and she will do it."

During their exchange, the man with the bullhorn was shouting at them to get out of the truck or they would fire on them.

Brad pushed another button. Then spoke over the trucks speaker system.

"You have no authority to stop us. If you are law enforcement, show us your I.D's. Otherwise, we will be forced to take drastic action against you."

Tired of talking, someone in the group took it upon himself to fire at them. He had a shotgun loaded with buckshot. He fired at their windshield and the pellets bounced off. As if that was the signal for the rest of the group, several others began firing at them as well.

The men were staged on both sides of the road with a clear lane between them and the vehicles in front of them.

"Computer! Missiles to the first three vehicles," Brad calmly stated.

Almost before the command had left his lips, three vehicles in front of them exploded into fireballs. The men before them leapt aside, panic quickly setting in as they began to retreat towards the remaining vehicles parked just behind those on fire. A few of them kept firing at the truck as they retreated until it finally sank in that their bullets were bouncing off the truck.

Just as they were approaching the remaining vehicles, they too exploded, then burst into flames, showering the men with sparks and flaming materials. Brad knew what had happened but General Neagle did not.

"How," he exclaimed. "You didn't give a firing order."

"We have friends," Brad replied.

It was then that Aden spoke to Brad via his headset. "The authorities have been notified and someone should be arriving shortly."

"Thanks, Aden. You and Trainer are much appreciated today."

The men outside realized they were no longer in control of the situation. Several of them were already fleeing across the fields headed for some cover north of the road. Moments later, the remainder of the group was joining them.

Brad no longer considered any of them a threat. He drove around the burning vehicles and stopped about a 100 yards on the other side.

"Don't get out," he said to Neagle. "We'll wait for the authorities to arrive. We don't want to make a target for the rifles back there."

"Suits me," Neagle replied. "Did our friends call them?"

"Yes, they did. Speaking of which, I wish you would consider the communications implant."

"As soon as we get back," General Neagle stated. "As soon as we get back and that is going to include my new staff as well."

"Good," Brad replied. "You won't regret it."

#

Ten minutes later, a Utah state police car could be seen approaching with another not far behind. As the driver pulled up alongside them, rolling his window down, Brad did the same. He was alert to any trickery as he knew they could trust no one simply because they wore a uniform or drove a government vehicle.

"We got a call saying men ambushed a black truck from the proving grounds. From here, it looks like things didn't turn out as expected."

"No, officer. They did not. The men have fled into the brush on the north side of the road. There are ten of them and they are all armed. Several with rifles, so I wouldn't get too close."

"Any suggestions as to how we get them?" the officer asked.

"A video of the encounter as well as individual photos with I.D. will be sent to the Utah State Police dispatch in Salt Lake City."

"You can do that?" the officer asked.

"Yes sir, we can. It will likely save a few lives. Those men are all part of a right wing group who won't hesitate to shoot anyone attempting to arrest them. Better to catch them individually when you can. I would stay well shy of them right now. Of course, you have your orders so I guess it's up to you but again, that is a dangerous group."

"I haven't received any specific orders just yet and what you say makes good sense to me. Yes, I think that's the smartest path to take. We'll arrange for some equipment to come clear the road. We can haul off the scrap later. I'll get my partner coming up behind us to turn around and we will allow this group to make their own way out."

"That works for us too, officer. We'll be on our way now. You have a safe day," and Brad proceeded to drive away.

"You went through all of that like it was a simple walk in the park," Neagle stated.

"General, once I learned that Trainer and my friends within his reach were only trying to help us, I learned to accept that there are many ways to fight a battle and getting oneself hurt or injured in the process is not on the agenda. We have a big battle brewing ahead of us but in the end, I'm confident we will win out."

"I have to admit that I feel a bit insufficient right now, having seen what you and your teams can do."

"Well general, you always have the option of changing that. It's your decision and yours alone but perhaps you might want to consider speaking with one of the med techs as to how you could be enhanced, so to speak. You have time before the space ship is completely unearthed to make some changes. It is entirely up to you."

"I may just take you up on that," Neagle said.

They drove on into West Valley City and located a shopping center they used once before. Once their shopping was done, they decided a steak dinner at the Stockmen's Steakhouse would fit the bill.

Some hours later, they headed back to the base camp for the big dig. They didn't call in to alert anyone as to whether or not they were staying overnight or coming back. Both knew they had one or more moles working there that would simply pass on the information as to their whereabouts.

#

Trainer was working on finding the location of the Montana group's base. He had the area narrowed down to being near to Wolf Point, Montana. They earlier located a decoy bunker and now it was a matter of locating their active bunker or whatever they used as a base to coordinate their plans of attack.

With the recent attempt to kidnap or kill Brad and General Neagle and with the demise of the group in Maine, there had been some communications between the intern in Washington and the Montana group. It was apparent that the intern had not been with the group that picked up the girls and delivered them to the bunker in Maine.

Trainer began to monitor all communications between the big dig facility base and outside contacts. He picked up several calls between cell numbers on the base and nearby in Salt Lake City as well as others in Wolf Point, Montana that appeared to be suspect.

He placed some of his team members on alert to the callers and notified John Michael with the FBI. He hoped between the two, they could get some details and locations before any further attempts were made to kill or harm someone else.

It was Monday morning at the big dig operation. No special attention was paid to the comings and goings of personnel through the main gate. Just the usual security checks to confirm the wearer of the badge was who they were supposed to be. Or at least that was the way it was supposed to work.

Security at the gate was not aware that a facial recognition program was in use and when a person checked in, the system compared the I D with the person bearing it. Trainer well knew that the system was only as good as the people manning the security booths at the entrance. Soon after they started operations, he arranged for additional remote security apparatuses to be installed.

Now, he had one of their team monitoring the input to shorten the time from gate entry to their being alerted. Otherwise the persons entering could be in and out of sight in no time.

After the installation of the office buildings which housed the administrative side of the big dig operation, Trainer had foreseen the need for a new group of buildings with a different design. Guests and visitors entered from one end and could only access his people directly by moving from one end of the building to the other end. No one, aside from his teams could get direct access to their offices. The other entrances only operated on voice command. There were no door knobs or handles to operate to access them and no visual access into any of the offices from the outside although there were windows in place.

#

The van drove up to the gate guard window. The men inside presented their I.D.s to the guard. He scanned them into the system and handed them back to the driver. The guard activated the gate and it slid aside to allow them to pass.

In the team's office, Ellen, one of the aides, alerted Brad that a group of people had been allowed entry into the base that did not match the issued I.D.s. It was obvious that the guard at the gate allowed them entry.

Brad immediately alerted General Neagle and the three man security team that arrived just hours after the attempt was made to take Brad and Neagle on the road. Neagle quickly armed himself and took a position in his office to help if needed. The security team split up with one inside and two just out of sight of the front entrance.

Trainer, in the meantime, ordered a Hawk to take a cloaked position near the entrance of the base if needed. He also activated the red light alarm in the security guard housing that meant a security breach had occurred. Every man there was required to report to the security chiefs briefing room for instructions.

The van drove directly to the administrative office. Six armed men exited the vehicle. Each man now wore a ski mask to hide his facial features. Four of them quickly made for the entry door and two took defensive positions outside. As soon as the four men entered the building, the one standing outside the closed door heard an odd sound.

He thought, "What an odd sound as if the door just locked."

He reached out and tried it. It was locked. "Hey," he shouted to the man by the van. "The door just locked."

"They probably locked it when they went in," the man replied.

He didn't get time to say anything else. He shouted as he dropped his gun from splintered hands.

The man by the door only had time to exclaim, "what the" before he too dropped his gun from splintered hands.

Almost as quickly as it had happened, both men found themselves face down with a knee in their back and tie wraps being fastened around their wrists.

The last man through the main door heard the door latching sound. It caught his attention for a brief moment then he shrugged it off and proceeded to follow the other men down the hall towards a glass door. They moved past two closed doors, pushing on them as they went by as there was no handle on either. Each was locked.

They could see a desk through the glass door at the end of the hall with a woman sitting at it. She appeared to be occupied as she had not looked at them as they approached. Just as they reached the door, she looked up, smiled and stood up.

Odd, thought the man in the lead. She is not at all scared of us or our guns. That by itself should have set off warning bells. He reached for the door handle. As he grabbed it to push it open, he got a tremendous electrical jolt. He couldn't let go of the handle as it continued to shock him. The only thing that let go was his bladder as he pissed all over himself.

The man behind him, unaware as to what was happening, placed his hand on the man's back wondering why he was not going on into the office. The shock he received knocked him back into the man behind him. Shouting in pain, he dropped his weapon. This got the attention of the remaining two men, who startled jumped back only to find some very sharp objects pressed up against their backs.

Very quickly, they were slammed down onto the floor of the hallway, yelling in pain as men stepped on them as they moved past them to the two men in front of them. The electrical charge was off now and the man at the door collapsed onto the floor only to find himself being cuffed and dragged down the hall by his collar. His companions preceding him.

At the guard window at the gate, another vehicle pulled up. While the guard was scanning the I D of the man inside, two men entered the guard shack. They identified themselves to the two men in the room, then instructed the man manning the window to come with them.

He was a bit hesitant at first but didn't realize they were onto him. Another guard, normally working a different shift, came up and punched in, saying he had been called in early. As the guard relieved of duty departed with the two men, the two guards exchanged pleasantries and wondered what was happening with their colleague.

An hour later, a van came through the out lane. The driver was one of the men who had taken their colleague. They recognized the van as one used for detention transfers. Behind the driver and his assistant, were seven men chained to their seats. They recognized one as the other gate guard.

After the van departed, they received a visit from the head of security. He proceeded to grill them on procedure and explained that the men being taken away in the van had attempted to breach security, being allowed in by their former co-worker. They were apprehended and being transferred to a federal facility.

While it was always possible that someone could fake an entry pass, it was their job to give each pass their utmost attention in order to prevent possible breaches to base security. The guards assured the head of security they would do their utmost to make sure it didn't happen on their watch.

Base operations resumed as before but newer more stringent security measures were put in place, especially for those in supervisory positions like Brad and General Neagle. In the future, any local trips off the base would be accompanied by at least one security detail. The idea wasn't too pleasing to either man but they could now see that circumstances had changed and they would have to go along with the new arrangements.

Brad himself decided that it would be easier to arrange for a Hawk to transport the two of them to a more secure area where they could have their break without outside interference.

Chapter 12 - On to Finnean

The two women were now back in the palace and their men were onboard the Phoenix, now on its way to the planet Finnean. By nightfall on the planet, they would be in position for Mathew and his group of Hawks and Marines to insert themselves without detection.

They went over their plan of attack including all the pilots and ground troops in a meeting to insure everyone knew what the plan was and how they wanted to carry it out. Everyone participated in the process and that helped insure that no one had any misunderstandings as to their part in the battle plan.

As they approached their insertion site, it was already dark on their side of the planet. They selected an initial set down location not far from the small inlet where the communications platform was supposed to be located. Mathew hoped someone would be close by, making initial contact easier and giving him a chance to interact with the Finns as they preferred to be called.

While Mathew hadn't yet seen a picture of the Finns, he was under the impression they were part human and part fish. He had no expectations and would reserve his opinions until after he had a chance to interact with them.

He did not doubt that it wouldn't be as simple as walking up to one and saying "Hi, I'm Prince Mathew."

Most likely, they wouldn't care who he was and he wasn't aware of any prophecies related to stopping the Pache from taking over the Finnean planet.

With a final word from Logan, to go with care and let him know how things were going, Mathew boarded the Hawk and took a seat next to the pilot. Soon after, they were outside the Phoenix and once all five Hawks were in position, they began their flight into the planet's atmosphere towards the area selected earlier as the best location to set up a command center.

An hour after leaving the Phoenix, all five Hawks were setting on the ground. There were several small hill or dunes separating them from the inlet or bay where the communications platform was supposed to be set up. While the marines were setting up a base camp a defense perimeter and a command center, Mathew chose to check out the location of the communications platform.

Before leaving, he made sure his communications set was working with the command centers communications officer. As soon as they confirmed that, he began to make his way carefully over the rocky hill that separated them from the inlet. It was still a good few hundred yards from there to the platform he was looking for.

In the low night light, Mathew could see well enough but paused several times to scan the area ahead for heat signals that might indicate someone was out in front of him. He was yet to see any life forms as he continued to move onward. The ground was rocky with some sandy areas throughout that made travel a little easier.

He was not aware of any animal life that might pose a threat to him but then they had little information regarding the planets life forms aside from the Finns themselves. He was not even sure how he was going to communicate with them, having decided he would cross that bridge when he got to it.

Moving slow and steady, it was a half hour before he got close to the final hilltop that separated him from the communications platform concealed in the inlet ahead. He wore his black skin tight armor and his cape. His princess swore he liked his cape better than all his other gear and went nowhere without it.

Mathew knew if he had to enter the water, he would have to leave the cape behind. His weapons pack was strapped to his chest and his other hand weapons were located strategically on his armor for quick access.

Mathew found himself at the top of the hill overlooking the inlet. He was lying down scanning the area ahead. He could see no life signs, no heat signals nor could he make out anything that resembled a communications platform.

After some time, perhaps fifteen minutes or so, he decided to move down into the inlet and try to locate the platform. As he made his way down, he began to notice a smell that was getting stronger as he moved nearer to the water. It was the smell of something dead and it came and went with the light breeze that was blowing in from the sea.

In a few minutes, he was near enough to the water's edge to get a bearing on the smell. It was much stronger to his right and he began to move in that direction. It was several hours before coming daylight, so he didn't feel the need to look for cover in this area. He would worry about that later. As he slowly moved down the beach, the smells strength increased. In another minute, as he moved carefully ahead, he could make out objects half in and half out of the water.

Mathew moved over to the bodies, as that was what they were. Kneeling down, he studied them closely.

"So this is what the Finns look like," he thought. "Very human with some exceptions, of course since they spent so much time in the water."

He observed gills beneath their jaw lines which blended in so well that he imagined they would hardly be visible if they were on land. They had all the normal human facial features as far as he could tell and the hair on their heads extended down to just in front of the ears much like human sideburns did. The hair appeared to be as fine as silk and from what he could see, long enough to cover the ears and the back of the neck if not longer. He thought he was looking at males and that was confirmed as he moved over to the third body. It was definitely a female.

"She had been very pretty in life," he thought."

Her facial features were very fine, her eyes almost Asian like. Her hair was longer than the others. She, just like the others, wore something like a leather harness although he was sure it wasn't leather but in her case, it was obvious she had breasts whereas the others did not. He was unable to make any other determinations as her lower body was still in the water.

Mathew stood and looked around. Something caught his eye further up the beach and away from the water. He moved in that direction. In a few moments he realized he was looking at what was left of the communications platform. It had been torn apart, no doubt by the Pache.

Something else was also evident. There were shell casings all around the platform. It didn't take long to figure out the Pache had used the platform as a trap to catch the Finns coming back to it, obviously killing the ones nearby before they even got out of the water to access the platform.

"Well, that screws that part of the plan," he thought.

He walked back to the water's edge, considering what his next move should be. While he stood there, he communicated with the radio officer at the base camp, telling him what he had found and instructing him to inform the marines and pilots that as soon as they were ready, they were to start looking for Pache positions they could return to later and take out. In each case, he instructed, they were to go in hard. They didn't need any prisoners and the men stationed on this planet were nothing but cold blooded killers as far as he was concerned.

He instructed the radio officer to forward the information to the Phoenix that the communications platform provided by the Tomarlins had been destroyed.

As he stood there scanning the waters in the inlet, he detected movement. Using his heat sensing abilities, he detected four subjects in the water. They appeared to be watching him. It was likely they thought he was a Pache, so how was he to convince them otherwise.

He decided he would make himself vulnerable to them and perhaps they would make a move on him, even to the point of trying to take him captive. It was worth a try.

Mathew moved back to the platform and moving around the back of it, found a place he could hide his cape, then pulling his head gear on, moved back to the water. As he left the platform he informed the radio officer he was going to attempt to contact the Finns.

He would be back in touch as soon as he had something to report. The marines were to continue on with the mission. The radio officer urged him to use caution and report back as soon as he could.

Mathew entered the water much as someone who was planning on washing off would. He detected what he thought were spears and a net with the Finns. Maybe they would try to take him but knowing that the Pache couldn't breathe underwater, he guessed that the best they could do was either spear him or drag him under with their net in an attempt to drown him.

"Let's see how this goes," he thought.

He waded out as far as he could and still keep his head and shoulders above the water. He made motions like he was washing his arms off. Then he heard one of them speak.

"Let's take him now."

They spoke telepathically or at least they did when they were in the water. The communications platform didn't work that way so they must also be able to speak verbally.

Another, likely the most senior spoke. "Take him alive with the net. Let him suffer and drown while we take his body out to the reef for the sharkfinns and crabs."

"Good plan, Lena," another female said, as they moved towards Mathew from beneath the surface.

Mathew continued as he was doing, waiting for them to move on him. It appeared, as near as he could tell that he was dealing with females. He didn't have long to wait.

Moments later, a net went sailing over his head and landed on top of him. He had only a second to brace himself before he was being pulled along by the others towards deeper water.

"Keep the net tight," the one called Lena ordered. "We don't want him to escape."

"If he does, we can always finish him off with our spears," another replied.

"Yes, Cassie, so maybe you should follow behind the net just in case he manages to get out."

"He is not even fighting, only hanging on to the sides of the net as if this was a joy ride," Cassis reported. "No, wait. He has turned and is facing me. He's just staring at me and he has some kind of hood over his face. Something's wrong. Maybe it's another trap."

The women stopped pulling Mathew and released the net. As it fell away to the bottom just below, Mathew allowed himself to drop to the seabed and stood there as they gathered around with their spears at ready.

"Which of you is Lena?" Mathew mind spoke them.

"He mind speaks," one of the women said. "How can that be?"

"Which of you is Lena?" Mathew repeated."

One of the women raised her spear, then spoke. "I am Lena. Who wants to know?"

"Thank you, Lena. I am Prince Mathew. I believe you sent for me."

The others lowered their spears. They were not sure what to say or do. As they stood there, Mathew sensed movement in the water. He moved to face from where he sensed the movement was coming. As he turned that way, one of the women began to frantically move away as another said to no one in particular.

"It's the killer sharkfinn. Separate, or he'll get us all."

Mathew was now able to make out a very large shark like creature bearing down on them from the deeper water. Its mouth open, its teeth showing as it swam towards them. Without leg fins, he was not as mobile as the others. He decided it was kill or be killed.

He pointed at the giant shark with his right hand and fired his photon weapon into its open mouth then dropped down to the seabed as it cruised past him leaving a trail of blood and flesh before coming to rest in the inlet.

The others looked on in stunned surprise. Mathew said to no one in particular when he spoke them. "I think we need to move on from here. This one will attract others."

Lena moved to Mathew's side. She instructed Cassie to take his other arm. "We can move him with us faster than he can on his own."

In a moment they were speeding through the water. Mathew had no idea where they were headed but at least he had made contact and for now all he could do was enjoy the ride. They traveled outward into deeper water then downward towards what appeared to be a reef in the distance.

Mathew could see other Finns off in the distance and they all appeared to be moving in the same direction he was being moved to. So far, the others had not questioned his appearance, as he had on his armor and the headgear.

"Perhaps, it is not so strange to them," Mathew thought.

Soon they were just outside the edge of what he called a reef. It was the largest coral reef structure he had ever seen, stretching for as far as he could see in every direction. There were small and large fish and sea creatures everywhere he looked. Some appeared to interact with the Finns while others just darted in and out of reef openings.

One of the Finns in their party moved ahead of them and Mathew was able to see how they were made from the waist down. He noted that they wore leggings something like shorts and there appeared to be small fin like protrusions along the outer sides of their legs.

It appeared their feet were wider at the toes and webbed although they could obviously walk on them as well, which would seem to indicate they had something like ankles that were possibly double jointed.

As they approached the reef, Mathew observed a larger opening near the base of it. There were other openings further down but it was soon obvious the largest one was where they were headed. Moments later they entered the opening.

He expected it to get dark inside but luminous growths or something similar lined the sides and top providing plenty of light to see with. Just before they entered the reef, he had tried to contact the radio operator at the base but got no response, so he figured he would have to be on the surface before he could get through. No matter now, as they moved on into the reef.

Mathew observed what appeared to be a light source ahead as they moved inward. The bottom appeared to be sandy and dotted with small shells and various kinds of sea life. The water appeared to be getting shallower and the bottom closer. As they skimmed just over the sand, he felt the water breaking over his head.

Suddenly the women on each side of him pulled up, allowing him to place his feet on the bottom and stand. As his head cleared the water, he realized they were in an open air filled chamber. Just ahead and before him, lay one of the most amazing sights he had ever seen.

"It's an underwater city," he thought. He could see windows and doors and all sorts of more modern fixtures one didn't expect to find below the surface of the sea. Nothing seemed out of place, yet at the same time it did.

Mathew began to slowly walk towards the area before him. The water was shallow and growing shallower. The room or pool they were in was ringed by a short stone wall. Perfect for sitting on or whatever one chose.

He quickly noted that the area behind the wall, much like a courtyard, was slowly starting to fill with Finns. Off to one side, was an area that could only be described as the courtyard of thrones.

It was not long before Finns, obviously some of great importance began to move in that direction. Till now, nothing had been said between Mathew and those that brought him here since their brief exchanges earlier. While he moved forward, the Finns who helped him there moved onward into the courtyard.

Mathew could now sense and hear in his mind many voices. It was as if everyone was trying to talk at once. Still trying to make sense of it all, he moved to the edge of the pool in the direction of the thrones. As he took stock of those before him, he realized that there were a lot more females than males, a whole lot more.

It would be in line with what he was told earlier about the Pache killing off so many male Finns. His attention was directed to several Finns now entering the courtyard. They were dressed more royally than most of the others.

There was an older male in a white robe carrying a staff and several women dressed in robes as well. He watched as the man and those with him took seats among the thrones. They were escorted by a group of what he could only call guards.

"Perhaps they are the royal guards for those individuals," he thought. Each of them was wearing the leather harnesses and carrying a spear and a short sword and each of them were females.

All, very attractive females, he realized after a moment. In fact, he had yet to see anyone in here who was not remarkably well featured and athletic looking.

As he sat on the stone wall and shifted his legs to the other side, the guards adjusted their stances to face him. He realized he still had his head gear on and decided it was safe to remove it. As he took the sides of the hood on each side of his neck and pealed it up and off his head, he could hear the gasps from all those nearby.

"They must have thought that was how I looked," he thought. "I hope they like this me better."

Apparently, they did as there were several remarks passed between those near the thrones and several smiles followed by laughter. At least now, they were not so unalike.

Mathew stood. All eyes were on him. As he was about to move closer to the thrones, a commotion off to his left got his and everyone else's attention. An angry young woman was pushing her way past several Finns. She was armed with a spear and a sword and was shouting something to the effect that his kind had killed her father and brother.

She broke free of the few trying to restrain her. Ran forward a few steps and flung her spear in his direction.

Mathew followed it as it traveled towards him waiting till the last second to turn sideways and catch the spear as it went past him. This brought a gasp of surprise from many but didn't stop the woman. She continued running his way with her sword.

It was apparent that she would get to him before anyone could intervene, if they were of mind to. He didn't try to stop her progress, only watched as she got closer with her sword raised over her head to strike him, then he sent a few splinters into her hand.

She screamed as she lost her grip on the sword and it fell from her hand. She quickly snatched a knife from her belt with her other hand and tried to stab him with it. He calmly reached up and grasped her hand then allowed his hand to slide down until he had a grip only on the knife blade.

She tried to wrest it from him but he wouldn't have it. As she stopped for a moment to catch her breath, the knife blade began to take on a blue glow. She looked at his hand and the knife. He released the blade only it was no longer there. As she looked on, he opened his hand and what looked like melted steel poured from it.

The woman dropped to her knees and broke into sobs of anguish. Mathew knelt beside her, his fingers pushing the silver white hair back and taking her face in his hands. Looking into her tear filled eyes, he searched her mind and quickly had what he wanted. Not sure how he had done it but sure he had it right.

"Reenae," he spoke loud enough for those near to hear.

"I did not take your brother and father but I can promise you that those that did will pay for it."

Then he spoke louder as he helped her to her feet.

"By this week's end, all who took part in the killings of your people will be no more. That, I can promise."

Reenae looked at him, her face showing her surprise.

"How do you know my name?"

"It does not matter," Mathew told her. "What matters is we make the wrongs right, and while I cannot give back what has been taken from you, I can make sure it does not happen again."

As she regained her composure, a friend walked up, spoke to her then led her away. Mathew turned to face those on the thrones. They were all attentive as he had, up to then, been the center of attention for everyone in the throne room. He walked forward closing the distance between himself and the thrones to about fifteen feet.

He could see the guards were getting anxious. The man in the robes mind spoke them, telling them to stand at ease. Mathew looked at the man and mind spoke him with a "thank you, Sire."

Chapter 13 – Aegis Daughters

He obviously had not been told by the others that Mathew could mind speak as he appeared surprised but before he could think to reply, Mathew spoke out loud.

"Your highness," he said, addressing the man in the robes. "Please accept my sincere apologies for not getting here sooner and my regrets for your losses and know that I will personally see to the destruction of all those party to this crime against your people."

The man in the robes stood, then spoke. "Who are you? What do your people call you?"

Mentally, Mathew suddenly knew what answer was expected of him, what the other wanted to hear but those words did not come easy for some reason and when he spoke, it was not the answer the man wanted.

"I am Prince Mathew."

The man in the robes stood there for a moment. It appeared as if his brows wrinkled as he was deep in thought. Then he spoke again.

"It appears your people do not yet know who you are but I do, so tell me again, who are you?"

Those crowded around listened attentively, knowing that his answer was important but not yet knowing how so.

Mathew did not hesitate to say, yet he knew that his life from this moment on was forever changed and he was not sure it was for the better but he knew there was a force that was starting to guide his life and there was nothing he could do about it.

"I am the Shadow Prince," he said, loud enough for all to hear.

You could have heard a pin fall in that courtyard. All but the man in the white robes dropped to one knee. Mathew looked around.

"Please no," he thought. "Not this." He spoke to all before him. "Please do not bow before me."

Then he mind touched the man in the white robes.

"Please command them to stand. I am not ready for this, Sire."

The man mind spoke back.

"As you wish, Prince," then he spoke to the others to rise and they did but still they looked on as if he was someone he knew he was not. At least not yet.

"Come, Prince," the man spoke out loud. "We have much to discuss. They will prepare a feast for everyone while you and I talk."

Mathew followed as the man and the guards led the way into the reef. His mind was racing as he knew there was much this man could tell him yet he was almost fearful of what it would be.

Once again, he knew he was being led down a path towards a future he obviously had no control over. A future, he knew was going to change his life and those he loved, forever.

They entered a well-lit corridor that narrowed to the point that only two or three abreast could walk down it. After walking through a stone arch, he found himself in a small courtyard with another throne room only this one had two thrones to sit on.

Facing the thrones were several rows of stone bleachers. He wasn't sure what they were going to discuss but did not doubt that by the end of this day he would know many things he needed to know, like it or not.

The man dismissed the guards. The senior of them questioned him as to whether she should stay.

"Just in case," she said.

He assured her that he was in no danger and would be just fine then appeared to relent. "If you insist," he told her, "just find a place down the hall and wait on my call."

"Yes, father," she said as she walked out.

"Your daughter," Mathew asked as he watched her walk away.

He couldn't help but notice her as not only was she a beautiful woman, but her silky silver white hair flowed behind her as if to say, watch me.

"One of them," he replied with a smile.

He observed Mathew watching her leave the room and smiled to himself. "This day has been a long time coming," he thought.

Mathew looked around the room. "Actually this room is kind of sparse, as if it was a room of secrets or for handing out sentences to wrong doers," he thought.

The man in the robe cleared his throat as if to speak or just to get Mathews attention.

"Where are you from, Prince?"

Mathew did not hesitate but said straight away, "Bara."

"No, before Bara?"

"Earth, but I was born of Eden."

"You are very young for a Shadow Prince."

"It is not my choosing," Mathew replied.

"It never is, so how long have you known?" the man asked.

"Would you be so kind as to give me your name," Mathew asked, then stated, "only a few months."

"Some call me Aegis, the others, well, it matters not but that will do."

"A shortened name for the older water gods," Mathew thought. No reason for him to question it. He had already been party to stranger things.

"Do you know what the future holds for the Shadow Prince?"

"No, I don't and I am pretty sure I don't want to know."

"I'm afraid, Prince, it is no longer your choice. You should know that this happens every thousand years. No one knows how the selection process works but somehow it does."

He went on to say that the Shadow Prince was tasked to travel from star system to star system stepping in to save those in the direst need. It was a given that he couldn't be everywhere at once so in many cases, he arrived too late for many but always seemed to leave with something accomplished.

As the years passed, his abilities increased and his life span increased with that. He outlived many civilizations and watched the birth and death of many others.

"What about my mate, my love and my children? What happens to them?" Mathew asked.

"I suspect that is why you are here, Prince. I have something for you and her. At some point, they all come here. I suppose it is foreordained. Anyway, before you leave, that will be addressed."

They talked for hours. He was full of information that was already shaping Mathews future in ways he couldn't even begin to imagine. After a while, his guard or daughter, most likely both, came to the arch.

"The food is ready," she announced.

"Excellent!" Aegis practically shouted. "I love a good feast. Come Prince, but don't eat too much, for you my young friend are going to have a busy evening."

"Christ, not again," Mathew thought as they walked down the corridor towards the main courtyard.

The courtyard was awash in lights. He would try to remember how they managed that as he knew there was no power source down here or at least none he was aware of. There were people or rather Finns, everywhere.

There was some kind of string music like harps playing in the background. Even a low drum beat could be heard. All the young women were dressed in silky flowing gowns that accentuated their own natural beauty. He instantly thought of mermaids and all the women had the silky flowing hair.

Mathew was led up to a stone table with stone beaches for seating. A place one seat removed from Aegis was indicated as his. Aegis told him with a wink, that while they didn't normally eat their fish friends, it appeared that a large sharkfinn died recently and was their main course. Mathew didn't reply, only smiled back.

As they were seating, he observed Aegis's daughter coming from the corridor. She wasn't in her military gear anymore but was wearing a beautiful red tinted silky gown, which with her silky silver white hair made her appear almost radiant.

"Her hair appeared to be part of the gown and she was," he thought, "the most beautiful woman he had ever seen."

She noticed Mathew was looking at her and smiled back at him, causing Mathew to look away. In a moment she took the seat between him and Aegis. She wore some kind of perfume Mathew couldn't identify but it smelled almost delicious.

Moments later, servers started bringing out dishes and offering what was on them to those seated. Aegis was the first to be served. He took liberally from the dishes offered. Mathew was next and he took a small bit from each offering. He remembered what Aegis said earlier and knew if there was any substance to what was said, then he did not need to overeat right now.

As he sampled the food taken, he found himself asking Aegis's daughter what he was eating. She laughed and began to tell him what each food item was, including the sharkfinn which was the only thing he actually identified. Mathew then asked her what her name was.

"I am Aegis' daughter, Syllium." She replied.

"A very pretty name," Mathew said, repeating it to himself. "I have never heard that one before."

"Really," she said. "Well I promise you won't soon forget it."

Mathew didn't doubt that was so.

A few hours later, he noticed the lighting was starting to dim and that, considering where he was, further increased his curiosity as to the source of their lighting. During the course of the meal and much conversation, several of the young women came by and introduced themselves, almost as if to say, I will see you later.

Mathew began to realize this was a replay of the nights he spent with the Zetans on the white continent. One of the women that spoke to him, Mathew recognized as the woman who had tried to kill him earlier. She was dressed in a purple tinted gown and like Syllium, had the silky silver white hair.

Mathew noticed she was favoring her right hand as if it was bothering her yet she carried on as if it didn't. Before she could leave Mathew reached out and took her hand. She went to jerk it away but he mind touched her. "Your hand hurts. Let me see it."

She stopped resisting and stood patiently as Mathew traced his finger over her hand stopping lightly over the small red spots his keen eyes could see.

He gave her the lightest of injections and when he had finished, released her hand. She flexed it, clenching and unclenching it, smiled and spoke to him.

"Thank you, Prince. It no longer hurts." Then she turned and walked away.

Shortly after, Aegis stood, looked over at Mathew and informed him that he was calling it a day. "Syllium will show you your room for the evening," he said.

"We will resume our talk tomorrow if the Prince is able. He paused for a moment then added. "We've lost many men recently. I'm sure you can understand."

Mathew looked after him as he walked away. He wasn't sure but somehow it seemed to Mathew that Aegis wasn't just a few years old, he was centuries old. He suspected that even that assessment might not be close. His mind was wandering as so many thoughts ran through it. The brushing of Syllium's gown against his hand as she stood up, got his attention. He stood up beside her. She looked up at him. She was a few inches shorter than he was.

"Are you ready?" She asked.

"When you are," Mathew replied.

"Good. Follow me, please."

Mathew realized he hadn't followed Aegis's departure and didn't know in which area he had reentered the reef. Syllium led him off in the opposite direction of the thrones into an area that was less well lit or had dimmed earlier. She led the way, walking briskly in front of him, her silky hair flowing behind her.

They entered a smaller archway. There was plenty of light in this corridor. They walked past numerous doors and up to the last door at the end of the corridor. Syllium opened it and indicated he was to enter. Located in the center of the room, larger than life, was a large oval bed. It was loosely covered with many colored silk clothes draped across the bed.

As he entered the room he sensed Syllium had closed the door but remained inside. She walked across the room to a bowl and lifted it off the stand it sat on. She returned to stand in front of him with the bowl.

"My lord," she said. "Take one and eat it now."

He picked one of the small objects up. It felt soft and doughy. "What is it?" he asked.

She replied. "You are but one man and there are many of us. This sponge will help you perform for each of us. It is not harmful, but don't take more than one per woman."

Mathew almost said he would manage without it but remembering the Zetans, he decided perhaps it wouldn't be a bad idea. He placed the bit of sponge in his mouth and chewed it up. He could feel it tingle in his throat as he swallowed it.

He walked over to the open archway to the left of the bed. Sure enough, there was a toilet inside as well as a shower. He noticed the shower was running and he didn't see any valves with which to cut it on or off. He stuck his hand under the water and found it to be pleasantly warm.

It was, he decided, time to take care of his toilet needs and he began removing his armor until he was down to his shorts.

First he visited the toilet and afterwards decided a quick shower wouldn't hurt either. There was something like soap and plenty of sponges for bathing. As he stepped into the shower, he sensed then felt a body next to his.

He assumed it was Syllium as she started washing his back. Soon that part was done and he turned to repay her with the same, only, it wasn't Syllium. It was the woman who had attacked him earlier.

"She's in a different mood now," he thought, as he finished washing her back sides and began on the front. She was definitely in the mood as he finished with her front side as her nipples were just about as hard as they could get. As they moved out of the shower, he realized something else was hard, then thought. "Oh well."

The woman took his hand and led him out of the bathroom to the bed. As they passed the bowl, he took another piece of the sponge and tossed it into his mouth. When they reached the bedside, he went to sit but the woman pushed him back onto the bed, following him down as he landed on his back. She wasted no time mounting him and guiding him into her.

As quickly as they mated she began to work on him, giving him no time to think about anything else. In a very short while, he had given her what she wanted and she moved off of him and Syllium took her place. He was still erect and she began just as the other had.

He wondered how long it would take for him to satisfy her and soon discovered that she wanted the pleasure as well as his seed. It took a bit longer this time and while they came together, he felt a hand on his shoulder.

There was a tap as to say look here. He glanced up. It was another woman. She held her open hand out to him. He realized she was offering him a piece of the sponge and took it from her, into his mouth.

It was obvious the sponge not only gave you an erection but gave you the strength to use it as well. After a while, he no longer tried to keep up with time and he felt Syllium shudder as she was finally satisfied and had his seed. He on the other hand, still had an erection and as Syllium moved over, the new woman took her place.

They had just begun when he felt the tap on his shoulder again. It was of course, another woman with a piece of sponge.

"No need to wonder how many," he thought. "Just have to hope my heart holds out."

Mathew had no idea how many women he had been with and it had long before moved past the point of being pleasurable. It had become simply something he had to do. At one point, there was no woman to offer him a sponge.

When the last one left, he stepped into the nearby bathroom and relieved himself then walked back into the bedroom. Curious, he looked into the adjoining room. There was a bathroom and another door. He opened that one. He only glanced into the room briefly. There were rows of beds in the room and a woman was on each one.

"So that was where they came from," he thought.

He moved back to the bed, and sat on the side of it. He was starting to get sleepy. Then a message from one of the women entered his mind. He wasn't sure which one.

"Get some rest," she said. "We will be back."

"Thanks," he replied.

"Get some rest," was the reply.

Mathew thought for a second, then standing, stepped over to the sponge bowl and took another one, chewed it up and swallowed it and made his way back to the bed. Best to be ready for later, he thought as sleep overtook him.

He wasn't sure how long he slept but sure enough, someone was in the bed with him. He rolled over. It was Syllium. She smiled and touched her finger to her lips then to his.

"Rest," she said."

Mathew smiled and went back to sleep.

Chapter 14 – On to Waardin

The Phoenix was positioned over Waardin. From the planet they likely looked like another star in the night sky but from where they were, they could see many fires burning across the planet. It looked almost as if they were looking at a giant wasteland below. They had no idea how much destruction and loss of life the Pache had caused below but it had to be pretty severe if what they could see from space was any indication.

They took a position that gave them a good view of the largest city on Waardin. It must have held over a million people at one time. There were smoldering fires all across the city. Even from here, they could see where once tall buildings were now rubble.

Logan and Commander Borne completed their plans for the initial attack on the pache positions. In a few hours, just as it was coming dawn, they would launch twenty Hawk fighters. Logan would be piloting one with a co-pilot to assist.

They were now actively radar jamming the planet to prevent them from seeing the Phoenix. They didn't know what systems the pache were using but on the off chance they did have a system that could detect them, their jammers would not allow them to see the Phoenix nor any of the Hawks once they launched towards the planet.

They picked their initial targets. Upwards of ten airports located across the planet that were being used as military bases for the pache. There was constant movement of the new fighter jets as they came and quickly departed to carry their cargos of death.

Logan wondered how things were going with Prince Mathew on Finnean but knew there was little he could do right now, no matter how things had turned out. The radio officer on Finnean had contacted them earlier to say that the communications platform had been destroyed by the pache and there were way too many dead Finns.

The Prince had gone off to make contact with them. Since the last time they communicated, the radio officer had yet to hear from the Prince. Logan suspected that Mathew was likely somewhere underwater as that was where the remaining Finns would be.

At daybreak the Hawks were launched. Each pilot had his assignment with two each assigned to the ten identified airports. They were cautioned to be mindful of the local populace as they had already suffered greatly at the hands of the pache.

Logan chose the largest airport which was near to the city they had been watching from space. He instructed his wingman to take a position near the end of the runway in cloaked mode and if any fighters got past him and off the ground, to take them out.

As he came in over the end of the largest runway, he observed dozens of the pache fighter jets taxiing to take off positions. It was apparent they planned to get another early start. Each jet had what he took to be a single bomb mounted beneath the underbelly and one smaller one mounted beneath each wing.

"Let's do this," he said to his co-pilot.

"With you, my Lord," his co-pilot replied.

Logan came in slowly above the runway. Targeting the plane nearest to him, he allowed its pilot to engage power for takeoff and as it began to move down the runway he sent a small missile straight into its nose cone. The ensuing explosion from his missile set off the three bombs the plane was carrying.

The fighter jet behind that one was forced to come around it as there was a large hole in the middle of the runway. A third fighter jet was taxiing to the other side of the destroyed jet. Logan had planned it that way. He wanted the other pilots to think that local insurgents had destroyed the first jet and then hurry up their departure to get off the ground.

The next two planes came around the burning jet, then began to accelerate for takeoff as the runway was wide enough for both to go at the same time if they were careful, Logan fired off two more missiles. So fast were those missiles they weren't even seen before they struck their targets.

In seconds there were two more explosions and now the main runway was blocked. Logan moved on past the burning jets to get access to the jets lined up behind them. Several jets were already moving to use the other runways to get into the air. One was moving past them as it roared towards the end of its runway. As it lifted up, it exploded in a massive fire ball. Still others continued to accelerate as quickly as they could to get off the ground.

Logan targeted another jet that was just lifting off a side runway with another jet practically in its wash. His missile struck the first one just behind the pilot's seat and the jets engines lifted upwards right into the path of the following jet. There was debris and fire covering the end of that runway.

Several more jets managed to get into the air via alternate runways. The other Hawk was working on those. There were so many now and some were getting a good start. The pilots of the jets still had no idea from where their attackers were coming from, only that they needed to get into the air and away from the airport if they were to live to see another day.

Pache ground troops were being mobilized onto the airport runways. There were several armored vehicles taking up positions at both ends as they tried to source out the locations of those shooting down the jets.

Logan moved into a position above the airport control tower then fired several missiles into two of the armored vehicles. His co-pilot was monitoring the radio chatter between the tower and the pilots and between the military officers in charge at the airport and their ground troops. Logan didn't want to give up the element of surprise just yet and decided they would target as many of the jets already airborne before they could drop their bombs.

It wasn't hard to locate the jet fighters. They left a trail of smoke from their engines as they burned off extra fuel putting as much distance as they could between themselves and the airbase. They were all calling on the ground troops to locate the insurgents before they were forced to return to base for more fuel.

Logan instructed the other Hawk to make one more pass over the airport and light up some of the heavy equipment rolled out to clear the runways. Then he was to pursue some of the jets already departed. Logan gave him his flight path so they wouldn't be on the same one.

Across the planet, the Hawks inflicted serious damage to the fleet of jet fighters stationed on the planet. In some few cases, mainly the smaller airports, there were no fighter jets left to fly nor were there any major ground resources remaining for the pache to use. Throughout the day, no one had a chance or opportunity to interact with the Waardins.

Logan and his flight crews stayed busy the whole day, locating and destroying jet fighters and ground vehicles where ever they found them. They didn't target any warehouses or buildings as they suspected Waardins were being forced to do maintenance or just perform upkeep for the pache and they had no idea how many they were holding hostage.

As darkness set in, they returned to the Phoenix. The Phoenix command center was monitoring all planet communications. There was considerable chatter between the pache at the various airbases but soon they began to pick up other chatter that was obviously from the Waardins.

Logan asked if the radio techs could triangulate some of the communications to give him an idea of where they might be located. Then he could attempt to make contact with them. One of the radio communications specialist told him he could make contact with one or more of them.

After a while, he was able to break in on a conversation between two men who by all indications were Waardins. They were talking about what they had seen today regarding the destruction of many of the pache war planes and equipment at a smaller airport a few hundred miles from the larger city.

The one said that following the airport attack, his small ground force engaged the remaining survivors left there and now there were none. For now, he told the other, the airport was theirs. One of the men called the other one Captain Maran.

Logan chose this moment to attempt to contact one or the other.

"Captain Maran, this is the spaceship Phoenix. Please respond."

There was silence for a while. The radio officer said he was still there as he could hear one of them breathing. Likely, he still held the comms button down.

Logan spoke again. "Captain Maran, this is Lord Logan from the spaceship Phoenix, calling. Please respond. We are the ones responsible for the destruction of the airplanes and airport equipment."

"How do I know this is not a trap?" Was the response.

"Captain Maran, all I can say is that we are here to help you destroy the pache invaders as we did on Tomarlin. It is important that we meet as we do not want to cause any needless bloodshed among your people."

The communications officer came up and handed Logan a note that gave him the location of the airport nearest to the party they thought to be Captain Maran.

"We have lost too many people to be caught in another trap. The pache are very clever as you no doubt know."

"Captain Maran. I am going to land at the airport near to where you are right now. I will be standing on the runway with no weapon in my hands. I will be there in twenty five minutes."

"How do you know where I am right now?"

"I guess if I'm right, you will find me on the airport runway. Twenty five minutes," Logan said, then walked off the bridge and headed to the hanger.

"I will need a co-pilot and two marines," he said to no one in particular.

They were waiting beside the Hawk when he got there. In less than two minutes they had completed their checks and were leaving the hanger. In ten minutes time they were hovering over the airfield the communications officer said was nearest the location of the transmissions. Logan instructed the co-pilot to scan for heat signatures in the area.

The scans found several with some movement on the opposite side of the airport and additional movement near the end of the runway. Logan guessed it was the Waardins scouting for any Pache fighters following the destruction of their planes and ground equipment earlier in the day.

He had the Hawk set down on the runway. The hatch was opened and he walked out onto the tarmac. The hatch closed as soon as he was clear and the Hawk lifted clear of the runway and took a cloaked position nearby until needed.

It was five minutes till time and Logan stood there expectantly. By all appearances, he had no weapons but then looks were deceiving. At twenty five minutes, men began to appear from both sides of the runway. Logan was forewarned. There appeared to be twenty but no indication as to who was the man in charge.

The men closed to within ten feet, their weapons trained on him. His co-pilot informed him that three other men approached from the end of the runway in a vehicle. Logan turned to face that way. In less than a minute, a vehicle, much like a small jeep pulled up. It had no lights but Logan was sure it likely had some type of night vision equipment to help them navigate.

A man stepped clear of the vehicle, then strode up to just in front of Logan. He was all military in appearance and Logan judged it wasn't just for show.

"Captain Maran, I presume."

"How did you find us?" Captain Maran asked.

"Our communications officer triangulated your radio signals and made a best guess."

"Tell me again, who you are?" the officer asked and before Logan could answer he added, "Are you responsible for the destruction of the enemy jets and other equipment here?"

Logan thought for a second then answered. "No, not at this airfield or eight others like it. Just those at the main airport near the large city about three hundred miles from here. My troops did this one and the others.

"How many men do you have, and where are they? We haven't seen any indication of forces on the ground. In fact, was it not for the explosions some of my men heard, we wouldn't even be here."

As he spoke, Logan's co-pilot alerted him that three men were approaching very slowly from the opposite side of the runway. They didn't act as if they were with this group.

Logan spoke quietly. "The three men approaching from that way," and he pointed. "Are they with you?"

A very brief exchange between the men and the captain before he stated. "This is all of us."

"Light them up," Logan instructed his co-pilot out loud.

Suddenly a very bright spot light illuminated three men who had been sneaking up on them. The light was so bright; the men could only hold their hands up to block the glare. They were all armed.

The men near Logan quickly moved towards them and seized their weapons. In just a minute, it was clear that they were locals and not Pache. They thought they were sneaking up on a group of Pache.

They all returned to stand near Logan and the Captain. Now that they were aware that something was near to them, Logan had the Hawk set down just ahead of where they stood. It was no longer cloaked.

"What kind of plane is that?" One of the men was heard to say.

"It's not a plane," another said. "It's a spaceship. It has to be. It was just hovering there all the time and we couldn't see it."

"You're very observant," Logan said to the man. "It is a Hawk fighting ship which we will use to take back your planet."

"Is that the only one?" Captain Maran asked. "They have hundreds of fighter jets and lots of ground equipment."

"No," Logan replied, "there are many more of them but in all honesty, that one could destroy all their jets. According to my pilots, we destroyed over sixty of them today as well as ground equipment.

We intend to destroy a lot more tomorrow but we need to make sure we don't harm any of your people in the process."

Chapter 15 – Freeing the Hostages

The captain turned to one of his men and asked him to contact Captain David. In a moment there was a radio conversation between the man and someone else. He handed the radio set to Captain Maran. Maran spoke to someone, then asked him what information he had as to the location of the hostages. There was a reply which Logan couldn't quite follow. Afterwards, Captain Maran turned and spoke to Logan.

"At present, they hold thousands of our people prisoners under threat of death if we attempt to attack them. I don't know what will happen after today and what you have done to their planes and equipment but I'm sure it's not good.

According to our source, the pache from the city have said they will gather up a thousand of the prisoners' tomorrow at the stadium and if we have not all surrendered by 10:00 hours, they will start mass executions."

"Can you show me this stadium you speak of?" Logan asked.

"There is no time to get there," Captain Maran stated. "Look at the time. It is only a few hours before daylight now." Then he said under his breath, "they have my family too."

"Not if you ride with me," Logan said, indicating the Hawk. He then instructed the communications officer on the Phoenix to have a team ready to depart the Phoenix in fifteen minutes. He wanted two shuttles. He wanted one to come to his present location and pick up the men here then bring them to a location they would decide soon. He wanted marines ready to land on his command as soon as he gave a location.

In minutes, Logan had Captain Maran and his radio man buckled in the Hawk and he joined the co-pilot. He left his two marines with the men on the ground. They departed the location but not before he informed the other men that a shuttle would be landing soon to pick them up.

In minutes, they were near the city. By the few lights that were on, Captain Maran gave them directions to the stadium. They set down in the parking area just outside of it. They were still cloaked so as not to attract unwanted attention. There was a pache ground vehicle parked near one of the entrances.

Captain Maran asked if they could see them. Logan informed him that they couldn't as long as the Hawk remained cloaked.

"You mean like invisible," he stated.

"Yes, like invisible," Logan replied.

Captain Maran remained quiet for a short while as Logan passed on instructions to the Shuttles and other Hawk pilots. When Logan paused from giving orders, Maran spoke again.

"Your technology is much further advanced than the pache. You give me reason to hope that with your help, we can overcome them."

"You just keep thinking that way," Logan replied. "In a few days' time, we plan on being able to hand you the keys to the city, and speaking of the city, does it have a mayor and how do you govern your people?"

"I'm not sure what a mayor is," Captain Maran replied, "but we have a city council with a council leader chosen every two years. Our government is run by governors from each province. They select one from among them to be the council leader with two beneath him just in case something should happen to him."

"Whatever works for you," Logan replied. "So where are these governors?"

"They are being held in the government's main council building. The council leader is there as well. The Pache took them as they were in session soon after they invaded us. They cannot leave and it is up to the people to see to it they are fed and looked after.

"Several have taken sick and died because the Pache refused to let them seek medical treatment. They said doctors could come to them but could not leave. The first few doctors that went there were never released to leave so others won't go there."

"And where, pray tell, is the council building," Logan asked.

As it was starting to grow light, Captain Maran pointed to a tall building not far from the stadium.

"That is the building. They occupy the upper floors. The Pache occupy the lower ones. They don't protect the top as we don't have access to it."

"You do now," Logan replied.

"Think of a safe place we can take them and I will see to it they get there. I will need a few of your men or yourself to assure them it is okay to leave."

"What do we do first?" Captain Maran asked.

"It is another three hours till 10:00 hours. How many governors are there?" Logan asked.

"At least sixty plus twenty or so assistants I'm guessing." Captain Maran told him.

"Okay," Logan said. "But first things first," as he moved to the back of the Hawk. "Let's wake up the pache in the vehicle over there."

He quickly moved down the now open ramp and trotted towards the vehicle. It appeared the men in it were resting. Best to leave them that way, he thought as he stepped up to the door. The window was open and the two men inside were fast asleep as he suspected. He saw to it they wouldn't wake up ever again, then relieved them of their weapons which he carried back to the Hawk. He had no use for them but the Waardins might have for the time being.

"What did you do?" Asked the Captain.

"It appears they will sleep their lives away," Logan replied. "Now let us move on up to the top of that building there."

They were soon hovering over the top of the building. Logan received a call from one communications officer on the Phoenix stating the Hawks were planet bound. Were there any new instructions or were they to continue as the day before? Logan informed him he needed four Hawks positioned over the large city ready for instructions but the rest could take up where they left off the day before, only he wanted them to pursue a different mode of attack on the jets.

"How do you wish them to proceed," the radio officer replied.

"Let the jets get airborne then see if the Hawks can send a directional pulse that shuts down the jets electrical system. The jet pilots would lose control and ground control for them would think it was a mechanical problem. Perhaps, they would ground the remaining if enough fell out of the sky.

"They will be there shortly," the communications officer replied, "and we will do as you suggested."

"The other four are to wait for my commands," Logan told him.

"Yes sir," was the reply.

Logan found a position on the building where the Hawk could set down. Just enough room to land and get the hatch open. They exited the Hawk and Logan walked around sizing up the available space on the building. There wasn't enough room to physically land a shuttle but if it held position, they could board through the aft hatchway.

Captain Maran walked over to the door that led to the escape stairway. It was chained off. He turned to Logan who was approaching. "I don't have anything to remove this with," he said.

Logan took the chain in his hand clenching it as he did. There was a blue glow and he opened his hand as the chain came apart and he began to unfasten it.

"How did you do that?" Captain Maran asked. "That's good chain."

"I'll tell you later, now let's see to these people inside and start moving them out."

They moved down the stairwell to the floor Captain Maran said they were located. Logan tried the first door they came to. It was not locked and he checked for guards. There were none to be seen.

Captain Maran moved down the hallway to the next door. It had a glass insert and he could see several people inside sitting around a table. He opened the door and stepped inside, his weapon at ready in case there was a guard with the group. There wasn't and one of the men spoke up.

"How did you get past the guards down below? They only allow the food deliveries."

"I didn't come from below," Maran replied. "I came from the roof."

"What good is that going to do?" Another man asked. "We can't escape that way."

"You can now," Logan said as he stood in the doorway. "We need to leave in groups of twenty five at a time and the sooner the better."

"Leave to where?" another man asked as he stood up.

He was obviously ready and willing but unsure where and how they were going.

Logan took that moment to speak to his co-pilot. "Have the shuttle hover near the Hawk with room enough for us to load it from the rear. Send Captain Marans men down the stairs to help us move the people out. We'll be there shortly."

He turned to Captain Maran, instructing him to start moving the people up to the roof. His co-pilot would meet them and board twenty five at a time onto the shuttle. He was to send his men to collect the rest of the people in the building but they were to try and avoid alerting the pache.

Moments later, the soldiers were coming down the stairs and Captain Maran began giving orders as to where they were to go while he continued to urge the governors up the stairs. As they exited the door on the upper deck, they were directed to the shuttle.

Soon there were twenty five inside and with the door shut, the shuttle lifted off and was away to the small airfield they had been at earlier. It was decided that was the safest place for the moment.

In a few minutes the shuttle landed. They offloaded twenty three governors and two soldiers who had been given guard detail for the governors. The shuttle departed as soon as the last person was off and the aft door shut.

Soon, all the governors as well as their assistants were up on the roof waiting their turn to depart. The shuttle returned, loaded up and departed again. It would take two more trips to get them all off. While they were getting the men and women onto the roof, there was a disturbance as several people entered the floor they had occupied.

The pache guards opened the door for them to enter, not taking the time to check on those inside. They were bringing the governors breakfast and lunch meals. This had become a routine which was likely why they didn't think to check inside as they let them in.

As the two women and one man entered the hallway, they called out to someone to let them know they were there; only that person was not there, just the soldiers guarding the rear as the governors departed. As they moved their cart down the hallway, one of the soldiers stepped out and spoke.

"Just keep coming," he said, "and be quick about it."

Startled, one of the women jumped back. "Oh," she said, "who are you," then realized it was one of their soldiers.

"How did you get in here," she said a little quieter. The others just looked on.

"No time for questions and answers," he replied. "Let's get this food up to the top and you three will have to leave with us."

"Leave where?" The man with the group said as he looked around. "Where can you go from up there and where is everybody?"

"They're upstairs, now come on, get a move on, we don't have all day."

Another soldier joined them and helped them gather up the food as they made their way up the stairs.

By now, the shuttle was picking up for its third run. Logan was giving instructions to two of the Hawk pilots to monitor all movements to the stadium. The other two was to take up positions to be ready to destroy any pache equipment moving towards the stadium that wasn't hauling people.

Logan asked the man with the two women how long before the Pache would check on them. The man replied that they generally allowed them about ten or fifteen minutes. It always depended on which ones were on duty.

In a few minutes, the shuttle was back. The remaining people were loaded up including the three with the food. That would come in handy, Logan told Captain Maran. As the shuttle lifted up and away, Logan refastened the chain on the door.

"Let the pache figure this one out," he thought. He instructed his co-pilot to take them over to the stadium as there should be some activity over there by now.

Sure enough, as they approached the stadium, he could see large vehicles unloading people at the entrance and herding them inside. He called the shuttle and told him to load up the captain and his men and head back to the stadium.

He was looking at their options for getting into the stadium and taking up positions that wouldn't alert the pache. He requested the other shuttle from the Phoenix with the Marines proceed to the stadium and standby for his instructions.

Commander Borne spoke to him via his Hawk communicator telling him they were loading now and the Phoenix was standing by to assist as needed. Logan said he would get back to him as soon as he had some targets pinpointed. He hated to destroy anything the Waardins could use later but this was war and you couldn't always afford the luxury of being able to pick and choose your targets.

Chapter 16 – The Retaking of Finnean

Mathew felt something touching his face. For a moment he thought he was in his bed at the palace and it was Alexis teasing him as she so often did, then his mind reminded him he was in a different bed on a different planet. He opened his eyes and found himself looking into Sylliums eyes. She was smiling as she lightly stroked his forehead and face with a bit of silk cloth.

Time to wake up," she said. "You have work to do."

"I do," Mathew replied. "Okay, but bathroom first," as he went to get out of the bed.

"Don't forget the sponge," Syllium said laughingly.

"How could I," Mathew replied. "You girls hand them out like candy."

He picked up one from the bowl as he went into the bathroom, observing as he did that the bowl had been refilled since the last time he had passed by it.

Soon after, he had taken care of his personal needs and even taken a moment to rinse off in the never ending shower, as he thought of it. By the time he got back to the bed, he was feeling a rise below and she was simply smiling and finding a comfortable spot.

As she was the first, this time, it didn't take long before he was spent. She got up but instead of leaving went over to the bowl and took another piece of sponge, then came back to the bed. He took the sponge as she crawled on top of him.

"We're not done," she said as she positioned herself above him and began a slow movement that was, he knew, designed to give her the most pleasure.

It didn't take long coupled with the earlier session for her to start getting where she wanted to be. She began to work faster and harder and suddenly she was like jelly, quivering and slowing down so she could get off. Mathew surprised her by rolling her over and taking the top position and control of her. He began to give her more than she had bargained for as she struggled to get free. In seconds, she couldn't stand anymore and passed out into a deep sleep.

Well, she asked for it, he thought as he pulled her over to the side of the bed. He walked over to the bowl and took a few more pieces of the sponge. Sitting on the bed, he wondered when the others would begin to show up. He didn't have to wait long. The door to the bathroom opened and another girl came in.

"Oh, she is still here," she said.

"Come on," Mathew replied.

"She is sleeping and will be for a while."

"Sleeping," she said with a giggle. "What did you do to her?"

"Only what she asked for," Mathew replied. "You should be careful what you ask for. Sometimes, it is more than you can handle."

"I'll remember that," the girl said as she lay down beside Mathew.

He didn't waste any time with her as they came together. She was ready to quit as soon as he had given her the seed.

"I'll send another," she said as she left the bed.

Mathew reached under the pile of silk that served as a pillow and took another sponge. Beats going back and forth to the bowl, he thought. Before long, the day was half done, all the girls had been in his bed and Syllium still slept but more importantly, he was getting hungry.

He lay beside Syllium. Taking his finger, he traced around her face, then down her chin and neck. He let his finger trace down between her breasts. She was smiling yet still asleep. As he traced around her breasts and then around the nipples, she started breathing heavy yet she was still asleep. Suddenly, she sat up.

She sat there, breathing heavy, then looked at him. "What did you do to me?" She whispered.

"Just what you asked for," he said.

"But it has never been like that before," she said.

"I guess it depends on how far you are willing to go," Mathew replied.

"I need to go now so the others can come in," she said as she scooted to the edge of the bed.

"You're a little late," Mathew replied. "The other girls have all come and gone."

"While I was lying there asleep. Oh, I will never hear the end of this," she muttered.

Mathew stood beside the bed. She looked at him, then at him again.

"You're still ready, aren't you," she said.

"It appears," he said, "that the last sponge has not yet worn off" and she reached for him as he spoke, laying back onto the bed and pulling him down onto her.

As soon as they started, she began to quiver. Mathew knew her female senses were at their highest now. He was slow and gentle but even then, it was only a few moments before she had reached her high point. Fortunately for her, Mathew had too.

They lay together for a few minutes. She didn't want him to move. Any movement at all simply coursed through her body causing sensations she had never felt before and it was almost painful it felt so good. Mathew knew what her problem was but he couldn't fix it. The only option was to separate or wait.

He told her to hold on to him and then he rolled over onto his side. Slowly, he withdrew from her and that was that. After a moment, he got up and went to the shower while she went off her own way.

As he washed off, he thought or rather he hoped the sessions were over. Things were getting too personal and he had other things to do. He finished his shower and began putting on his armor as that was all he had to wear. He heard a sound at the door and turned to find Reenae, the girl who had wanted to kill him the day before, standing at the door.

She had in her hands, a robe similar to what the Aegis wore.

"Put this on," she said. "You can wear the armor later when you go back to land."

"Thank you," Mathew replied as he took the robe. He removed the armor and put on the robe. He was glad to see it fit remarkably well.

"If you are hungry, follow me," she said. "They have set out some food for us. Afterwards, you and Aegis can talk."

They left the room and walked down the corridor. Mathew realized she still had the purple tinted gown on. He wondered if that was normal wear here or for occasions. They exited the corridor and walked through the small arch that was now well lit. In a moment they were back into the courtyard. He could smell and see platters of food as many others were gathered around taking what they wanted.

There were small shell dishes to eat off of and fresh water to drink. As he moved nearer to the food he noticed that some of the women he thought he remembered from the night before were dressed in the leathers while others still had on the silk like gowns.

He picked up a shell dish and began to place a few items on it. Mostly those he remembered from the night before. About the time he thought he had selected enough for the moment, he observed Aegis walking towards him. He too carried a small shell dish with food on it. As he drew near, he spoke to Mathew.

"Walk with me, Prince. We can converse while we eat."

Mathew joined him and they walked towards the area he referred to as the thrones. As they went, Aegis asked him how his evening had been. Not sure how he should answer the question, Mathew replied.

"Pretty busy, would be accurate. I hope that I have satisfied everyone's needs. Mine certainly have been."

Aegis laughed, then directed him to one of the throne seats. As they sat, he spoke.

"I am told that a few of the women need your attention just a little bit longer but at least one has said she has had enough for now to last a long time."

Mathew knew whom he was talking about but he chose to change the subject.

"Have you been here a long time, Aegis?"

Aegis grinned then looked at Mathew.

"I suspect you have two questions and I will answer both. I have been here a few thousand years and yes, I can still father children and still do but the women you slept with are all my daughters. They require another man's seed as you are no doubt aware."

He looked at Mathew a few seconds and then followed with another statement.

"No, I don't know how long I will live but life here is good and I cannot find fault with it and to answer the question you have not thought to ask. I was once a Shadow Prince. You might consider this my reward for my work."

Mathew could think of nothing else to say or ask. At that moment a male and female came forward.

"Sire," they said. "There is some kind of ship outside the reef entrance. There are two humans inside it. They appear to be waiting on something."

It was at that very moment that Mathew heard the call on his communicator. "Prince Mathew, can you hear us." To the surprise of those around him, he spoke back to someone they couldn't see.

"Yes, I am here inside the reef."

"You are okay, then."

"Yes, I am okay. How goes the battle."

"It has been pretty one sided so far. It appears they pulled most of their people off and took them to Waardin. They left a small contingent here.

"After we destroyed all their equipment and the remaining warriors they left behind, we went through the few documents we were able to locate and the messages they received indicated that they no longer considered Finnean a threat and planned to come back to set up more permanent bases after they finished on Waardin.

"We have been unable to locate any other Pache. We have flown over most of the planet till now and it appears our job here is pretty much done. How goes yours?"

"It appears I will be down here at least one more day," Mathew replied. "Set up a new base camp near the shore by the inlet. See if anything can be done as far as repairs to the communications platform. You will find my armored cape beneath the back side of it."

"We already found it, sir. We were able to locate you by tracking your communicator's locator. We will do as you command and set up near the beach. Do you want us to come back for you or will you return on your own?"

"I will return on my own," Mathew replied, "and thanks to all of you for a job very well done."

"Thank you, sir. We return to the shore now."

"I got most of that," Aegis said as the others looked on.

"Am I to understand that the pache forces on the beach have all been destroyed? All of them?"

"That's what I am told," Mathew replied. "They didn't have many people here apparently but it was enough to do some serious damage to your people. My people will set up near the beach and attempt to repair the communications platform. If they cannot fix it, someone will return that can."

"Fair enough," Aegis said. "We still have much to discuss once you're finished eating."

Mathew said he was for now and the two of them headed off to the smaller room they had discussed so much in the previous day.

They remained there for the rest of the day until Syllium came to the door to say that the evening meal was ready. Aegis thanked her and told her they would be there soon. She smiled at Mathew then turned and left.

After a half hour, they entered the courtyard. Just as the evening before, there was light music in the background and plenty of well dressed women and a few men. Mathew felt really bad that he hadn't arrived sooner to stop the slaughter of the Finns. Aegis must have sensed his thoughts as he spoke directly to Mathew.

"We do not control our own destinies although we like to think we do. You could no more stop what happened here as I could. While I am now blessed with a long and productive life, I am no longer as an immortal and can be killed. That in itself only lasts until the next Shadow Prince arrives.

For some reason, they all come through here sooner or later, even if just for a few minutes. It is like the moth drawn to the light. Tomorrow you will know the reason for it. I am just glad I can help and perhaps it is why I am still here."

"Perhaps you are right," Mathew replied, "but I have always felt that in some way or another we do control our own destinies and right or wrong, I will continue for as long as I live to think that way. Now, what say we have something to eat as I am feeling pretty hungry right now."

Aegis laughed, then led the way to the food. As they were filling their shell platters, he reminded Mathew that it was best not to overeat.

"Your night will be long, young prince."

Mathew didn't even bother to answer. He withdrew his hand from the platter before him, looked down at what he had and decided that would be enough. Aegis just grinned and pointed at a place close by where they could sit.

All throughout the meal, the women would stop by for just a moment to say hello to both of them. Most carried on a brief conversation with Aegis while they managed to stand close to Mathew at the same time.

Each one had a different aroma and Mathew was sure he recognized the smell even if not the woman. As they left, they made sure their gowns brushed against Mathew.

"It was beginning to appear like a ritual," Mathew thought.

Before long, it was evening again. The lights were dimming and once again, Aegis stood and said he was calling it a day. The woman Reenae was standing nearby and walked over offering her arm. Mathew didn't have to be told twice to know it was time.

As they walked through the arch and down the corridor to the door at the end, Mathew observed that all the women in gowns had left the courtyard. One was so easily distracted by all the beauty around him that he often missed the little details. Something he needed to remember in the future as it might not come with benefits like this time had.

The night was long, just as Aegis had foretold. There were many participants and a lot of sponges were consumed. It was well past midnight before the women began to taper off. He knew Reenae had been with him twice and a few others he remembered from their perfume had been there more than once as well.

As he was sitting on the edge of the bed, he thought, well I hope I have taken care of everyone that needs it. He went into the bathroom. He was intrigued by the never ending shower. After taking care of his toilet needs, he stood in the shower for several minutes. He was reaching for a sponge when he felt one on his back. At first, he wondered which woman it was, as he could not smell an identifying odor. Then he felt the finger tracing his neck and around to his cheek and he knew who it was. He turned to face Syllium.

"I thought you said you had enough," he said with a smile.

Taking the sponge from her and beginning on her front side since she faced him. She didn't answer right away. She allowed him to wash her front then before she turned around she reached for his mouth. He saw the sponge and accepted it. Then she turned to offer her back. When he was finished she turned and taking his hands, led him back to the bed. As she lay back pulling him down towards her, she spoke. "I said you would never forget me and now I'm making sure you don't"

Mathew awoke hours later. She lay sound asleep beside him. He rose and showered then put on his armor. When he left the room, she was still sleeping, and her silky white hair only accentuated the smile on her face.

When Mathew walked into the courtyard, Aegis was standing there. "I have two things for you, Shadow Prince." He held in one hand a small pill like object. In the other, he had a small silk bag. He handed the pill to Mathew.

"Swallow it," he commanded. "Do not bite into it."

Mathew did as Aegis instructed. He couldn't see that it made a difference but the evening before, Aegis had spoken of the pills of life. He said Mathew would need to take one before he left and he would explain what the other was for just before he did leave. Two Finns approached and Aegis told him they would assist him in getting to shore. Mathew thanked him for his help and all the information he had given him.

"You thank me now, Prince but maybe later, you will curse me. And who knows, perhaps someday, you will return. If for no other reason than to see your offspring and," he said laughingly, "perhaps their mothers."

Mathew turned to go and Aegis spoke.

"Forget not this, young prince," and he held up the small silk bag. This is the other pill of life. It is for the one you love. You will be separated many times for long periods. While this won't keep her safe, it will give her long life while she awaits your return.

I wish we had some for the children but there are just so many and they have to be saved for the ones that need it the most. Go, my friend. I will look forward to your return some day, as will another.

Mathew donned his head gear and began to follow the two Finns to deeper water. As the water reached to his shoulders, he turned to look back. There in her leathers, was Syllium. She raised her hand to her lips and smiled. Mathew raised his armored hand to his, then pointed at her before diving forward into the water.

The Finns each took a forearm and began to move rapidly towards the shore some distance away. In less than thirty minutes, Mathew was walking out of the water towards the beach. His co-pilot stood watching as he stepped out of the water onto shore.

"I trust all is well with the Finns, now," he said.

"Yes," Mathew replied. "I believe it is for now."

Chapter 17 –The Retaking of Waardin

Logan looked on as the pache trucks drove up and unloaded their human cargo. Before long, by his estimate, they had delivered at least eight hundred people to the stadium. Several times, he witnessed scenes of brutality as many were prodded and kicked as they made their way inside. He didn't doubt that if they didn't intervene soon, this day was going to end in bloodshed for the Waardin citizens in the stadium.

He was looking for some way they could develop an element of surprise and in a few minutes he discovered it. On the back side of the stadium was an access corridor that allowed the stadium goers to move freely beneath the seating areas down to the toilets and vending areas. It appeared the pache were ignoring this area as they thought they had control of all the people out on the stadium field.

Logan immediately instructed the incoming shuttle with marines come to the backside of the stadium in cloaked mode. The shuttle could only get so close but by lowering the aft ramp, the marines were able to leap across a short gap and enter the stadium just below the highest seating section.

Logan instructed the marines to spread out and take positions where they could fire upon the pache before they could fire upon their hostages. Due to the distance involved, some would be using hand held e-displacer splinter guns. It was regrettable they didn't have the longer range assassins' weapons.

As the morning dragged on and 10:00 hours arrived, there was no indication as to what the pache were going to do. There were several different pache involved in conversations with others via radio and other communications devices.

No doubt, they were getting updates on fighter jets falling out of the sky, but they couldn't figure any way to blame the Waardins for it. At one point, there appeared to be an argument between two groups of pache. Logan watched as there was shouting and pushing and then the one group charged over to the hostages who had been forced to stand the whole time.

Logan, sensing something was fixing to happen, instructed one Hawk to take position on the opposite end of the stadiums field from him. "If anything starts to happen, take offensive action against any and all the pache you can target," he ordered.

He ordered another Hawk to take a position that would prevent any other pache from entering the stadium once things started happening. He hoped to be able to catch them off guard and then free the hostages but it looked like that was going to be a long shot.

As he watched, the pache soldiers began seizing individual hostages, dragging them away from the crowd and forcing them onto their knees. It was obvious to Logan it was time to act.

"Engage," he ordered the marines. "Use extreme measures, now."

Immediately there was a change in the action in the stadium as some marines moved onto the field and others took positions above it. You could not hear anything as the e-displacer made no sound.

As the pache soldiers began to drop to the ground from no immediately visible cause, some of them observed the approaching marines. They moved to engage with them, but it was too late as the marines were far too quick and ready, not to mention the fact that all the marines wore body armor.

Outside the stadium, the second shuttle offloaded the rebels and the few marines accompanying them. They engaged the pache foot soldiers, while the Hawks destroyed the trucks and armored vehicles. Most of the pache had been loitering outside as if this was just another day with no thought to the next minute unless someone gave them orders.

Today, those orders would not be forthcoming. In thirty seconds time, there were no living pache outside the stadium. As the few on the inside were cut down by the marines, many in the crowd of hostages decided to make a run for it.

Unfortunately, this gave many of the pache some cover from the marines and a few of them used their final moments targeting anyone around them. Dozens of hostages were wounded before the marines could bring the remaining pache soldiers down.

Logan had little leeway to fire on those inside with his heavier weapons. It was the same for the other Hawk pilot. In a few minutes the marines had cleaned the site of pache. None remained alive and now they could attend to the wounded hostages. Several received serious wounds.

The marines wasted no time calling in a shuttle and loading them onto it. Logan landed inside the stadium. The other Hawks maintained watch. As soon as the worst cases were onboard the shuttle, it left the stadium and headed to the Phoenix.

Logan received a message from one of the Hawk pilots outside the stadium. A large force of vehicles was headed their way and they were pache. Logan instructed him and the other pilots to coordinate an attack on the front and back of the convoy.

"Eliminate the threat," he said, "but let one vehicle escape."

Far off in the distance, Logan could hear a roaring sound. Not sure what it was, he asked one of the Hawks to check it out. Seconds later, he got his answer. The pilot informed him a rocket ship had launched and was now entering the planets outer atmosphere. Logan knew it wasn't one of theirs, so he asked his co-pilot to ask the Phoenix if they could target and take it down.

Soon after, the co-pilot informed him that the Phoenix was tracking the rocket. Seconds later, he reported the Phoenix had launched a missile to track and destroy it. Moments later, he advised Logan the target had been eliminated.

"Good job," Logan replied. "Let's make sure this is a one way trip for the pache."

The firefight outside the stadium resulted in a mass of vehicles on fire with pache bodies scattered all over the streets. It's a sad sight, Logan thought but then they brought it on themselves.

He sent his Hawks to follow the one vehicle they allowed to escape. He hoped it would take them to their base. Soon after, they were rewarded as about thirty miles outside the city was a massive base, with troop barracks and equipment.

It was about a mile across and well dug in. A massive operation and a big target for the Phoenix, once they confirmed the base coordinates.

He ordered the Hawk to send up the base coordinates to the Phoenix but advised against any action until after he had met with the Waardins. He was concerned that they might have a lot of Waardin slave labor at the camp.

The Hawks were instructed to keep a close watch on the base as Logan expected reinforcements to be sent to the city. It was not long before his assessment was correct as a larger contingent was being formed with heavier equipment and more men. The convoy hadn't yet left the base but his pilots reported that there was a lot of activity within the base.

Logan made a quick trip to the airbase where the governors were standing by. He wanted a quick meeting with them and Captain Maran. As soon as he arrived, they were ready to meet, having been alerted by his people there that he was coming. His first question was as to the status of their people that might be at the Pache main base. The senior councilor came forward and stated.

"We know they have a base but we have never been able to locate it."

Logan informed him that they had located a large base about thirty miles outside of the city. His concern was for any Waardin hostages that might be on the base.

The councilor advised him that he was not aware of any Waardins being kept on any bases and he thought the destruction of the base far outweighed the loss of a few Waardin lives when compared with how many they had lost because of the base.

"Give us a moment to decide," the councilor requested of Logan.

Logan asked Captain Maran if he could contact other rebel groups and see if they would consolidate their forces once his forces located the other pache bases. Maran told him they had remained separate till now to prevent the loss of more rebel lives by sudden attacks from the pache but with the help of Logan's marines, they would be able to band together and take back their cities and the planet. While they discussed strategy, the senior Councilor returned to inform Logan of their decision.

"We believe the total destruction of this base is in all our best interests. Across the planet, the Pache are stretched pretty thin now and your arrival has already begun to have a major effect on their ability to launch attacks on us. Perhaps it's the element of surprise as we have been unable to maintain a drawn out campaign against them."

He spoke further about the war and the pache having the advantage of air power with their war planes. The Waardin had an air force before the pache arrived but they were able to mount an attack on all of our bases planet wide and we no longer have that ability. Even our space vehicles were destroyed with the exception of those they chose to use themselves.

That has been difficult for them as our pilots have all gone into hiding and aligned themselves with the various rebel forces. They have been unable to master all of our space vehicle flight controls. They're earlier attempts resulted in many crashes and the loss of their pilots.

"Then, with your blessings, we will start a campaign to totally destroy their bases as we find them," Logan stated, "but if you learn of any significant numbers of your people being held at any of these bases, you must let us know.

"When we strike the bases, we will be doing so with low yield solar pulse missiles from our ship in space. They are designed to kill people with minimal damage to infrastructure. Normally, we wouldn't even consider using this type of weapon but in this case, against the pache, we have no second thoughts on the matter."

When they finished talking, Logan contacted the communications officer on the Phoenix, requesting Commander Borne speak with him. Once the commander was on line with him, he passed on the information regarding the Waardin governor's agreement to authorize the strikes against the pache bases using the solar pulse missiles.

The commander informed him that they had just finished preparing the first missile with the solar pulse warhead. It had taken some modifications to their normal weaponry to prepare this one as it wasn't part of their normal arsenal.

"It would be ready to fire within the next hour and we have the base coordinates for the first missile."

Logan asked that the Phoenix advise him as soon as they launched the missile as he wanted to do a fly over soon after the missile impacted the base.

"I would wait at least a half hour," the commander advised.

"I will do as you suggest," Logan replied.

"One more thing," Commander Borne stated. "Prince Mathew has informed us that there are no pache left on Finnean. There was only a small force there and they have all been eliminated. He is eager to rejoin us as soon as we can get close enough for their Hawks to meet us."

Logan thought for a minute, then replied. "As soon as we have eliminated a few of the pache bases here, I'm sure you'll be able to leave long enough to rendezvous with him. We could use some more firepower here. Please pass that on to the Prince."

"As you wish, Lord Logan," the commander replied.

As Logan waited for word of the missile launch, he ordered the Hawks near to the base to pull back at least three miles to avoid any effects from the incoming missile strike. He observed the Waardin governors were having a session together on the airport runway.

There was plenty of open discussion, and on occasion one or two of the men began to shout and disagree verbally with what was being discussed. Logan wasn't close enough to hear what they were saying but at some point, the ones most agitated appeared to calm down and they all came to some kind of agreement.

Logan looked on as three men approached him. He noted that one of them was the senior counselor. The first man to speak introduced himself as the governor's council.

"Lord Logan," he said, introducing himself and the others. "I have been asked to petition you in regards to the ongoing destruction of the pache bases and the soldiers. We do not doubt that with your superior firepower and that of your ship in space, you will soon have the pache subdued and we realize that because of their crimes against us and others that you have taken the position that they should all be destroyed."

He paused for a moment then continued.

"Lord Logan, many of us at one time or another have had encounters with several of the solders including their officers. Yes, we agree that many have committed unspeakable crimes against us but we would also like to say that many of the soldiers are young boys and men who don't want to be here and have resisted participating in the killings some of the older men have carried out.

"We are asking you to develop some kind of campaign that will give those boys and men a chance to surrender to your forces. They can be moved to secure areas until you can arrange their transfer back to your planet, if in fact that is where they want to go. If they can prove their worth and wish to remain here, we won't object to that either but they should know that if they choose to stay, they will be on probation and subject to restrictions for many years."

Logan was impressed by the offer of forgiveness these men had presented to him for many of the pache on their planet. He well knew that there were conscripts who were here against their will as that had been the way of the former ruling family.

He had even been told this by the pache military officers on Bara. He hadn't brought this up to the Waardins before now as he didn't believe it was his place to do so and he was glad they had presented him with options going forward.

"Lord Logan," he heard over his communications set. He recognized it as the communications officer from the Phoenix.

"Logan here," he replied. "Go ahead."

"Missile launched," was the reply. "Missile launched and on the way to the coordinates provided."

Logan turned to the men he had been talking to. "Gentlemen, I have room for three passengers. Would any you care to come with me to witness the destruction of the base near here? We will watch from a safe distance, then afterwards we can enter the base if you choose or just do a flyover."

The three men agreed and once they were seated and fastened in the Hawk, they lifted off and moved a few miles closer to the base. Logan knew the missile would be arriving at any moment. He gained altitude until he felt they could see what was about to happen. The base was a scar on the landscape before them. The senior councilor asked where the missile was.

Logan told him and the others it was moving too fast for them to see it but if they would watch the base far ahead of them, they would see its impact.

As they watched, there was a flash and it was like a giant wrinkle of air hit the base. It was in fact the shockwave from the solar pulse explosion. It struck pretty near the middle of the base and the wave carried on well past the base's perimeter before it seemed to break up and dissipate.

They were too far away to see its physical impact on the ground and those near to it. Logan told them they would be able to over fly the location in thirty minutes.

After thirty minutes, Logan began to move closer to the base. As they drew closer, they could see the convoy that reached outside the base on the road that ran through it. Where they could see bodies, they were just lying around the vehicles or in rows as if they had been mustered in ranks before boarding their vehicles with many more still inside the vehicles.

The only physical damage to infrastructure was that nearest the impact point. Some overturned vehicles, some tents with their covers pushed flat but the most revealing thing was all the bodies lying all through the base.

One man said it was incredible and terrible to see at the same time. Logan did not attempt to land the Hawk. From where they were, the number of dead told him all he needed to know. Logan ordered another Hawk to fly over, taking photos of the base.

They will be used on flyers we will be dropping onto the other bases after today, he told the pilot. He instructed him to take the photos back to the Phoenix for printing. He contacted the Phoenix to request the photos be processed upon arrival with a message printed on the front and back of each. They were to be mass dropped on the remaining pache bases overnight.

By late evening, the Hawks on missions had returned. They reported good success in creating the pulses that effectively shut down the jets in flight, causing many to just drop out of the sky when they lost power. Many of the pilots bailed out but others fought to keep the planes aloft until it was too late.

Eventually, the pilots refused to take to the skies. As the Hawks returned to the Phoenix for the evening, they were prepared for night action. Cases of boxes with the flyers were placed in the Hawks to be dumped out over the bases. Some were to be dumped out over the cities and anywhere pache soldiers might be located.

Two shuttle loads of rebels and marines were taken to the base where the personnel had been killed by the solar pulse explosion. The rebel soldiers and marines were there to move the bodies and take possession of the base. Everything was just as if the dead were still living or coming back. Food laid out, gear and equipment ready for use all around the base.

Communication devices were found to be open with incoming calls going unanswered from other bases. Logan attended the base and assigned several of his marines to take the calls and inform the parties on the other end of the call that this base had fallen to the Waardin with no survivors remaining.

They were told on numerous occasions that what they spoke of wasn't possible. The marines advised the person on the other end of the call to be on the lookout for photo proof in the coming hours.

Overnight between 10:00 pm and 02:00 a.m. the Hawks distributed the flyers to the remaining airfields and any bases they had discovered during the two day assault on the pache.

The flyers told them what the pictures depicted of the now overtaken base outside the city. What had happened to the soldiers there and what was expected of them. No planes were to be in the air or they would be shot down or disabled so they couldn't fly. No convoys of military vehicles were to depart the bases without permission.

Logan managed to get the Phoenix to download pictures of the now destroyed royal palace on Bara to let the soldiers know they were fighting a war for a government that no longer existed. There could not be and would not be any rewards for what they were doing aside from death if they didn't surrender.

By 10:00 hours the next morning, the bases that could, were in contact with the marines at the former base requesting more information regarding the fall of the former Pache government and what they could expect if they surrendered.

Logan had already informed the marines to tell them if they laid down their arms and surrendered as instructed, they would be provided with shelter at one base or another and then as quickly as it could be arranged, be given transport back to Bara.

They were also informed that the Waardins would allow those that chose to do so, to remain there on the planet as long as they intended to be law abiding productive citizens.

By 14:00 hours that day, all the bases they had discovered were flying the white flag of surrender. Flyovers by Hawks revealed weapons stacked in the back of transport vehicles and men gathered around waiting for further instructions. On one occasion a fighter jet took off but when the pilot saw a Hawk fighter just off the end of his wing tips, he lowered his flaps and came around for a landing.

He was not carrying any bombs and they learned later he had been ordered to take off against his better judgment by a superior office who wanted to see what type of response he would get. Lucky for him, the Hawks weren't shooting first and asking questions later.

Chapter 18 – Salt Water Lizards

With the pending surrender of the entire Pache contingent on Waardin, the Phoenix had not had time to meet Prince Mathew near enough to Finnean for his squad to rejoin it. They were instructed to stay put.

Mathew used the time to do some flyovers of Finnean. He wanted to learn more about the planet just in case it became important to know later on. Earlier, he asked Aegis if there were other Finns across the oceans on the planet. Aegis said he wasn't aware of any others but he certainly couldn't rule it out.

Mathew used two Hawks to start photo mapping the continents. Both Hawks flying an east to west flight pattern and then one Hawk moving closer south while the other moved closer north and continued their flight paths. The remaining Hawk maintained an alert status in case any of the Hawks encountered any problems.

They found deserts and mountains and massive forests. There were the usual forest animals as well as a few in the deserts and mountains. They saw rat like creatures, large and small lizards and of course numerous bird species. There was horse like creatures as well as those similar to cattle and sheep on the plains. They never once encountered any overly large beasts.

There were also some very large fresh water lakes that eventually ran to the sea. The poles were uniform and there was a lot of land mass surrounding them which aided in preventing the melting of the ice caps. There was some melting and the water flowed from the ice caps to the lakes and on into the sea.

As they continued the photo mapping, they remained in cloaked mode. They wanted to make sure if they did encounter any humanoid life forms they didn't send them running for the hills or down into the water depths.

Mathew and his co-pilot were a thousand miles from their base camp when they came upon another river entering the sea. One side was bordered by a high steppe or cliff that extended out into the small bay. As they crossed over the beach area near the mouth of the river, they observed a small settlement of Finns or rather a small settlement on the beach that was being used by Finns.

Mathew was curious as to why these Finns didn't live underwater but mainly used the water to keep them alive and spent equal time on the beach. He noticed that the few men and women were very gaunt and ragged as if their diet was poor.

They definitely needed help but he didn't want to rush in until he had spoken with Aegis. He knew he needed to know more before he approached them and decided to go back to the reef and speak with Aegis.

It was late evening when they positioned the Hawk above the waters above the reef. Mathew now wore flippers he had not carried with him before. With them strapped on, he exited off the ramp. He didn't use a skimmer as they were okay to a certain depth but this would likely tax its limitations. The Hawk maintained its position for a short while then moved back to the base camp.

Mathew swam steadily down towards the reef. In the distance he could see some Finns coming and going. Soon, several spotted him and swam to meet him. They instantly recognized him when they got closer. No doubt they were letting the others know he was back.

Two swam up to him, a male and female and offered to take his arms and help him down to the reef. Mathew held his arms out and each took him by a forearm and began swimming down to the reef. Mathew was able to make a difference this time with his flippers and they moved rapidly through the water.

The assisted Mathew as far as the shallower water inside the reef opening then signaled they were returning outside. Mathew waved at them and continued onward. Soon, he was walking up to the stones that separated the water from the courtyard.

At first there was no one in sight but after a few minutes, Aegis and Syllium could be seen coming out of the reef quarters and into the courtyard. Mathew removed his head gear and awaited their arrival. A few others came through but did not hang around. It was, Mathew thought, business as usual. He was not the special guest any longer. That was okay with him.

As Aegis walked up, he greeted Mathew, then asked to what they owed his visit. Syllium only stood there as if of stone while the two talked. She was, Mathew noticed, as pretty in the leathers or whatever they were, as she was in the silks, but back to business and he returned Aegis' greetings with one of his own but included Syllium.

"Sire," he said, "while I've been waiting to meet up with the spaceship, we have been mapping the continents just so we have an idea of what is there."

"And did you find anything aside from the rats, lizards and larger four legged animals," Aegis asked, "oh and let us not forget the birds."

"That is why I am here," Mathew replied. "We discovered a small settlement of Finns living about a thousand miles up the coast near the mouth of a river." They appear to be living on the beach and spending enough time in the water to provide what they require for their bodies.

We didn't spend a lot of time there as I wanted to confer with you regarding this." They did not see us as I did not want to panic them."

"Did you get any kind of count on them," Aegis asked.

"From what we could see, maybe twenty or so and we did not see any children and everyone we saw looked really gaunt and poor as if they had a very poor diet."

"Was it open accessible beach or rocks or cliffs," Aegis questioned.

"One side, the side across the river and our side, was blocked by high cliffs that ran out into the water. They had the river and the inlet. It would require them a long trek to get around the cliffs to the other side. Maybe too long for them to be out of the water, but couldn't they swim around it?" Mathew asked.

"What you have described is the perfect habitat for the large killer sharkfinns and salt water lizard. It is likely they are unable to venture long in the water and so they live there, kind of like prisoners to the beasts, unable to venture too far for fear of dying out of the water or dying in it.

"I can bring them out, sire, but we would likely need someone to come with us to help prevent panic among them."

A very good plan, Prince," Aegis stated and then suggested they take Syllium with them so she could help persuade them that you meant no harm. It was agreed they would go in the morning.

Mathew noticed that food was being brought out near the serving area and it reminded him that he had not eaten since early morning. He felt his stomach rumble.

"Would you join us for a meal?" Aegis asked, adding. "It would probably be easier if you spent the night and got an early start in the morning."

"Thank you, Sire," Mathew replied. "You are right. It would be easier if it is not too much trouble for you."

"No trouble at all, he replied, except that we will have to make other sleeping arrangements for you tonight as tonight is the children's story night. We use the big bedroom to gather them in and read stories to them and when they fall asleep, we just shift them around and tuck them in.

"No problem, Sire. I will gladly sleep here in the courtyard if it is okay with you."

"Nonsense," Aegis replied. "I'm sure Syllium will find a place for you," and then with a chuckle, said, "let's eat."

Mathew looked at Syllium as Aegis walked over to the serving area. She was, it appeared, not really focused on him at the moment but rather on her own thoughts. She must have realized he was looking at her, as she quickly smiled and spoke.

"Sorry, Prince, but for a moment there I allowed myself to wander off. Are you hungry, but then you must be for I heard your stomach rumble a while ago."

"Was it that loud," Mathew asked, then followed that statement with a question. "Are you sure I am not being a bother, I can have the ship pick me up at the surface and I don't have a problem sleeping here on the beach."

"No, my prince. Actually I was thinking of how nice it would be for just the two of us to live on a beach somewhere, away from all the problems of the world. Kind of like wishful thinking, I suppose."

Mathew was not sure why he said it, but it came out before he could think about what he was saying.

"Careful what you wish for, my lady. Wishes have a way of coming true and you don't really know all that much about me and moreover, who in their right mind would want to spend their life with a Shadow Prince."

Syllium looked him hard in the eyes then spoke. "You, my Prince, have no idea of your real value. I know you have a wife and a love but I also know that most of the time in the past when they have been given the choice between a life with family and a life only with their man, the women have chosen family.

"Aegis has told me this as he knows I have feelings for you. He says you have feelings for me although you don't yet realize it nor will you put me over her. He has said I must not get my hopes up and perhaps I have but then, that is how I am and I would have no problem giving up my family for a life with you."

Mathew didn't know how to respond to that. She was right. He did have feelings for her in his own way but he was sure that Alexis would choose him. But then, one never knew the true feelings of a woman and he wouldn't know either until he had put the question to her.

He returned Syllium's look as she hadn't given ground. He knew that his life was going to change soon and he did not feel it was going to be for the better but he also realized that it was going to be what it was and they would have to cross that bridge when they got to it.

"Syllium, I would ask you to leave us see how things turn out. Sooner than both of us realize, our lives will change. Either for the better or worse or even both and your father is right. Like it or not, I do have feelings for you."

"That is all any of us can ask for," she said. "Now, how about we get something to eat?"

"Lead the way," Mathew replied and followed as she led them over to the serving area.

#

The next morning, they were up early. Syllium and a male Finn assisted Mathew to the beach. They made good time with him using his fins. When they came up out of the water, the co-pilot was standing there waiting.

"Good to have you back, my Lord," he stated. "Do we have a plan for the day? Noting, as he asked, the two Finns who remained out of the water.

"Yes," Mathew replied. "I will take a Hawk and you will pilot a second. The other two, with a pilot only will follow behind. We will approach the area we discovered last evening."

He indicated Syllium and the male Finn and continued.

"We will make contact and once they have agreed to come with us, you will follow with the other Hawks and we will return them all to this location."

Very soon, Mathew was hovering over their small village. As soon as he was close enough, he could see the villagers were having real issues on the beach. There were several salt water lizards on the beach. The villagers were holding them off with spears and several of the men had been injured as indicated by others dragging them away from the beach to safety further ashore.

Mathew wasted no time setting the Hawk down. He instructed the other pilot to take up a defensive position and destroy any lizards that appeared to pose a threat. He hated to kill needlessly but these creatures had nothing but feeding instincts going for them.

He didn't try to approach slowly as planned. There was no time and Syllium and the male Finn were right behind him. She hadn't brought her spear but she did have her sword. The male had his spear. Their landing momentarily distracted the Finns and the lizards sensing this, charged forward. There were six of them and they were hungry and eager to feed.

Mathew was close enough to intervene and fired upon the nearest lizard, nearly cutting it in half. The beasts were monstrous in size, easily reaching twenty to twenty five feet in length. They were also very quick. The blood from the first one he killed brought on a feeding frenzy from two of the others but the remaining three were determined to have a Finn for breakfast.

As Mathew drew closer, he again fired upon the closest lizard. On Earth, these would be called salt water crocodiles but no matter, they were just as deadly. As that one churned up the sand he fired once more killing a third one. The remaining lizard in front of him turned back to the water.

The Finns on the beach gathered together now, as they confronted those they recognized as like them with the exception of Mathew. He slowed down to a walk. He could sense Syllium behind him as they approached the others.

The blood of the dead lizards in and near the water brought on a massive feeding frenzy by both the salt water lizards and the sharkfinn. They seemed to coexist quite well together when there was plenty of food. As they advanced towards the Finns on the beach Mathew observed a look of fright come upon the faces of the ones in front of him.

He wheeled around to find a giant lizard rushing forward, its mouth open and only a few steps from Syllium. She must have realized her danger as she wheeled with her sword at ready. The problem was the sword was like a toothpick to the lizard as it leapt at her. Out of the corner of his eye, Mathew saw the Hawk begin firing at the lizards, realizing this was an attack even if unorganized.

Later, they would say Mathew screamed the word "No!" as he engaged the giant lizard.

The lizard had taken Syllium in its mouth but had not yet bitten down on her as Mathew leapt forward firing just behind the jaws of the lizard and severing them from the head. He didn't stop there, slashing fire at the body to make sure it made no advances then pulling the jaws apart as they crashed to the sand with Syllium sandwiched between them.

The remaining Finns rushed forward to help but were afraid to get too close as there was so much blue fire coming from Mathew's hands. Mathew used his fiery blue hands to slice off the snout, then as the blue fire winked out he jerked the rest of the jaws apart.

The force of the attack knocked Syllium unconscious. Mathew lifted her clear of the bloody remains of the lizard and carried her up towards dryer ground. He was not in a panic, yet one could say he was surely distressed for the moment.

Behind them, the other two Hawks arrived and were keeping the beach clear of any lizards that ventured out of the water.

Mathew checked to see if she was breathing. He hoped she only had the wind knocked out of her but she was not breathing. He quickly took her face and positioning himself above her, began to give her breaths.

After three quick breaths, he checked to see if she was breathing on her own. She was still unresponsive and he resumed breathing for her.

By now, one Hawk had landed and the pilot was approaching with a med kit. Mathew's efforts had yet to get her breathing. Thinking quickly, he remembered he could give her an injection but it took a lot force for him to do it with his fingers as the needles there were so small.

He quickly parted her harness and found a tender spot on her chest. He punched his finger into the spot giving her what he hoped would get her back.

As he withdrew his hand, thinking what to do next, her eyes opened and she gasped for air. She went to rise and he held his hand on her chest telling her to lie still. She lay there staring at him, starting to feel some pain in her chest and ribs from the attack.

"In a moment, I will give you something for the pain," he said. "Let's just wait and assess your injuries."

She tried to smile then closed her eyes. For a moment, Mathew thought she was passing out again but she didn't. Mathew looked up at the male Finn that had accompanied them and spoke.

"We need to get these people away from here. Get them into the Hawks and get them back to our base."

The other pilot along with the Finn took charge. The other two Hawks landed. They were able to get three adults each into three Hawks and left to drop them off at the base camp. One Hawk remained on standby for defense if needed.

The lizards were approaching again. The scent of food was too overpowering for them to stay away very long. As soon as the three Hawks returned, one with a stretcher for Syllium, they loaded up the remaining Finns and moved to the shore base.

Upon arriving at the base, Mathew requested the man who had accompanied Syllium return to the reef to see if they could treat her injuries. Several of the Finns they saved from the beach moved to go with him. Mathew asked them if they were strong enough to make the swim as help would be coming back and they would have some assistance.

In the end, only two took to the water with the other Finn. Syllium was awake and Mathews co-pilot, also a medic, was giving her a good examination. Mathew remained by her side although she insisted she was okay.

In twenty five minutes, a large group of Finns, mostly female began emerging from the water and coming ashore. Several of them immediately began offering the weaker ones saved from the beach some nourishment. Some kind of seaweed, Mathew thought.

Others, came to check on Syllium. She kept insisting she was okay but suddenly she doubled over with pain from her lower abdomen. The medic, continued to check her vitals and examining her for other injuries. Moments later, as she cried out, there was a bloody discharge from her female organs and she passed out.

The medic continued to check her over, requesting another female Finn who indicated she knew how to help, assist him in cleaning her up. Once they had her cleaned up, Mathew asked what their assessment was, even though he already knew. They stated her body, so recently traumatized, had rejected any fluids from her female organs including any recent eggs that had been fertilized.

In other words, the medic said, "Even if it was at a very early stage, she has miscarried. She will be okay after some rest, but I wouldn't move her like she is unless it is via transport."

Mathew thought for a moment then instructed that she be put in the Hawk. The medic asked him what he intended.

"I am going to take her down to the reef," Mathew replied.

"But you can't open the Hawk underwater," the medic stated.

"I won't need to. I can take the Hawk into the reef to the air chamber."

Mathew asked the medic to accompany him as well as the Finn who had been assisting.

In a few minutes, the Hawk lifted off and traveled the short distance to sea above the reef. Then slowly, Mathew took the Hawk down. His passengers watched as they sank down to the seabed in front of the reef. Then moving slowly ahead he moved towards the large arched opening and entered it. As he moved ahead, he could see the roof was going to allow him only a few feet of clearance but it was enough.

As they broke the surface of the water inside the chamber near to the courtyard, the entire yard was full of Finns looking on, including Aegis who began giving orders to those around him. The guards moved forward as Mathew opened the hatchway. They immediately took charge of getting Syllium out of the Hawk.

The medic and his Finn assistant followed them into the chamber with the large oval bed. It gave them room to move about and allowed others to come and go as needed.

Mathew sealed the Hawk and moved over to speak with Aegis. As he started to apologize for what had occurred, Aegis held out his hand and indicated he wanted to speak first.

"I have been made aware of what happened, Prince. We both know it was not your fault, so apologies are not necessary. It was simply an unfortunate set of circumstances and I understand you reacted to it immediately with what I am told were unbelievable results.

"It was said that you physically ripped the giant lizard apart to free Syllium. We cannot begin to thank you enough for bringing her back to us. I have been told that she has miscarried but she is young and there will be other chances. Perhaps, not like she had recently but most certainly other chances."

"Now, what say you and I go check on our girl?"

Mathew followed Aegis into the room. She appeared to be asleep but as soon as she heard Aegis speak she turned to look up at him. She made an attempt at a smile but you could see her heart wasn't in it.

"What are the medics saying," Aegis asked her.

"I will be fine," they said. "Just bruised and banged up a bit, and of course, I lost the birth cells. The medic said it was just my body's way of fighting the trauma and that otherwise all systems, as he put it, are working well and I will be just fine."

"That's my girl," Aegis said. "Yes, you will be just fine and in a few days, it will be as if it had never happened."

"Yes, father, I'm afraid you are right," she said as she looked away, tears running down her face. "Just like it never happened."

Aegis turned and started walking out. He had others to look after. Mathew stood to leave and Syllium spoke.

"Would you sit with me a little while? She asked.

Mathew glanced at her and said he would be back in a few minutes after he sent the Hawk back to the base."

"You will stay a while," she asked.

"Yes," he said. For a while, so you rest and I will be here when you wake up."

"Thanks," she said and closed her eyes. Just for a moment, she told herself but soon after, she was asleep.

Mathew went back out to the courtyard. The medic was talking to the Finn who had assisted him. When Mathew walked up, he told him he was leaving the med unit with Leah, indicating the Finn who had assisted him with Syllium.

"They don't have anything this modern and we have more where this one came from."

"Good idea," Mathew said. "Now, are you okay with taking the Hawk back to the surface?"

"Yes sir. Are you staying here for now?"

"Yes, for now. We aren't going anywhere up there and perhaps I can be of some help here."

"Very well, sir. If anything comes up, I will come back down and let you know."

"Thank you," Mathew replied.

He stood there as the co-pilot come medical officer slowly maneuvered the Hawk to the opening then exited the chamber. Then he turned and walked back to the room where Syllium slept.

Chapter 19 – A Shadow Prince Retired

Logan was pleased with all that was happening so far on Waardin. The pache were surrendering as quick as they got word. Few of them had the stomach for the war and most if not all of the ones who were the most pro-war minded had died in the earlier attacks by Logan's forces.

As luck would have it, the base they destroyed was the center that controlled all the other forces on the planet with all the hardliners stationed there.

The Pache had no issue with the Waardin being their jailers. The Waardin allowed them to remain on their bases without any weapons as long as they maintained the base and did not leave it.

Now there was the logistical nightmare of getting what appeared to be nearly a thousand former pache back to Bara.

The men on the bases had lots of questions as to what had happened to the ruling family and who was the ruler now. Many were glad to hear that none of the former would be their leaders.

As more than one said several times over. Those people were some really sick bastards and we were nothing but cannon fodder for them. Now, at least we can live our lives like we choose.

All the pache soldiers were presented with the opportunity to remain on Waardin but in the end, none of them wanted to, many stating that after what they as a nation had done to the Waardin, it was certain that the Waardin would not be forgetting or forgiving any time soon, no matter what they said.

After several consultations with the Phoenix, Logan decided that the best thing to do was to start the transfer of pache. They shuttled 300 up to the Phoenix and she departed for Bara. Logan was in contact with the communications officer with Prince Mathew's squad, who informed him of the rescue of the Finns and that several had been injured. He stated that Prince Mathew was assisting in their recovery.

Logan didn't question what that meant just accepting that it would be a few days or longer before Mathew was ready to depart Finnean and that gave them a breather from going back to the Finn planet and allowed them to transit back and forth to Bara which saved a lot of time with the transfer process.

It was a two day process one way by the time they offloaded and returned. After the third trip, they would be ready to drop by Finnean and pick up Mathew and his squad. Logan did not want to leave Waardin until the last pache was off the planet.

The Waardins began rebuilding their planet and the infrastructure that had been damaged by the war. After several long and intense meeting between Logan and the governors, it was agreed that sometime in the near future, they would exchange delegates just as they planned on doing with Tomarlin.

The Tomarlins built a new communications platform for Finnean as the one destroyed couldn't be fixed. They sent it from Tomar via a cargo ship to Waardin and it was expected to arrive in the next few days, which would fit perfectly with their travel to the Finn planet to pick up the squad there.

#

Syllium woke up to a semi-dark room. She felt something on her arm. Looking down she realized it was a hand and belonged to Prince Mathew who was asleep on the other side of the bed. He had laid down with his clothes on, lying close to her while she slept.

He looks so at peace, she thought when she knew he had so much going on in that mind of his. She turned to face him and repositioned her arm slowly so as not to wake him. Then placing her hand on his, she closed her eyes and went back to sleep.

Both of them slept for several more hours. Outside it was already mid-evening. As she went to sit up, she uttered a low ouch. A voice beside her suggested she move slowly as she had some serious bruises.

She looked over at Mathew. He was laying there watching her. She looked down at her chest and ribs. There were several large ugly bruises. She realized she was completely unclothed.

"What the heck, he's seen all of me already."

Mathew reached over and pointed down at a particularly large bruise.

"My apologies but I caused that one."

"Oh," she said. "I thought I could blame the lizard for all of them."

"Sorry," Mathew replied. "That wouldn't be fair to our now departed lizard. I poked you there trying to inject you with a heart stimulant."

"What for?" She asked.

"You weren't breathing and I wasn't getting a heartbeat. I think the blow to the ground just short circuited your body, kind of like the miscarriage."

"And you did what then?"

"I breathed for you," Mathew said, "and then I gave you an injection to stimulate your heart."

"Is that something like what you call kissing?" She asked.

"Yes, kind of like but for different reasons."

Mathew realized that the Finns had never practiced the art of kissing. He hadn't witnessed any doing it and of course he had not done it to any of the women he had performed for. Kissing was, after all, a personal thing and not freely given, except for the occasional peck on the cheek.

"Is this kissing a personal thing?" She asked.

"Mostly," he replied. "In my culture, it can be anything from a casual greeting to what some would call foreplay."

"What is foreplay?" She asked.

"Well, aside from kissing, it is like when I gave you a bath before sex. It is meant to get you in the mood although it doesn't always end that way."

"You mean it doesn't always end with sex."

"Right," Mathew replied. "For example, lots of people kiss when they are leaving each other. Like say going to work in the morning, or sending a child to school or just for no other reason than to say they love each other."

"I think I like this kissing thing," she said.

"When done right, most people do," Mathew replied.

"Perhaps," she said, "you could show me how this kissing works."

"Perhaps," Mathew said, "knowing that it was only going to heat up their relationship and it was already hot enough."

"Okay," she said. "So when?"

"Don't rush it, girlfriend," Mathew replied. "Let's see about getting you some lunch and later, we can agree to talk about this kissing thing."

"Why do we need to talk about it?" She asked with a giggle, "and what does this girlfriend mean."

Son, Mathew told himself, you are digging a very big hole here.

#

The door opened and Reenae entered with a large shell platter with food enough for three or four people.

"I hope you two are hungry," she said. "I took the liberty of bringing enough for now and later as I didn't think you would feel like getting out just yet."

She looked over Syllium's chest and ribs.

"You really took a beating, didn't you?"

"Yes, and it is really sore," Syllium said, but I guess if this is the reward for getting to live then I am really very lucky."

"Yes," Reenae replied, "you are and I am too."

"You mean?" she asked.

"Yes, I missed my cycle today. I'm so happy."

"I'm happy for you too," Syllium replied but there was a tear in the corner of her eye which she wiped away.

"I'm sorry," Reenae said. "I shouldn't have said anything."

"No, I'm glad you did, so how about the others?"

"I'm not sure but most of them will know by the end of next week, now you need to eat something, to get your strength up."

Mathew hadn't said anything as he listened to the girls talk. He supposed he should be glad for the women but it was hard to see it as something to celebrate. Perhaps, if he was making his own family like he was with Alexis, he would see it different but now, it appeared that too was in jeopardy.

#

In a star system far away and not yet named by man, a woman stood next to her mate. They shared a home and there were three kids in various ages and stages of growth off in the distance laughing and playing together like any parent would wish their kids to do.

Both adults were old by man's standards but not old for them. Up until recently, he had traveled a lot, sometimes staying away as long as several years.

She had their home and the kids to look after. She was alone when she gave birth to them but managed as best she could which was actually remarkably well. They had waited late in their lives to have their children, choosing to spread them out so as not to overburden her as she was responsible for both herself, the child and their living while he was gone.

There were not many residents on this planet. It was unique as it was completely unspoiled by man. Unspoiled that is, if you didn't count the small holdings the individual families had for themselves.

There were two other families which were much larger than theirs. That was because they had been here longer and had more members. The only thing lacking was the daily ability to interact with others.

The families themselves lived about a thousand miles apart. It had only been recently that members of the other two families had agreed to meet in order for their children or young adults to interact and consider the prospects of taking a mate. Prior to now, they couldn't and they simply lived until death or some accident took them.

There were no predators on this planet that anyone was aware of aside from those in the sea. For good or bad, on land the humans were the only hunters and there was a limit to what was available with fish being the primary source of protein.

As they all lived near the water and not wanting to take any chances, they each built their own catch basins to fish from as well as swim. The basins allowed the smaller fish in but kept the larger ones out. It was basically a safety zone for them without the worry of predator fish attacking them.

The couple was the newest to the planet. They had been living here a few hundred years short of a thousand. Yes, a thousand. They had been directed there by a source who knew of the planet and knew as well that it would be a safe harbor for their kind.

The man, until recently, had been the only working one of his kind but the years were taking their toll and he had been home now for over two months. Off in the distance was a giant rock that rested against a hillside which was the backdrop to their small holdings. The rock itself was the most impressive thing in the area and looked more like a giant piece of lava or perhaps a meteor.

If it was here, then so to was the man as the giant rock was in fact his mode of transport. That was why he called it the Transporter. His woman and kids called it the rock. It only worked for him and opened on his command or on its own if there was a new assignment for him.

Within the rock were two chairs or perhaps command seats. They were for the man and woman only she had only used it once and that was when she came to the planet. She had never asked or wanted to leave since then, only remaining there and waiting for the man to return.

They knew it was time for him to leave when the rock opened. It was a signal that it was time for the man to travel once again. She had asked him once if he knew where he was going before he got there and he had replied that he was given the information he needed during travel from here to wherever it was he was being sent.

Today was different. As they stood together watching the sunset with the kids nearby they heard a loud boom. They looked towards the rock. As they watched, the rock opened up to allow them to see inside.

As usual, there was only the chairs which were more like lounges, surrounded by darkness which were more suited for resting than anything else for they had no control over where the rock went.

The woman almost broke into tears as she realized it was calling the man to go away. So many years and of course they weren't getting any younger. She had been hoping that soon it would leave without him, signaling that his work was done and another would take his place. They could then live out their years here together.

As the man embraced her, the kids began running towards them as they too knew what it meant.

"I'm sorry dear," he said. "Maybe this one will be the last one. At least we can hope."

"I know" she said, trying to put on a brave face in front of the kids. "We can always hope. Anyway, I will be here waiting for your return."

Anything else she was going to say was shut out as the rock slammed shut. The loud boom reverberated across the land. After a few seconds the rock lifted clear of the ground and without a sound, shot up into the atmosphere and off into space.

The woman clung to the man, crying and laughing at the same time. Finally, his work was done. They stood together trying to see if they could see where it was going but already it was blending into the darkness of space and gone from their world and their lives.

Perhaps, in a few hundred years, they would see its return if the new Shadow Prince chose to live on this planet.

#

The Phoenix was departing with the third load of Pache from the planet Waardin. Its communications officer contacted the squad on

Finnean, informing them that they would be back in three days and allowing for one or two days on Waardin, would be coming to meet them for pickup.

The radio officer on Finnean, part of Mathew's squad confirmed he had received their message and then spoke to Mathews co-pilot, passing on the information. The co-pilot proceeded to take the Hawk up and out over the reef. Then settling down into the water, he allowed it to sink to the seafloor.

Once there, he tried to reach Mathew on his communicator. On his second attempt, Mathew answered him. The pilot passed on the information. Mathew thanked him and said he would be on the beach in five days' time.

Mathew was sitting in the courtyard talking to Aegis. He always seemed to have some new information for Mathew regarding the work of the Shadow Prince. It was a hard but rewarding job and once the Transporter came for Mathew then he would begin his work as the real Shadow Prince.

He told Mathew that one had to learn to distance themselves from the work. He was or would become the savior and destroyer at the same time. He would save many lives but take many more. There was no real balance or at least there had never been before. It was up to him to decide which side of which conflict he would become the judge, jury and executioner for.

Most times, they made the right decision but he knew that on more than one occasion he himself had made mistakes and allowed emotions to shape his decisions and even been fooled by those that tried to use him for their own gain.

He admitted to Mathew that his weakness back then had been the women, especially the pretty ones who it seemed were almost always the most devious.

Mathew heard the co-pilots call but didn't respond until he had made a second attempt. Once he had acknowledged the call and replied, he turned back to Aegis and their conversation.

"Do you think you can put up with me for another four or five days?" He asked.

"I look forward to it, my young Prince, as will several others," he replied with a big smile.

He signaled for one of the female guards and whispered in her ear. She smiled and quickly departed. Mathew didn't ask what it was about. He was sure that sooner or later it would all become clear.

Chapter 20 – They Speak of the Shadow

On Bara, the ground work for the next chapter in the lives of Princess Alexis and Prince Mathew was about to be laid out. The Houns, those closely attached to the royal family, requested a meeting with the queen and princess. Shadow and her parents would be there.

This request was, in itself, very unusual and had never before occurred in the history of the relationships between the Houns and their Baran mind mates.

The Houns met several times recently to discuss the soon to happen transformation of their young Prince Mathew into the Shadow Prince. They didn't know if he was yet aware of it but they did know the time and moment were fast approaching and he had no control over it.

They knew what was expected of him. What they couldn't determine was how the princess would react to her part in the developing situation. It was going to be a hard decision for her. One that many before her were forced to make and they well knew her case was all the more difficult as she was the heir apparent to the Baran ruling family and that carried a great deal of responsibility.

Alexis was less than a month from giving birth. The Houns had first thought to wait until after but time was not a luxury any longer and they knew that the Prince could be called away at any time. Even before he returned home from this mission he was on now.

As they gathered in the royal chamber, Queen Marie asked if anyone required any form of refreshment. The Houns indicated that they did not but they had a request if it was acceptable with the queen and princess. The queen said it was okay. What did they need?

Shadow spoke. "We would like to bring in two others who will speak for us. She will tell this story we wish to relay to both of you but she will have no control over her tongue, rather we will control it. She will not be harmed by this. It is better this way as the mind talk can be slow and burdensome.

"So who is it you wish to have join with us?" the queen asked

"They are outside," Shadow spoke. "It is the Red Guard Commander, Maxim, his Houn Flame and the Zetan woman, Kieran."

"Why Maxim and why Kieran? Both of them have suffered losses recently and might not be up to this."

"It is because of their losses that we have chosen them. After today, they will need to be comforted and they will become a pair. It is decided."

"So, you Houns decided this," Queen Marie said with a smile.

"No, the prince decided this but has not been here to see it through."

"And you say this cannot wait for his and Lord Logan's return?"

"Yes, your highness, it cannot wait," Stone spoke.

Kieran and Maxim were ushered in. Neither knew what this was about. The Houns asked that they be seated together. Then Shadow and her mother stood before the two. Shadow mind spoke the queen.

She told Maxim to take Kieran's hand. He took her left into his right. Then the queen spoke to Kieran.

"They are going to use you to tell a story. You will not know what you are saying but you will remember it afterwards. You will not have any control over what you will say, only know that it will not hurt you but you may experience a lot of sadness.

Do not be ashamed to allow your emotions to take over. Maxim's job is to be there to comfort you. Someone for you to lean on."

The queen paused then asked. "Are the two of you okay with this?"

As if already one, they replied, "we are."

Alexis spoke. "I have to say that I sense I am not going to like where this is going and I also sense that this has more to do with my prince."

Shadow and her mother stood before Kieran and Maxim. They both seemed to stare right through Kieran.

Then Kieran spoke. "You are right, princess. It has everything to do with you and your prince and yes, you are not going to like where this is going but what is coming cannot be stopped."

There was a pause in the room. Alexis was sitting next to her mother. She reached over and took her mother's hand as if she too knew she was going to need comforting. Her mother placed her other hand above the one she was holding as she waited for Keiran to continue.

"I will start with a story and end with where we are now," Kieran said and began.

"Many thousand years ago, from some source not yet known, came a man. Some called him a savior, others the prince of death and many other names have been given over the years but the name that has always remained the same is the Shadow Prince."

"Oh my God," Alexis muttered. Her mother only held her hand tighter.

"We don't know how this began but every thousand years, another Shadow Prince is chosen and the one chosen has no say in the matter. The old prince is retired to live out his remaining years.

In years past, they have chosen to live on an unspoiled planet many galaxies from here. Even we do not know its location."

Shadow turned to look at Alexis. Her head was bowed and the tears ran freely down her face. The queen had now placed one arm around Alexis' shoulders and pulled her closer.

Kieran continued the story. "It is the Shadow Prince's mission to travel the stars from planet to planet stopping the wars and fighting that go on between the inhabitants and between the planets. As he grows into the job, so too does his power. It is said that he can destroy a planet if he chooses.

"We have not heard if this is true only that it is possible. We do know that in times past he has been deceived by some and when the occasion occurred he has gone back to make things right and destroyed those who had deceived him. He is after all, still human.

"We know he meets with another former shadow prince who has lived, we are told for many thousands of years and guards the seeds of life. Something necessary, rumor has it, to allow the shadow prince to carry out his mission.

He is allowed one extra seed to bring to his mate but she may only take of it if she chooses to go with him. This meeting I have just mentioned has already occurred."

Alexis sobbed out loud. Even the queen was crying now and tears ran freely down Kieran's face. Each of the women knew where this was going and the telling and listening to the story was becoming very difficult. Kieran continued.

"Very soon, the prince will return home. This home but it is no longer his home for life. He will be here this time for a visit only. To spend time with those he loves. If he will ever return is not known. For some reason, it seems to create a rift in the fabric of time that works around him.

"That is the reason we are here now, to tell this story and prepare each of you for what is coming. You are fortunate that we know what is to occur and can prepare you. Many don't get the chance."

Alexis spoke then. She had to catch her breath several times but she managed.

"You are saying that my prince is," and she paused before saying, "the next Shadow Prince. How do you know this?"

Shadow mind spoke her and her mother.

"Two things gave it away, princess. On the day he rescued you from the Pache, one of them asked him who he was. He started to tell that man whom he later killed that he was the black prince but something came over him and he said he was the Shadow Prince.

I don't think he had any choice at that moment. It was the beginning of the shadow taking over."

"Later, when he named me, it was because the name was on his mind. Something he couldn't escape from."

"But how does that mean anything?" Queen Marie asked. "How can you be so sure and why must he become this Shadow Prince. Can he not refuse it?"

Shadows mother mind spoke then and all there could hear her.

"Queen Marie, our kind have known and kept these secrets and stories for centuries, handed down from mother to daughter and so forth. Many nights as we stare out at the stars as is our nature, we hear the voices and more stories coming across space and time.

"Perhaps it is why we are here but we do know that we have never been wrong and still the stories come to us and as for the prince refusing to become the next Shadow Prince. Understand this. He was selected by another and while we might call him the Shadow Prince, he is in fact a God Warrior and the choice is no longer his."

Alexis spoke again. She managed to control her voice for the moment.

"So you are saying my prince will bring back with him a seed, this seed of life or long life or whatever it is and I have to choose if I will follow him before I can take it. So what happens to our children, our families, our future, this kingdom?"

Kieran spoke again.

"You must decide princess, if you can give up all the other things you have mentioned. Your family, your children and yes this kingdom. It is going to have to be your choice and yours alone. No one can make that decision for you but I will tell you this. Most choose not to go. It is a lonely life.

"He will take you to a safe place at first. Likely not of his choosing, where you will be on your own, waiting for his return and very likely giving birth on your own to more children. That is possibly the only plus.

"The worst part is that he will be gone for months and even years. You will have the advantage of a long life but you will not be immortal. He will very nearly be, for at first he will heal himself when injured but over time as he grows older, he will try to avoid injury as the healing will come more slowly."

"I cannot make such a decision," Alexis cried. "It is too hard and I love him too much."

"And he loves you just as much, but he cannot stop what is coming, nor can you and yes, you can make the decision and you have to. Not today but very soon now," and as she finished Kieran broke into sobs and clung to Maxim who only pulled her closer.

He too was crying now, for he had lost much lately and felt the need to comfort the woman next to him yet he didn't want to go too far and offend her.

Maxims' Houn Flame stood up. "Come, Maxin," he spoke. "Bring the woman. She is in need of a man and you are in need of a woman. The prince said this would be so and he was right."

Kieran raised her head. She had heard the Houns words in her mind. She looked up at Maxim.

"Are you sure?" she asked.

He looked down at her and said he was, then he rose and said to the others.

"I think our work here is done. We will take our leave now. If we are needed, do not hesitate to call."

He looked directly at Princess Alexis and spoke.

"When he comes back, thank him for me. He is a very wise man and we will miss him."

"I will," Alexis murmured. "I will," she repeated as she lowered her head onto her mother's lap.

The Houns all positioned themselves at the feet of the women as if to offer comfort. Comfort that was not coming and they all knew it. Shadow sat up. Speaking to no one in particular when she mind spoke.

"They return in five days' time."

#

Far away, in the Zeta system a war many years old raged on. Many had died never knowing for what reason except that for as long as they could remember, they had fought each other. Others spoke of treachery several hundred years old yet none could say what it was, only that the other was to blame.

During the night, a roar filled the skies above the planet as a meteor passed through the planet's atmosphere. It did not strike the planets land mass but it created such a disruption in the atmosphere that storms began to form like none ever seen before in all recorded history. Even those at war were forced to stand down and take shelter as the storms raged all across the planet's surface.

The strong winds, rain and lightning continued for days with massive flooding and damage to infrastructure all across the planet. For the time being, those who had been fighting were forced to redirect their efforts to saving their own people.

Yet, they knew that once this had passed, they would once again resume where they had left off. The meteor continued across space and time and only he or those who controlled it knew where it was headed.

Chapter 21 – Presidential Assassins

Brad and General Neagle stood on the observation tower watching the work ongoing before them. The dig had long since reached the top of the space craft Eden Seven and was now clearing its top and digging around its sides. The news channels practically turned the big dig into a soap opera. They chronicled the life of the digging team much like television had done with those non to famous alligator hunters and moonshine makers.

Some of the antics they pulled to get their ratings up were a bit farfetched but they had allowed them to film it with the one stipulation that there would be two shows and two different networks doing the filming. This gave equal time to other networks and a chance for more people to profit from it. Plus, the big dig got a cut of the money generated from the advertisers.

Trainer was still hot on the trail of the group from Montana but they had become even more elusive than it had been believed they could. Even Trainer was concerned with his own inability to locate them which only reaffirmed how dangerous they could be as a home grown terrorist organization.

If the government had been under siege, then their actions would have been applauded but since it wasn't, except to those within the group, they knew they had a serious problem on their hands.

To make matters worse, the president refused to limit his travel even with the threat to his life and those around him ever present. This forced the government to go into overdrive trying to locate and contain the threat the group presented.

Trainer had even changed the trajectory of some of the satellites flying overhead to give more coverage to areas that posed a threat to the president when he was traveling.

Trainer learned that morning that the Presidents helicopter was being transferred to Denver to be used as a ferry during his ongoing campaign for re-election. The presidential plane would take him and his entourage to Denver and depending on where they were going, they would either use the helicopter or travel by motorcade.

This was an invitation to the group who had been looking for such an opportunity to strike. They wouldn't need to make detailed plans to strike, only position themselves in multiple locations and wait for that so called golden opportunity.

Trainer could do little other than target the area with satellite coverage and look for any significant changes to the area such as vehicles out of place or anything that could be used as cover for an attack.

Once again, he was able to pick up short bits of conversations over the telephone exchange that mentioned Eagle One but none gave up any concrete information or stayed on long enough for him to develop a pattern or a telephone number with the exception of those calls from legitimate operations.

The days for the trip in Denver dragged on until it was now the Presidents last day. Those around him convinced him a trip to Colorado Springs with a tour of the Garden of the Gods monument park was in his best interests as select members of the media and local politicians would be accompanying him.

Trainer himself couldn't think of a worse way to expose oneself to danger than that would and his council to the president fell on deaf ears, since the worst thing that had happened so far had been a few protestors flinging eggs at his motorcade.

Trainer had his Hawks on standby and even had one with a stretcher in case it was needed. Each Hawk had medical personnel onboard. He convinced Brad to allow him to use some of the new team members now fully recovered, as scouts to see if they could spot any potential threats. The evening before, team members took up their positions and with their special gear, they wouldn't be sighted unless they wanted to be.

The day began as any other presidential affair with the media and politicians doing their thing, then the flight to a pre-selected location near the Garden of the Gods Monument Park.

The authorities didn't try to limit the president's exposure by minimizing the number of day trekkers motoring or hiking in the park during the president's visit, saying that the public should be able to share the park with the presidents group and this would make him appear more a people's person

As the motorcade moved through the park, one of the scouts noticed a small pickup truck with a camper mounted on the back had stopped ahead of the convoy.

There appeared to be three people with the truck and one was looking at the passenger front tire. One of the men was removing a jack from the back of the truck and placing it under the front bumper while another removed a spare tire from the back of the truck. The scout observed that the front tire was not flat, which was all the information Trainer needed to send in a backup detail.

The problem was the motorcade was only a few hundred yards from the truck and slowly getting closer. Trainer messaged one of the senior security men with the president via his headset, advising him of the situation ahead.

As the motorcade moved closer, one of the rear vehicles moved around and took the lead as it sped up towards the truck parked on the side of the road ahead.

Two men got out and advanced on the truck. They were met by one of the men and the woman, who laughingly indicated they had a bad tire and were preparing to change it. One of the men asked if he could see in the back of the truck while the other looked in the front of the truck. He seemed oblivious to the man who appeared to be using a wrench on the front tire.

The woman opened the back of the truck, allowing the man to look inside. He only glanced in then backed away and spoke on his headset. The motorcade only slowed down then resumed its speed at his instructions.

It appeared they planned on remaining with the truck until the motorcade passed by. Trainer heard the security man say to another that it was another false alarm. It was at that moment that the Presidents car came up alongside the truck.

The woman pulled a pistol from her skirt and shot the man near her in the back of the head, while her companion shot the other security man.

The man with the tire iron jumped up and reached in his pocket for something. The scout shouted the alarm but it was too late. He took aim as the man held what appeared to be a hand grenade to toss under the car. The scouts shot took him in the head but he had already pulled the pin on the grenade which fell from his hand.

He had moved to the side of the Presidents car to toss the grenade beneath it. As it rolled towards the car, it exploded. The explosion was enough to flip the car onto its side. The woman reached into the back of the truck and retrieved two automatic weapons, one which she tossed to the other man in their party.

The Hawk was now in position and fired into the truck causing it to explode in a ball of flames knocking the man with the gun down.

The woman was already moving to the side of the overturned car and firing into the roof top. They would later learn that the bullets were specially made to penetrate armored steel plating that was supposed to protect the occupants inside the car.

Before the man could recover, the scout had put a bullet in his skull. He couldn't get a shot at the woman behind the car but the Hawk could and in a few seconds she was incinerated by a photon blast from the Hawk.

Trainer was watching the whole thing unfold before him. He wondered why the security personnel in the other vehicles had not responded yet but was later to learn that the only two to accompany them into the park were in the lone car at the request of one of the politicians and those running the park service.

As the vehicles in the motorcade sat there with politicians cowering in fear behind their car windows, a Hawk landed and several members of Brad's team began working frantically to get into the Presidents car. After a few moments, they all gathered together and were able push the car back onto it's now shredded tires

The men jerked the doors open to come face to face with what could only be the sight of calculated carnage. The woman had known where to target and no one had been able to hide from her bullets.

The force of the bullets blasting through the roof of the car had been diminished after they penetrated the steel armor but it was still enough to cause serious damage, made even worse as the bullets were no longer in rifled shapes but damaged shrapnel.

Trainer ordered them to retrieve the president. By now, news helicopters were everywhere covering the thought to be assassination of the president by some group who phoned in to say they were responsible for killing this president who they believed was under the control of aliens.

"He was just the first," they said.

The caller made the mistake by staying on the phone with a reporter for fifteen seconds too long. Trainer not only had the number but the location of the call. He sent a Hawk with a team to follow up. It would turn out to be the biggest break they would get.

Not only was the call from the groups bunker but most of the group was there as was evidenced by all the vehicles parked around a large lump in the ground.

Trainer realized that they must have television within the bunker and one of the members had called from there to gloat and tell the news reporter they were responsible. He only realized his possible error after he hung up but chose not to say anything to anyone, hoping he had gotten away with it.

Trainer knew it would be better if the authorities were to clean up this mess and placed a call to the Montana State Police advising them as to where the terror group that had attacked the President's motorcade was located.

In short order, groups of state police cars followed by a quickly alerted swat team geared up and boarding helicopters were on their way to the location provided.

Trainer ordered his people to take up positions and not let anyone leave that bunker until the State police were close enough to take over.

At the attack site, the team was slowly extricating the President. He was badly shot up but upon getting him in a stretcher, they discovered he was still alive.

"Activate the stretcher and get him back to the base," Trainer ordered. Trainer then called Brad via his communicator informing him of what had transpired till then. Brad asked him if it might be in all their best interests if the president was brought to Area 51 for treatment if in fact he could be saved.

It only took Trainer a millisecond to agree that was a better plan and he instructed the Hawk pilot to take the president to the Area 51 base as soon as he was loaded up.

Brad and General Neagle were at the big dig site. Brad informed Neagle of what had happened and said they were bringing the president to their base.

"I'm going to the base," Brad told him.

"I'm right behind you," Neagle shouted as they ran over to the truck. Brad put in a call for a Hawk to pick him and Neagle up. He contacted the base and told them a priority one patient was coming in and was going to need the expertise of every capable medic at the base. He then spoke directly to Trainer.

"You know the best person for this is Van," he said.

Trainer acknowledged that he was probably right and that Van was already on his way.

"Thanks," Brad replied, then said he would be there to meet the patient and Van.

By the time the President was loaded up, several local police and ambulances were on the scene. No one else had survived the attack on the president's car and no one had any high expectations of the president surviving this, not even Trainer.

The news channels continued to say he had been assassinated as they had not been told that life signs had been detected. At that moment, the Vice President was being sworn in at the capital.

The group in Montana was still celebrating their successful attack on the president's car and the drink was being passed around. One man went outside, paying no attention, his mind on the other cases of beer in his truck. He had only made a few steps before he found himself flung to the ground, a weapon at his back and him surrounded by a swat team.

"Oh shit," he thought as he was dragged away. It was the perfect set up for the swat team to enter the bunker as those inside would be expecting the man coming in with more beer.

Moments later the door was jerked open and as quickly as they could enter, the swat team was inside, weapons trained on those who had their backs to the door watching the big screen television.

They knew they were in trouble when they heard the shout, "On the floor, get down on the floor with your hands out, your legs apart."

One man turned, reaching for his pistol. He went down with a head shot, blood and brains splashing on the front of the television. Only one other person made an attempt to resist, drawing his big Bowie knife, but his reward was a chop to the arm which was now broken and a lot of pain with it, for his actions.

Five minutes after the swat team entered the bunker, all the men and women had been shackled and were being led out. While this was going on, a virtual convoy of police and news people was converging on the bunker having been alerted by the Montana state police as soon as they had feet on the ground at the bunker.

Trainer's people withdrew quietly in the background and were now making their way to the base at Area 51. All of them were concerned as this was going to be a bad blow to their work with the governments if the president was in fact dead.

In the Hawk, the emergency stretcher was in control of the president's body. He was now in a coma, a combination of the trauma he had suffered and the meds he was given. All his vital signs were being controlled and monitored by the stretcher.

At the base, they were getting everything ready for the president's arrival, well aware that if anything could be done for him, they could do it.

Van was already there coordinating everything they might need for this president. He well knew how important it was to keep this man alive and he was prepared to do whatever it took to make sure he lived. Perhaps with a lot of new parts and pieces but as a whole fully functioning human being.

The news picked up on the fact that the president's body had been moved to the new base at Area 51. Many wanted to know why they were taking the presidents body to the base, while just as many wanted to know why he wasn't being transferred to a nearby medical facility for what was standard procedure, that being an autopsy to determine the exact cause of death.

Trainer contacted General Neagle who now had a communications device and asked him if he could arrange for the medical people who were normally at the presidents bidding and looked after him to be delivered to the Area 51 base.

"Trainer," Neagle asked. "Do we have a corpse or a body," suspecting that the president might still be alive if Trainer was wanting medical people brought in.

"Neagle, you're very deserving of the trust I have in you and very much tuned in to what is going on around you and yes, the president is still alive and we are going to try and make sure he stays that way.

The purpose of having his people there is to give the media updates if in fact we have something to provide."

"Thanks, Trainer," Neagle replied.

"I will have them here in a few hours," and he immediately contacted his opposite, the general that worked out of the Pentagon and was being prepped to take his place, giving him instructions as to what he needed and requesting that those needed were quickly forthcoming.

"I will send out officers and escorts to collect them," the general replied. "We will handle transport as well."

"Thanks, Grant," Neagle replied. "We will be waiting their arrival."

"Neagle," the other man said.

Neagle answered with a statement.

"In answer to your question, Grant, yes, the president is still alive but we are not putting that out until we have something to say."

"Understood," Grant said, "and thanks," then he hung up to look after Neagles request.

Chapter 22 – The New Shadow Prince

Mathew spent many more hours with Aegis. He asked many questions about his former life as a Shadow Prince. How he had handled various situations and had he developed any relationships in any of the places he had visited. Aegis never tried to skirt the questions. He knew why Mathew was asking them and he had no problems with providing the answers.

The first thing he said was that the prince needed to understand that he was no saint. He had never wanted or tried to be. He knew what his assignment was even though he was never told until just before he arrived. The only thing provided for him was transport to the location chosen by whoever did such a thing.

At first, he had begun to think that the individual or deity had a sick sense of humor as everywhere he went he was fawned upon by the women or most of them and as for the men, well if they couldn't kill him, then the sooner he left the better.

He had many women and had no doubt fathered many children. Enough, he suggested, to populate a small planet during all those years.

"At least," he said with a smile. "I left them with some good breeding stock."

He stated that on more than one occasion, he had allowed good looks and feminine charm to sway his decisions resulting in the unintended deaths of only God knew how many.

Once he had realized his mistake he had tried to make it right by first destroying those who had so misled him and trying to help as best he could the ones he had inadvertently wronged. In some cases, that was fathering more children.

"It can," he said, "become a vicious circle."

Mathew asked how he was able to defeat so many in war and battle. Aegis replied.

"You have not come into your powers yet but I assure you they will come and most likely you will have many more than I did from days past. In my day, I carried a staff. I used it to rain fire on my enemies."

He continued speaking, saying that after a while it became almost a crutch for me as I became too reliant on it. Once, it was smashed from my hands and I thought I was lost. I forgot my own powers until the one in front of me began to boast of what he was going to do to me. He too thought my powers were in the staff.

I grew angry and simply pointed at him as if to say, not today and he burst into flame and it was then I remembered that the staff was only a tool I used to channel my own energies. After that, I never used a symbol such as a staff again unless the culture I was working with were more accepting of such. Addressing Mathew, he said.

"You already can issue fire from your hands from your implants. I think I can say with all confidence that soon those implants will become immersed with your body much more so than they are now and you will never again need to have charges or more ammunition.

I could never fly on my own but you are more resourceful than I was and have more assets at your beck and call."

He spoke of the Transporter, saying that he would be moved from place to place numerous times and that while it might look small from the outside, within was a small world that would be able to provide most anything he needed if he asked for it.

"I used to find the time to make things that made my life and my battles easier," he said.

"Things you think up during the course of a battle and later find the time to perfect them only to toss them aside later and never use them again."

As the few days remaining passed Mathew realized that he still had to convince Alexis to come with him yet he already knew in his heart that she would not. He was undecided if he should wait for her or simply pick another. He also wondered if that other was the one here and now or if he should wait and see what he encountered on other worlds.

The more he thought on it, he knew that he could but would not make any decision on the matter until after he and Alexis had talked. The one thing he did know was that he loved Alexis, no matter what her decision was.

That evening, when it began to get dark, he ate a small bit at the banquet that was available every evening. He had been with Aegis most of the last few days. Each evening he had gone back to the room with the big bed only no one was there. He guessed Syllium had moved back to her room, wherever that was.

He had slept alone every night since his return. He wondered how Syllium was doing and if she had healed okay but there was no one to ask. Everyone seemed to be somewhere else. Perhaps, he thought, the new had worn off, meaning him.

He sat on the side of the bed for over an hour, every now and then he heard noises in the adjoining room but paid them no mind. After a while, he decided it was time to get a shower. He undressed and went into his bathroom with the never ending shower. He was going to miss that, he thought.

As he began to put soap on the sponge he sensed that someone had entered the room. He started to turn but felt a finger on his back and a voice he recognized say, no, no, no, indicating he was not to turn around. Then a hand reached around and took the soapy sponge. Out of the corner of his eye he could see the silver white silky hair he knew belonged to Syllium.

"Are you well," he asked as she began to slowly wash his back and backsides.

"Yes, my prince," she said. "I am well. And you, are you well," and she added, "in body and spirit."

"My lady," he said, causing a giggle from her.

"My body is well but I will not say my spirit is."

"Why is that, my prince," she said as she began to wash his lower legs and had him lift a foot but still not letting him turn around.

"As per your father, I only have a few days before I become this Shadow Prince being. After that, my life is no longer my own. Oh yes, in some areas but as for a life with someone special, well that will be a different story and right now I see no way forward."

She had finished washing his backside and slowly urged him to turn. She had on the thinnest silk gown he could imagine. It was soaked and clung to her now wet body. All there was to see of her was there before him, yet he just looked as she began to wash his chest. It was hard not to be aroused by such a sight and of course he was quickly becoming that way.

As she slowly washed her way down past his crotch she knelt down and for a moment took him in her mouth. He pulled her upright and closer to him.

"Who taught you that," he whispered, fighting to maintain his control.

"No one," she said, but my father told me that it was something men liked and explained it to me.

"Did you not like it? Did I do something wrong," she asked, putting a little bit of space between them.

Smiling, he said, "Of course I liked it, what man wouldn't and no, you didn't do anything wrong. I just don't want to hurt you anymore than you are already hurting."

She moved back against him. "Let me be the judge of what is hurting me and what is not."

Mathew took the moment to raise his finger to her face. He traced around her eyes and nose then around her mouth and lips then slowly leaned forward and placed his lips on hers. Her eyes widened as he slowly kissed her lips then realizing what he was doing, she pressed hers harder against his.

He pulled back a little and she must have realized that the slow tender movement was what he desired. They kissed for a moment and then he pulled away.

She looked up at him and said, "More, please."

He met her and they kissed for a good while then she pulled away and spoke.

"Someone once said you will never forget your first kiss. Until now, I did not know what that meant. Now I do and I promise you I will never forget this moment."

Mathew took the sponge from her, then slowly began to lift the wet gown from her body. She helped and soon it was free. Then he took the sponge and began her bath. When they were finished, she led him to the bed.

Mathew saw the sponge bowl was back. He reached as they walked by and took several in his mouth. He already was erect. He wanted to stay that way for a while at least.

"Are you sure you're okay?" He whispered as she pulled him down to her.

"I will be okay in the morning," she said. "Right now I need you."

They came together many times and in the morning she was not ready to wake and he lay with her until she was.

They were having a light lunch in the courtyard. It seemed they were the only ones there but then it was well after noon. Mathew heard the pilot call him. He answered. The pilot informed him that the ship would be there around noon tomorrow.

"Thank you," Mathew replied. "I will be there in time for us to rendezvous with the ship."

The pilot thanked him and departed.

"You will leave tomorrow then," she said.

"Yes," Mathew replied. "I will meet the ship and we will return to Bara sometime the following day."

"Prince," she said. "We have the evening and night. Let us not waste it."

"Are you sure this is how you want to spend my last few hours here. "

"What better way than to share the time with each other. If it is our last time together, then I will have something to remember you by for the rest of my life. If it is not our last time together, then it is the beginning of something that will last the rest of our lives."

"I can't argue with that logic," Mathew said, as she led him down the hallway to the bedroom.

The next morning, they skipped breakfast. He came out around 0900 hours by his estimate of time. She still slept. He let his fingers trace the side of her face then kissed her on her forehead. There was a smile on her face when he left the room.

He entered the courtyard to find Aegis and several others near the stone wall.

"It is time, is it not," Aegis said.

"Yes, it is," Mathew replied as he approached. He reached out and the two men clasped hands then forearms.

"I will miss you, Sire," Mathew stated.

"And I you," Aegis replied, then indicating behind him, said, "As will another."

Mathew turned to find Syllium standing there in her leathers.

"I will assist you to shore," she said pointing to Reenae. "She will help me."

Mathew looked at Aegis, then spoke what he knew was in his heart.

"I will return, Sire," he said.

Aegis smiled at him, then replied.

"Yes, I know my son. It was spoken long ago before you even knew it."

Mathew didn't try to answer that. He walked to the stone ledge, looked at the two women and said, "Ladies," as he began to walk to deeper water.

They in turn looked at each other and back at Aegis who winked at them then turned away, his job done for now. By the time the water was passing over Mathew's head the women each had a forearm and were moving him under the arch into deeper water.

Mathew had taken a moment before to put on the fins. They moved swiftly through the water to near the beach. There, Syllium pulled him down, indicating she wanted to kiss him before he surfaced. He met her and they kissed a long slow kiss, then he pulled away and touched her lips and surfaced.

He swam to shore, not looking back. When he was wading out of the water, he looked back. Nothing was to be seen but the wash of the sea. He turned back to the beach and waded ashore.

The pilot was waiting for him.

"We are ready, sir," he said.

"Then let us go," Mathew replied.

"We need to wait a bit longer," the pilot stated. "A Hawk is headed this way with the new communications platform. It will only take a few minutes to have it installed and ready."

"Very well," Mathew replied. "Let two of the Hawks proceed and we will follow as soon as the platform is installed."

The pilot spoke to two others and in a moment two lifted off and headed for space. A few minutes later, a Hawk set down near where the old platform had been. The pilot and a communications specialist began unloading equipment. The other pilots moved over to help. In ten minutes' time the platform was assembled and the specialist indicated it was working as required. Mathew turned to the sea and mind spoke Syllium. He knew she was there as he had seen her silver white hair bob up a few times.

"My Lady," he said. "The communications platform is working again when you need it."

She replied. "Thanks to you, my prince. Safe journey," and there was a splash as she swam away.

Mathew was on the bridge of the Phoenix within a half hour. Logan met him with a greeting and a smile.

"I trust everything went well here," he said.

"Yes, Logan it did, and now I would like you to come with me to the ships library for we have much to discuss."

As he passed through the bridge he greeted Commander Borne and told him where they were going and that he was welcome to join them.

When they reached the library, Mathew asked the computer to bring up anything related to a Shadow Prince.

The ships computer replied that it was searching its database. After a short while, a good bit longer than it normally took for the computer to find what was requested. The computer replied that it had found a few items of interest. Including a file that was sealed and as the computer stated, it did not have the pass code to open it.

That brought a few looks from the three men.

Displayed on the large monitor was the first of several lines that gave either an answer or a statement regarding the subject?

One stated it referred to a mythical being believed to be a saint or martyr.

The second stated it was another term for the one referred to as the savior or bringer of death. The answers were of course a conflict with each other.

The third was a report taken from a former space pilot who stated that he had been on a planet where the inhabitants said a man, they referred to as the Shadow Prince had restored order on their planet. He had stopped a war that had raged across their planet for hundreds of years and shown the inhabitants how they could live together and rebuild the planet. They also said before he left he had told them that if he had to come back, he would destroy all of them and start with a new world.

The former pilot said the planet was a virtual wasteland but they all seemed to believe they could repair the damage and rebuild their society. There was a vast dead glassy plain off to one side of the badly damaged city he landed near. When he asked them what had caused that, they all repeated the same story. The man they called the Shadow Prince had stood there as two armies fought and killed each other. He had approached both sides trying to stop the fighting. They had tried to kill him but for some reason it was as if they could not touch him.

They said he stood on the hill overlooking the plains where the fighting was taking place. He raised his hands to the sky, one man told the pilot, then lowered them. Putting his hands together, he slowly spread them apart all the while pointing towards the plains. A vast fire like torch spread across the plains. When he stopped and lowered his arms, there was nothing left but the glassy surface for all else had melted. Both armies were gone.

They said he turned back to the people gathered behind him from the city and surrounding areas and told them they could either live together like the brothers and sisters they were or he would destroy them as he had their armies. It was their choice.

They all fell to their knees and promised him they would rebuild and learn to live together if he would give them a chance. It is said he picked up a small child who stood near him, then told them that they like the child, had one chance. It was important for them and the child that they didn't mess it up this time.

It was reported that he left and walked towards the mountains on the other side of the glassy plain.

The sentence ended there.

Mathew looked at the screen, at the unopened file that the computer did not have the password for. There was a line for words or numbers to be input.

Commander Borne said he had never heard of this before. Logan replied that he had not either. The communications officer entered and stated there was a transmission from Bara. Logan and the commander left.

Mathew stood there for a while looking at the monitor. His mind was racing as he stared at it.

"Computer," he said. "Type in the word Aegis" and he spelled it.

As the computer did as commanded, the file changed. Numbers and pictures began to flash across the screen. There was a glow, an almost unearthly glow from the screen then suddenly there was a bright flash and Mathew collapsed onto the floor. On the screen, was a picture of Prince Mathew in his black robe? Across the bottom of the picture were the words.

"Welcome, Shadow Prince."

For a few moments, all was quite in the library. Then the computerized librarian sensing something was not right sent a signal to the bridge. The signal indicated something was wrong in the library.

A man at the command center (none were called aides any longer as per Prince Mathews orders. They were all men.) Shouted across the bridge that something was wrong in the library. Logan and the commander looked at each other then began a fast trot in that direction as did several others.

They arrived to find Prince Mathew collapsed on the floor and there on the monitor was the lifelike picture of him and the words below it.

"Computer," Logan commanded. "Did the Prince open the file?"

"He did sir. I can report that there was a glow from the screen and a bright flash after which the picture that is on there now appeared. The prince collapsed after the bright flash and before the picture came up."

The commander ordered med techs to attend the prince. He was immediately moved to sickbay. Once there, they hooked him up to their standard monitoring equipment.

Immediately a senior med tech questioned the readings they were getting.

"There must be something wrong," he stated, instructing the others to disconnect those units and bring in another.

Logan and the commander stood outside the sickbay waiting on a report.

They noticed the frenzied activity among the techs. It was baffling as they were unaccustomed to seeing any kind of disorder among the personnel. Shortly after they hooked him up to new units, the senior tech walked over to the door and suggested they might want to come inside.

"You need to see this," he said

He instructed that the patients reading be displayed on the bigger monitor. As they brought the reading online, both Logan and the commander could see that this was not normal human readings. A tech was attempting to insert a needle in the Princes thigh where he knew there was no artificial implants. The needle would not enter. It bent every time he attempted to push it in.

"I cannot get a needle in him, sir," he said to the senior med tech.

The senior med tech stepped up and said, "Let me do it."

It was obvious he couldn't understand why the other man could not. As he attempted to do what the other man had been unable to, he found the same problem. After several attempts, he gave up.

"It will not go in," he said, stepping back from the prince.

Something is happening to his body. It is as if he is being transformed into something else.

Suddenly all the displays on the monitor began to flat line as if the prince had just died. They stood looking on. Not believing what they were seeing. Logan walked up to Mathew's body.

"What am I going to tell the princess?" he said.

He felt Mathew's body and it was as cold as ice. The senior med tech ordered the others to clear the sick bay and they all began to depart.

The Commander said to no one in particular.

"How can this be? He was fine a few minutes ago. What happened in the library?"

The two men exited the sick bay and walked directly to the library. As they stood looking at the monitor, Logan asked the computer was there anything else other than the picture on the monitor.

The computer replied that the picture could be scrolled up for the print below it.

"Do it then," Commander Borne ordered.

The picture slowly moved up and text began to show below it. It went so far and stopped.

The words there caused the two men to look at each other for they were a contradiction to what had just happened.

"Fear not, for he cannot be killed."

Logan, not one to curse, said, "What the hell does that mean?"

"I have no idea," Commander Borne stated.

"Did I miss something?"

Both men turned around, shock on their faces and that was asking a lot for an android.

Prince Mathew stood there just inside the door. He looked perfectly fine.

"I guess I took a nap," he said.

"I don't remember anything after I told the computer to open the file, other than just now waking up in sick bay. That's a scary thought," he said.

"Are you feeling okay?" Logan asked.

"Why, never better," Mathew replied. "Why do you ask?"

"Because, my young prince," he replied. "We found you collapsed on the floor in here right after you opened that file and speaking of which, have you seen what was on the monitor."

"No," Mathew replied. "I don't think I have."

Turning, he pointed at the monitor. Mathew could see the print then watched as the computer as if on cue scrolled back up to the picture of Mathew and the label below it that said, "Welcome, Shadow Prince."

Mathew stared at the screen for several moments then spoke to no one in particular when he said.

"I guess the cat's out of the bag now."

Chapter 23 – To Save a President

The transport tunnel doors were open when the Hawk arrived at Area Base 51. The pilot flew into the corridor and landed in front of the medical team already alerted and ready. They quickly unloaded the stretcher with the president encased inside. This stretcher wasn't your standard unit found on earth. It was an all encasing unit that took over control of the body's life giving organs and kept the person within alive or as close as their condition would allow.

As they moved the stretcher into the prepared operating theater, Van was moving alongside it assessing the readouts and making preparations for his patient for the next few minutes while they transferred him to an operating chamber. They now had a sterile chamber ready and as the stretcher was aligned alongside, they made the transfer.

As quick as they were cleared of the stretcher, it was wheeled away to be cleansed. Now, more invasive systems began to connect to the president's body. The first thing Van did was insure the president was heavily sedated and pain free. It was, he observed, going to be a touch and go process as the president was only alive because of the medical advances their stretcher and now the operating chamber gave them.

Assisting Van would be the one of the Army doctors who had asked so many questions when they introduced the units to the military and U.S. government. He had become well educated on the surgical chambers use, but till now had not had a lot of opportunities to use it.

Another few persons would be there to assist as needed and a whole team stood by to prepare any artificial replacement parts. Trainer spoke to Van via his communicator.

"Don't ask me how to proceed, Van. Just do what needs to be done and please try to bring him back to us. No one is expecting miracles so if we happen to get a few, then so much the better for all of us."

Van acknowledged him and continued his assessments.

He already had a good idea of what he was going to be doing first and began instructing those in the room with him, exactly what they would need once the surgery started. He moved over to stand beside the military surgeon he knew as Todd.

Pointing at the screen on the side of the chamber he spoke.

"We have damage to the main aorta leaving the heart. One of his kidneys is in pieces as is his appendix. I see three punctures to his lungs and a wound to the back of his skull. Aside from that, his arms were badly damaged because he used them to shield his head and shoulders."

Todd looked at the monitor for a few seconds longer then spoke.

"I believe you are correct and of course the arms are the least of our worries, right?"

"That's right. They will keep till we have taken care of the critical issues. So, if you are ready, let's get started."

Todd nodded he was and Van instructed the chamber to open up the chest cavity and install the clamps. The clamps would keep the cavity open while they worked on the inside. Saline solution and blood expanders were being connected as the chamber went to work on the patient.

A robotic arm made a mark on the president's chest then followed with an incision. The incision began above the breast bone and sliced through it as if it was butter yet it only went as deep as was needed and not a fraction more. It continued to just above the naval and stopped there, then made short incisions across the lower stomach from left to right. More arms moved in and gripped the inside of the rib cage where it had been separated and spread it just enough to give everyone working room and good sight of the insides.

Van could see a massive pool of blood within. He called for suction and as the blood was suctioned with most of it to be filtered and reused, they could see the wound in the aorta.

"Todd," Van said. "It's all yours."

Fluids were being administered while Todd began applying the patch to the aorta. Van began removing the damaged appendix and the kidney. He had them out and closed up by the time Todd was finished with the all the heart related repairs. He discovered some near blockages in the veins near the heart as he worked and fixed those too.

Todd spoke. "Sorry I'm so slow, Van."

"You're doing fine and you will get much faster as your confidence builds. It was the same with me and all my kind."

"You can't tell, by watching you," Todd replied. "I hope if I ever need a surgeon working on me, it's you."

Todd began to seal the wounds in the lungs. The bullets had gone through and through and they were fortunate that none hit the spinal cord. Todd suspected they could probably fix that as well but he didn't ask.

"So, how's his pressure now?" Van asked.

"It's building up and brain waves are good and steady," Todd replied. "I still don't understand how these machines are able to keep the brain alive and well when there is hardly anything left in the body to circulate and feed it."

"Some things are a mystery to me too," Van replied. "Remind me later to show you something we hope to introduce to all your military and police personnel. It's no bigger than a nickel yet it does those things for a limited amount of time and is monitored by a remote computer system that alerts those watching after it that the person is in trouble."

"Van," Todd said. "You and your kind are giving us a whole lot more than you'll ever get back. We will never be able to repay you."

"It's not about paying or owing," Van replied. "It's about insuring that we all live and co-exist into a better future for everyone."

They finished cleaning up the insides, making sure they had not missed anything. When they had everything looking good, Van instructed the chamber to close the president up. The clamps pulled the rib cage back together and a sealant was used where the breast bone had been separated. Then the folds of flesh were brought back together from above the breastbone to the naval as well as those that were cut to each side. In minutes, as the sealants took hold, it was hard to tell there was ever an incision.

Both men walked over to a monitor. Displayed on the larger one was a rotating view of the president's bone structure. Markers indicated where any damage to his skeleton was located. It was hard to find anything salvageable on either arm.

The only plus was no damage was above the shoulders aside from the wound to the back of his skull. They had already determined he suffered a concussive blow but he would recover from that. The legs were only slightly better than the arms.

It was late evening. They both knew the president would live. Now they had to decide what types of repairs to do to his arms and legs. It was then that Trainer broke in on Van's communicator.

"I've followed the operation but I would like you to tell me what the prognosis is for him."

Van replied.

"He is going to live. We have completed the repairs to his internals. He is slowly stabilizing and should only get stronger. I would like Todd to help me with the arms and I think it would not hurt anything if we waited till morning and let Todd get some rest. He was up early and has been at it all day. I could do it all myself but he really does need the experience."

"Sounds good but I have one more job for both of you before you retire for the evening. The president's physicians and press secretary are outside. I would like you to brief them on what has been done and what you feel is the recovery time for the president before he can resume some kind of routine."

"Very well," Van replied. "We can handle that."

He turned to Todd and informed him that there were visitors outside who needed to be brought up to speed on the Presidents condition.

"I think," he said, "it would be in all our best interests if you filled them in."

The Captain walked into the adjoining room to remove his gown and gloves. Then proceeded to enter the nearby conference room they usually used for training discussions. Several men and women were sitting at the table and they quickly stood as he entered.

"Please remain seated," he said. "I am going to sit with you. It has been a long evening and I am really tired right now. Before I say anything else, please let me introduce myself as I don't think any of us have met before now.

"I'm Captain Todd West but please call me Todd or Captain Todd. I recognize some of you as being the president's physicians although I do not know all of your fields."

He paused as he shifted in his seat, then continued.

"I'm sure you have questions, so let us get on with that, shall we."

One of the men raised his hand before speaking.

"Captain Todd. I'm John Turner, press secretary for the president. The American public knows the president was killed earlier today. We are unsure exactly why we are here unless it involves something other than the disposition of his body. None of us feel this meeting was necessary but we really didn't have a choice in the matter."

"Mr. Turner," Captain Todd said, pausing, before continuing. "We did not ask you here to tell you we have a body to dispense with. We asked you hear to update you on the president's condition."

He raised his hand as Turner went to speak.

"Let me finish, please. The President, contrary to public opinion and the news services is not dead. He is not a vegetable, if you're wondering and in fact he will be on his feet and able to resume some of his work in about six weeks.

"That is why you were brought here. Now, do you have any questions or do you think you have enough information."

One of the physicians spoke.

"We saw photos of the president as he was being moved out of the car. He was a virtual rag doll. Wounds to his head, his arms practically destroyed and you're telling us he lived through that and will be back on the job in a little over a month's time. What kind of facility are you running here? No one else in this country could bring someone back after that."

"You're right, sir," Todd replied. "No one else in this country could have but this facility is not from this country, in fact it is not even from this world but the ones that run it never even considered if the president would live or not. That wasn't an option. He had to live and so he will.

"I can tell you now that I assisted in the surgery that saved his life and while we are not yet finished with him, his vitals are all intact and he is out of danger. In the morning, we will start transplants of his arms. I don't know if anything else will be required for his legs but that will be determined overnight."

"In about one month's time, you will be able to see him and if he is willing, talk to him as well. In about six weeks' time, he will be mobile and although he will still require some physical therapy, he should be able to resume some of his presidential duties."

The press secretary and the physicians broke into their own conversation, trying to decide who was going to say what. One of the physicians asked Todd if he wanted to take part in the press briefing. Todd told them no. He needed some rest. He was available if they had any questions but he would leave the publicity to them.

The press secretary turned to Todd and spoke.

"When this is over, Captain Todd, how will we know that in fact this President is the same man we saw shot in the assassination attempt and not a replacement? I do not doubt that you have the ability to do such a thing."

"Your right," Todd replied, "but I assure you that this is your president and you or anyone else you choose will be free to check him out when the time for it becomes necessary as I know it will. Now, gentlemen, if you will excuse me, I have rounds to make and then I must get some rest for tomorrow is going to be a long day."

Todd stopped to check on the president. There were several men nearby monitoring the chamber he was in. He recognized one as Casey, another surgeon who usually worked with Van. He spoke to him as he went out. They exchanged pleasantries then Todd went on into the quarters.

He stopped by the workout area. Some of the team U.K. members were there. They waved at him then trotted over to where he stood.

He recognized Colin who spoke first.

"How did it go?" Colin asked.

"It went well," Todd replied. "Very well, considering and tomorrow we will replace the arms. They are evaluating the rest and will decide between now and then."

"Good," Colin replied. "Lucky for him, you guys are here and able to do for him what you did for us."

"Yes, lucky for him and hopefully in the near future, you guys will be on the front lines removing the threats we face, like the president faced earlier today."

Colin smiled and spoke. "That's the plan and I for one am looking forward to getting activated and becoming part of the force that will be shutting down people like those that wish nothing more than to harm others."

"All of us are ready for that," chimed in Graham, another team mate.

"Thanks guys," Todd said. "Now if you will excuse me, I'm going to get a shower and some rest. We've got another big day ahead of us tomorrow."

"Later," they said as they went back across the workout area to their earlier activities.

#

Trainer and Van were discussing the transplants for the president in the morning.

"Have you thought about what you want to give him?" Trainer asked.

"Yes, initially, I had thought that all that was needed was the standard type. Nothing extra, just new arms but then it occurred to me that he is always going to be facing some type of threat. Either now or later and it only make good sense if he has the basic abilities to protect himself and his family, so I plan on giving him the force ones with the water breather and the e-displacer. He will always have the option to use them and if they aren't needed then good but if they are, then better."

"Sounds good to me, Van, now what about the legs?"

"According to our scans, he is developing arthritis in his feet, and his knee joints are shot, so I believe it would be prudent to do his legs from just above the knees down and he won't ever have to suffer that in the future."

"Sounds like you have it all worked out then. Thanks for bringing him back for us."

"All part of the job," Van replied. "Now, I think I am going to get some hot tea and take a brief break."

Chapter 24 – Two Princes

"Cats out of the bag," Commander Borne said. "What does that mean?"

"It means," Logan said. "The secret is out or there is a story to tell. Is that not right, prince?"

"Yes," Mathew replied.

"That is pretty much what it means and I need to tell you gentlemen some things and I need to get some things done before we get to Bara."

"Let's go to someplace more private, say, Logan's quarters," Commander Borne said.

Logan had the former human captain's quarters. The one Mathew had kept when he was onboard before. They entered the quarters and Mathew took the first seat he saw. As the other two found a place, he started speaking.

"Earlier, I asked the computer to bring up any information it had on the mythical shadow prince," and he paused.

"The fact is, the shadow prince is not a myth but someone who does exist and goes from planet to planet, galaxy to galaxy stopping wars and fighting bad. That does sound a bit theatrical but it pretty much sums it up."

"According to legend, a new prince is introduced every thousand years or so. No one knows how the process works, only that it does and the chosen one has no choice in the selection. His life is no longer his own and he must march to the beat of another's drum, so to speak.

"I am told, that the prince will have a long life, become practically immortal and if wounded will heal himself and I suppose, both of you are wondering where this is leading. Gentlemen, you are looking at the next Shadow Prince."

Neither man sitting across from him spoke for a few seconds. Then Logan spoke.

"I'm not going to ask how you know this is so. I suspect something happened on Finnean that got you here. What I need to know is what about Bara and your wife, the Princes Alexis."

"Logan. That is the worst part. She can go with me but she has to leave behind Bara and our child. There will be more but she will live by herself waiting on me to return from wherever I have been sent. That could be months or years. It is a life of loneliness and not everyone is cut out for it. That is why I said earlier that I needed to get some things done before I leave the ship."

"What might that be," Commander Borne asked.

"I need to transform one of the men, into as near a likeness of me as possible. Someone to stand in my place once I leave, for I am pretty sure that the princess is not going to leave Bara and I want her to have someone at her side. If later, she chooses to take another, then that is her choice but at least for now, only you two, her mother and she will know it."

"You are certain of this transformation that is to occur to you, Prince Mathew?"

"Yes sir, I am. Already my body is changing. Merging with my transplants and soon it will be as if they don't exist. I feel different now and I am developing new abilities I can't even yet explain."

"That explains why the med techs couldn't get a needle in you earlier," Logan said.

"I hope you know what you are doing," Commander Borne replied "but if you are serious about this transformation, then we best get it started."

They all rose and followed Commander Borne out and down the corridor. The Commander showed Prince Mathew where to wait and left. Soon after, he returned with an aide, one that had been in stasis. Several med techs came with him.

Mathew allowed himself to be led to a chamber nearby. The aide took his place in the adjoining one. Mathew was positioned on the couch in the chamber. The aide was strapped in. Sometimes the recipient felt the need to move and so the restraints. A drop down scanner was brought into position over Prince Mathew. A head set was positioned on his head. A more extensive device was lowered onto the aide.

Mathew was told to close his eyes and not reopen them until instructed. In a few moments there was a subtle humming sound. Mathew sensed the machine was performing some type of scan and his brain was being scanned as well. That went on for over an hour, after which the humming stopped. Mathew was told he could open his eyes.

He did, then sat up. All the equipment had been removed from above him as had the head set and he hadn't even realized it.

He looked over at the other chamber. Lying there was an exact replica of himself. He wondered what the other was thinking. He didn't have long to wait as the aide sat up. One of the techs asked him his name. He replied.

"Prince Mathew, but my friends call me Mathew."

Mathew walked over to him. "Prince Mathew," he said.

"Yes, Sire," the prince replied.

"You know who I am?"

"Yes, Sire. You are the reason I am."

"Would you humor me?" Mathew asked.

"How so?" he replied.

"I want to look into your eyes," Mathew replied. "I will tell you some things which you should know about Princess Alexis."

"As you wish, Sire?"

Mathew stepped up to the new Prince. He reached out and took the new princes head in his hands and brought his own face to within centimeters of the new prince. Mathew then held him there for a half hour. When he was finished he released his hold on the new prince and stepped back."

The other Prince Mathew spoke.

"It will be as you command, Sire."

"Thank you Prince," Mathew replied. "I am sure you will make a very good husband and father."

He then turned to a med tech and said, "Now, he must be able to father children with my seed."

"Come this way please, both of you," and the med tech led them off to another room. In thirty minutes, both men returned.

Logan stood waiting. "Do you think this will work?" he said.

"It will work for as long as she wants it too," he replied.

The next day found them landing on Bara. Mathew and Logan took a Hawk up to the cliffs above the palace. Shadow met them there.

"Welcome home, Mathew," she sent.

"Hello, Shadow," Mathew replied. "Everything okay here."

"No, not really, Sire."

"Why do you say that? Did something happen while I was gone."

"I think you know the answer to that, Mathew," she spoke. Her eyes were ever so sad.

Mathew dropped down to his knees in front of her. Taking her head in his hands, he drew her close.

"I'm so sorry," he said, "but if you know, then you know I had no say in this."

"Yes," Shadow replied. "I know. We all know. It still does not make it any easier."

"You said we all know. You mean Alexis and the Queen as well."

"Yes. We had to tell her. This allowed her time to prepare."

"But how did you know."

"We always know, but in this case, you told us. No, not intentionally but the signs were there."

"How did she take it?" Mathew asked, standing and turning to see who was approaching.

"Not well, my prince but now she is here and you and she can talk."

Alexis slowly approached. Her swollen pregnant belly leading the way and she was, even in sadness, radiant and beautiful, he thought. She approached him slowly then quickened her steps and ran to meet him. They held each other close as she began to sob. He took her over to a bench and they sat together. She wouldn't let go of him, just lowered her head into his lap and cried. Finally, when she had cried all she could, she sat up. Her fingers tracing his face.

"I love you," she said.

"I love you more," he replied.

"Why?" she asked. "Why did this have to happen to us?"

Mathew took her hand in his then spoke. "If I had a choice, I would not be a part of this," he said. "You have shown me what being in love and having a family is about. I would never give this up willingly. I hope you know that."

"I do," she replied in a very low voice. "I do." She stood. "Come," she said. "Let's go in. Mother wants to see you."

"Are you sure," Mathew asked.

"Yes, she said once we had this part over with, we should come to her. We have, she insists, a lot to talk about."

They entered the royal quarters and walked to the central lounge area. Logan and Queen Marie occupied one couch. She looked up as they approached.

"Hello, Mathew," she said. Then pointing at the couch across from her, indicated that he and Alexis should sit.

"I would," she said, "like very much to be angry with you but I understand this is not your doing. It is hard to understand. Perhaps we never will but as hard as it is for me and as hard as it is for Alexis, I suspect it is harder for you."

Mathew could no longer stop the tears as they streamed down his face and he knew that for now, he couldn't speak. For a brief moment he fought the urge to cry and then finally gave in, lowering his head and letting his emotions out.

He could feel Alexis' arm across his back and her head on his shoulder and knew she had given in as well. After nearly ten minutes, he raised his head. Queen Marie lay across Logan's lap, for she too had given in to her emotions.

Mathew sat there for some few minutes gathering himself, for he knew they had much to discuss. Alexis rose and left, only to return a few minutes later with warm clothes for each of them to wash their faces and dry their eyes.

Mathew looked at Alexis then asked if she was feeling okay.

She said she was but the baby was really active.

"Is it time yet?" Mathew asked.

"Any day," she replied.

"Alexis, my Princess, he said. "You know I have to ask you this question."

"Yes," she replied, "and you already know what my answer is, don't you?"

"Yes, I suppose I do, but I need to hear you say it."

"I'm sorry, my love. I would die for you but I will not leave this world and my family to never return. It is something I just cannot do."

"I know and it's that part of you that I love the most."

Queen Marie spoke. "What do we tell the people? Mathew."

"My Queen," he said, looking over at Alexis. "I propose you tell them nothing."

"But you will be gone and they will ask questions," Alexis said.

"Bear with me please," Mathew said. "I have made arrangements for someone to stand in my place."

"But they will know, I mean, will he look like you?"

"Actually, my lady, he will. He is an exact replica of me. He has all my features, my voice and if you will forgive me, dear, he has been instructed on everything you and I like."

"Everything?" Alexis asked.

"Well, maybe I left out a few small things, but most everything."

"So, when do we see this other you," Marie asked.

"After I am gone, my Lady," Mathew replied. "Until then, I am still husband to my Princess here."

Alexis looked directly at him. "Everything?" She repeated again.

"Everything," Mathew replied.

#

A week later, Alexis went into labor and gave birth to their son. Mathew was there beside her and took him from the midwife. He bundled the young prince and walked out of the room. Moments later, he returned. Alexis was now cleaned up and held out her arms for her son. Mathew gave him up and sat in the chair next to the bed. The two of them chatted over how handsome he was.

They had long ago decided on the name of Mathew Trainer Farmer. They couldn't think of anything else suitable to add to it for the Barans only took one name, mostly a first name. Few ever had more than one. Mathew was sure once the people heard what the new prince's name was, a new custom would be born.

Everything went well for the next month, then Logan received a call from the ship. He was gone for half a day and then returned.

"We have a situation," he told the others at dinner.

"What kind of situation?" Queen Marie asked.

"There appears to be a meteor headed this way, according to the ships long range scanners. They say it is coming straight for this planet and on its present course, they believe it will hit us."

"What can we do?" Queen Marie said.

"We can try to shoot it down, before it gets too much closer," Logan replied, "but at the speed it is traveling, that is going to be very difficult and even if we do succeed in hitting it, the pieces will still hit the planet."

Mathew had kept quiet till then. Then he spoke.

"What is the estimated time of arrival of this meteor?"

"Three days, at its current rate of speed according to the ship."

"Then it will be here in four days' time," he said.

"How can you know?" Alexis asked.

"That is not a meteor," Mathew stated. "It is my Transporter. It is coming to pick me up."

"Oh," she said, "then it is nearly time. Could you arrange for me to meet this new you before your last day."

"Now why would you ask that, Alexis?"

"I want to get a feel for him. See if I am going to be able to get along with him."

"You get along with Lord Logan, don't you?"

"Yes, but he is not my stand in husband."

"Okay, if you insist but do you think you will be able to tell us apart."

Queen Marie spoke up. "I bet I can."

"How about you, Logan?" Mathew asked. "Can you tell him apart from me?"

Logan grinned, which usually meant he was on to something.

"Okay, Logan," Marie said. "What do you know, that we don't know?"

"I know the other Prince Mathew has been in this house for at least a week of the last month off and on and it's obvious that neither of you did," indicating the two women.

"Mathew," Alexis squealed. "Is he telling the truth, has the other prince been here?"

"Alexis," Mathew replied with a grin. "He has been in and out and even slept in your bed on two occasions."

"Oh, my," she said, then she hesitated. "You really did tell him everything, didn't you?"

"I guess I did," Mathew replied. "The point is, if you can't tell, then neither will anyone else."

"There is one that will know," Alexis said.

"Yes, I know," Mathew replied. "Shadow will know."

"Can you not take her with you?"

"I don't know," Mathew replied. "If I could and she would go, then I would."

"Have you asked her?" Alexis asked.

"No, I haven't," Mathew replied. "Truthfully, I haven't thought to."

"Perhaps you should at least ask her if she would like to go with the understanding that you don't know if she will be able to."

"I will tomorrow," Mathew replied.

"Okay, then, it is settled," Alexis replied. Then with that look in her eyes, she said. "Now, my prince, you and I need to retire to our bedroom. I want to make some comparisons."

"Do you now," Mathew said, all the time following her towards the purple door he knew he was going to soon miss.

#

Out in space, the meteor come Transporter continued on its fiery path towards Bara.

In another galaxy, light years away. In a star system named after the Zetans, a war raged once again between two nations of people. It had been going on for hundreds of years. Many died. There had been a few years when the fighting stopped but it was mainly just to regroup and replace those that died fighting. The reasons for the war were no longer clear although many said it was the other side's treachery that started it and now no one could see a way out. Eventually, one would have to win over the other but for now, it was pretty much a standoff with millions already dead and more to come if someone didn't step in to stop it.

#

On Finnean, the woman named Syllium suffered another miscarriage. The others told her she had tried again too soon.

"Fear not," her father told her. "He will return."

She spent hours near the surface of the water over their reef home watching the stars, wondering if in fact the Prince would indeed return for her. Many nights in the reef below, she cried herself to sleep.

Chapter 25 – Goodbye to Bara

The meteor was scheduled to impact Baran space within the next few hours. Even the locals could see it as it approached, prompting some to approach government officials expressing their concern that this was a bad situation. Having been previously notified, the officials assured the locals that all would be alright, although, as the bright light in the night sky got ever closer, they themselves began to have concerns.

Mathew and Alexis stood on the rock ledge above the palace watching it as it got ever closer. Shadow was there earlier, expressing her desire to accompany Mathew if it was possible. Mathew had put the question to her a few days back and asked that she discuss it with her family as it was unlikely she would be back if he could in fact take her with him. That had been three days before and it was just now that she had come back with her answer.

The day before, Mathew received what one could only call a revelation. As if he suddenly had received a call to tell him what he was to do next. Only this came to him as a thought. The Transporter would crash through the upper atmosphere then slow down and come to rest on the ridge overlooking the grounds where the festival was held. He was to make his way there and find the Transporter open waiting for his entry. There was space for two humans although nothing was said as to whether the other had to be a human.

One thing they had not talked about was whether Mathew would ever be able to return to Bara. Alexis chose this moment to ask him if he thought he might be able to return some day.

"Alexis," he said, "I cannot say whether I will be able to or not but I fear that when and if I am ever able to, it will be many years after you have passed. That is what I sense but I don't really know. I do know that a thousand years living is a long time and I don't know if it is something I can look forward to as a blessing or a curse."

"It is a long time but I want you to know that at this moment, I believe I am making the right decision for me and Bara. I may regret it later but for now, it is the right thing for me and our son and those who will come later."

"Yes, Alexis. It is the right decision and the one I knew from the start you would make. It is why I prepared the other me and I hope that over time you come to think of him as me and this moment in our lives will be just a fond memory."

"I will try very hard," Alexis said. "I will never be able to forget you, Mathew, but I will work very hard at letting the other you find a place in my heart."

"I know you will do just fine," Mathew said and paused as the Transporter entered the upper atmosphere. There was a loud sonic boom as its momentum carried ahead of it. It appeared as a giant fireball streaking towards the planet's surface. In the distance they lost sight of it.

It was late evening and Alexis asked if he could wait till morning. She wanted one more night with him if it was possible."

"We will make it possible," Mathew said and they turned and went back down to the palace quarters below.

The next morning, just as the first rays of sunlight touched the horizon, four people and five Houns boarded the shuttle waiting above the palace. The pilot for this ride was the other Mathew. He greeted each as they boarded then took a moment to move over to Mathew. He reached out for Mathews hand and then they clasped forearms.

"I will not let you down," he said. "May your journey be safe and all your battles see you victorious. We will not forget you, Sire or what you have done for us. I do not speak just for the Barans but for all the aides whom you have treated as equals. If ever we can be of service, just call and we will come," then he turned and went back to the shuttle controls.

In a few minutes, they set down on the slope below the Transporter. It looked just like a giant piece of lava or meteor. It's outer shell black, pitted and still smoking. One section was open and within, they could see two lounge shaped chairs. As they moved closer, it appeared stark and barren aside from the lounges but Mathew was certain there was more within than they were seeing.

"Say your goodbyes, Shadow," Mathew said as he turned and took Alexis in his arms for the last time.

Shadow mind spoke her mother, father, Tran and Stone, then she trotted over to the Transporter and trotted up the small ramp. Once inside, she hoped up onto one of lounges and sat there waiting for Mathew.

They held each other for a few minutes then Mathew kissed her a long slow kiss. Afterwards, he touched his fingers to his lips, touched her forehead and then hugged Queen Marie before turning to Logan.

"I will miss you my friend," he said.

"I pray your years ahead are peaceful and well spent and they clasped hands then forearms.

Mathew walked towards the Transporter then as he reached the ramp he turned and looked back.

"I will not say goodbye," he said. "Just farewell for now, as I start this journey. May God protect and look after each of you and those to follow."

Alexis turned and found the chest of the new Mathew. She stood there, his arm around her shoulder and waved at Mathew as he entered the Transporter. Mathew stopped only long enough to place a harness around Shadow then fitted his own. As he lifted his hand in farewell, the Transporter door slammed shut with a loud bang. Moments later it lifted off the ridge and with a sudden roar, shot up into space.

Mathew looked over at shadow. She was lying on the chair, her dark brown eyes focused on Mathew.

"Well, girl," he said. "It looks like it is just you and I for now."

"Yes," she replied, "but somehow, I sense not for long."

Chapter 26 – The Ark Awakens

The Presidents eyes opened and he tried to focus on his surroundings. Van had a warm cloth in his hand which he used moments before on the president's eyes to remove the matt. Todd held a water bottle in his hand and told him not to try to speak before he had taken a few sips of water.

He acknowledged and took the straw Todd offered. A few moments later he tried to clear his throat and speak. The first words out of his mouth were.

"I suppose this is where Trainer say's I told you so."

"A bit late for that, sir," Van replied. "Glad to see you still have your sense of humor."

"Can I ask what I don't have because I feel very heavy and in a bit of pain?"

"You remember the assassination attempt; I assume?" Van asked as he punched buttons on the med panel.

"Yes, it seems like it went on forever in slow motion. I remember the woman shooting the agent in the head and thinking, this is not good. There was an explosion and then bullets coming through the roof of the car. I don't remember much after that."

"That's probably enough. We had our people close by but not close enough to stop the assault, only to end it."

"What about the others? Did they survive?

"Sorry sir, but you were the only survivor."

"You got the bastards responsible for this."

"Yes sir, including the intern on a congressman's staff that was passing on all your travel details. It's not likely he will see the light of day for a while."

"So what about me and my condition and what did you have to do to me?"

"We had to replace your arms and your legs from just above the knees. In a few weeks' time, you will start therapy and soon after that, you won't know them from the ones you had before."

"What about the public?" He asked, his voice starting to fade. Van had already programmed the pain meds and his sleep period was extended for two more weeks.

"They're aware that you will be back soon, sir," Van said, then stopped as the President was asleep.

They closed the chamber and left him there to rest and heal and perhaps dream.

#

At the big dig site, Brad and General Neagle were watching as the excavators were removing the last of the dirt and sand from beneath the spacecraft's overhanging structure. On occasion one of the dozen excavators could be heard banging into the skin of the spacecraft but they had been told earlier they couldn't damage it with the machines.

"Tomorrow, General," Brad said.

"Tomorrow, what?" Neagle asked.

"Tomorrow, they will use their thrusters to lift the vessel up enough to let the loose soil fall away from the underside. Then they will set her back down and we can start setting up the access gangway."

"You mean we've completed the digging?

"Yes, general, we have completed the digging.

"Well, happy day," Neagle said. "I thought we had another month or so to go."

"Sorry to bust your bubble," Brad replied, "but tomorrow we start sending the excavation equipment away. The riggers will remain for a while as will some of the cranes and operators."

"What do you plan to do with all the laborers?"

"We'll give them a severance bonus and send them on their way. Some will be able to take the portable cabins with them which we will move at our expense as we agreed."

"So a win win for all of them but the work is over."

"Yes and no. We have some major infrastructure work we hope to convince the government to jump into. That will provide a lot of work for construction all across the country and most of these men and women should not be too long out of work."

"Great," Neagle said. "I'm glad someone has finally figured out how to drive this economy and as our friend Mathew would say, save the planet as well."

"Funny you should mention Mathew," Brad said.

"Why, something up with him?" Neagle asked.

"More than something, I'm afraid or so I am told. The details have only been forthcoming the last few days. I have asked trainer to add that to your training aid. It might be helpful to know one day and if not for you then perhaps your ancestors a few hundred years from now."

"Damn," Neagle said. "Whatever it is must have been pretty impressive."

"That's not the choice of words I would have used. More like earth shaking and life altering would come closer to fitting the bill. Have you ever heard of a mythical being called the Shadow Prince?"

"No, I can't say that I have but I am all ears now if you want to enlighten me."

"As they headed back to their office, Brad told him what he knew so far."

The next day found them once again standing on the tower. All the excavators had been moved from the pit. A line cordoning off the edge of the pit was in place. Team members were positioned at various locations to prevent anyone from getting too close.

The media was in full force, having been informed the day before that the vessel was going to come to life today. Up till now, the Eden Paradise 7 had been dark. No sign of life but in moments that was about to change.

Trainer had, several days before, sent the codes that woke the crew within the ship. Now, they were going about their duties within. About two hours after Brad and Neagle mounted the tower; there was a shift in the noise levels in the area.

At first, you could detect a subtle humming sound but you couldn't tell where it was coming from. As the tempo of the sound increased, lights began to appear along the outside of the ship. It was as if they had suddenly appeared out of the metal shell that made up the ship.

Soon it was obvious that the sound came from the ship and dust was beginning to kick up around the edges of the hull where it contacted with the ground. It maintained that position and sound level for about twenty minutes, then as they watched, the ship began to lift up from the pit.

As it rose about forty feet above the floor of the pit, large landing pads began to lower from the underside. As soon as they were extended, the ship began rotating first one way then the other and finally began to lower down until the pads were fully engaged with the soil beneath.

Earlier information had given the size of the ship but it hadn't said how tall it was and as the men looked on, making casual conversation, they both agreed that it was at least ten stories in height at its highest point.

The noise level began to decrease and the strobe lights slowed down until they only just appeared to move. After another ten minutes a hatchway began to open and a ramp appeared beneath the overhanging hull. In less than a minute, it was fully extended and all grew quiet except for the low range humming sound.

The hatch being open was very inviting and Brad asked General Neagle if he cared to accompany him onto the ship.

"Now," Neagle asked.

"Yes, now," Brad replied, "all the time in a conversation with someone else."

As they descended from the observation tower, one of the team members drove up on a gator with tracks. They got on with him and he began motoring down into the pit and up to the ramp. A minute later, they were parked at the bottom of the ramp. Already there to meet them on the ramp was Briant and Casey. They were sent by Trainer to handle introductions.

As they stood at the bottom of the ramp, several aides marched down it. These were earlier versions looking more masculine with tougher features but still able to pass as humans if you didn't know otherwise.

The first down the gangway stopped, saluted the General then spoke.

"Welcome sir, I am First Officer Christopher." He indicated the man behind as being Commander Robin.

Casey stepped up and spoke. "Please allow me to introduce," and he pointed first at Brad, "Brad Bowen, and General Neagle. They are your primary points of contact here and Mr. Bowen is the liaison between Trainer and operations."

Commander Robin reached out and shook first Brad's hand then Neagles.

"Gentlemen," he said, "would you care to join me on the bridge." He then turned and strode up the ramp. Brad and Neagle first looked at each other and then Neagle offered Brad the lead. They followed the commander up the ramp. The First Officer remained behind with Briant and Casey.

Brad had never been on a spaceship before and looked around with interest as they entered what appeared to be a portion of a hangar area. There was equipment stored nearby that he didn't recognize but he didn't have time to check them out as the commander continued across and up to a lift. He signaled for the lift and waited for Brad and Neagle to catch up.

"Right this way," he said, as he led them into the lift. There was a counter on the wall of the lift and it went up at least six floors by Brads estimate. The lift opened and they found themselves in a corridor. The Commander led them off to their left and around a gradual curve. They noticed several doors along the way but in a moment they approached a pair of double doors which separated, sliding apart in opposite directions.

Before them was the bridge with numerous control and command stations. As Neagle would later say to Brad, "every bit like what you would expect to see on a spaceship bridge and more."

The Commander introduced them to several officers and other specialist at various stations on the bridge. They all appeared to be running checks and commands on different systems.

Brad spoke. "They all appear to be very busy at the moment. System checks, I assume."

"You are correct," the Commander said. "The ship has been in sleep mode for a few hundred years and everything has to be checked out as we bring her back on line. It will take several weeks before she is travel ready."

The Commander spoke to General Neagle.

"General Neagle, I understand you and your staff will be traveling with us when we depart."

"Yes, Commander, that is the plan. I hope we will not be a hindrance for you."

"No, Sir," Commander Robin replied.

"It will give us all a chance to catch up on Earth routines and habits. I think it will promise to be beneficial for all of us."

"I look forward to it then," Neagle replied.

They stayed on the bridge for another hour after which, Brad asked how the Commander planned to handle the visitors that would soon be coming onboard.

"We planned for this, years ago, but a picture is more valuable so follow me to our secondary conference room. There we have a layout of the areas that contain either replicas or remnants of what we brought to Earth all those hundred years ago."

He led them down the corridor to the lift. They went down one level and soon after, found themselves in a large conference type room.

The walls had pictorial diagrams and the tables had miniature scale models of what they had set up in the vast storage bays down below.

It was all very well set up and an excellent guide to what was to be seen in the storage bays.

"Looks like you thought of everything," Brad said.

"I hope so," the Commander replied. "It is, I believe, human nature to be skeptical and so we have worked hard to cover all the bases. There are still locations that are, we believe, yet undiscovered that will further prove our point as regards the resettling of the Edenites on Earth. We will, when the time is right, disclose the locations. It will give researchers, scientists and of course the doubters much food for thought and investigations for years to come."

"Sounds great," General Neagle said, "and having said that, I believe Mr. Bowen and myself have an appointment with the news media, who are no doubt chomping at the bit so to speak to get a look at this vessel."

"You realize that some areas are not going to be accessible to everyone," Commander Robin said.

Brad spoke.

"We fully understand and will cooperate in all matters that pertain to ship safety and security. I understand you have a less than full crew here and if you need any additional personnel for ships security, just advise how many and when and they will be provided."

"Thank you for understanding. We will likely be taking you up on that offer," Commander Robin replied.

Chapter 27 – Ice Cream and Pie

Van and Captain Todd stood on each side of the bed the president lay in. Hours earlier, they removed him from the surgical chamber he spent the last month in. Now he was well on the way in the healing process and it was time to wake him. Van wiped away the matt from his eyes and Todd held the water bottle, as they waited for the President to wake up.

While they watched, he lay there, not yet opening his eyes but licking his lips. No doubt he was aware of how dry his mouth was.

"Probably thinking about all the presidential duties undone since his encounter with the assassins," Van thought.

After a few moments, he opened his eyes. First he glanced at Captain Todd and then Van. Todd offered him the straw end of the water bottle and he accepted it, taking several good sips before releasing the tip of the straw. He licked his lips some more then looking at Van, he spoke.

"I remember you," then glancing at Todd, he said, "Captain."

"Yes, Mr. President, welcome back."

"I vaguely remember you telling me you had to replace my arms and lower legs but I don't feel the prosthetics," he said.

"You won't sir," Todd told him. "They are a part of your body now. You just have to get used to the extra weight and that will come with your rehab."

"You mean they are connected permanently?" he said, then added, "I guess I knew that."

"Yes, sir, it's a permanent fix," Todd told him.

"Can I sit up?" he asked.

"Certainly," Van replied. "Let me raise the bed for you." In a few moments, the president was in an upright position. He raised his left arm then lowered it. He trembled as he did it. A moment later, he did the same with his right arm.

"You're right, they are a bit heavier. Is the red area where they are connected?" he asked.

"Yes sir," Todd replied, "but over time, the red will fade and it will all look natural."

"And my legs, they are the same.

"Yes they are. They were replaced just above the knees."

"They feel pretty heavy," he said.

"Don't worry, sir. In a week's time, you will be walking normally and before long, you won't even know they weren't your original legs."

"I hate to keep asking questions but you're saying I will have full mobility in a few weeks' time. Does that mean I will be able to resume my presidential duties?"

"Mr. President, as of now, your mind is working just fine, so if you want to conduct interviews and speak with the public, there is no reason why you cannot do so, but you still need to remain here until you have completed some of your rehab functions. If necessary, the rest can be done from the comfort of your home. The longer you are here, the quicker you will regain all your normal functions."

"Is my press secretary around," he asked.

"He is, sir. In fact, we were anticipating that you might want to speak with him this morning. He and your two senior aides are here as well as one of your physicians."

"Well, this ought to be one happy reunion," the president remarked. "Would you tell them I will see them at 1300 hours today? I would like to have some solid food first. I think that will put me in the right frame of mind and I would like some outside news if you don't mind. I'm sure one of the news channels will bring me up to date."

Captain Todd laughed, located the TV remote and promptly handed it over to the president.

"I will inform those waiting outside you will see them at 1300 hours. Please excuse me," and he left the room.

Van stood there for a moment then asked the President if he had a preference as to what he wanted for lunch.

"I think I would like some fish fingers and a few fries," he said, "if that's not a problem."

"No problem, sir. I will pass it on and you should have it within the hour. I will leave now but this evening, a medical technician will be around to take you to the pool for some exercises. I will be back afterwards to check on you."

"Thank you," the president said. Then added, "Your name is Van, correct?"

"Yes sir, that is correct."

"Thank you, Van," he said. "Thank you very much indeed and please convey those sentiments to Trainer for me."

"That won't be necessary, sir. You can speak to him anytime you want simply by doing it."

"He's here?"

"No sir. On his instructions, we implanted a communicator in the back of your head and neck, sir. You can talk to him right now if you want. You just have to speak to him."

"Trainer," the president said. His eyes lit up.

"I hear you," he replied.

"Yes, it will take some getting used to but I'm glad you thought of it. It saves me having to hold that damn telephone to my ear when I want our conversation to be private. Yes, I'm feeling much better now. I really don't know how to thank you. You saved my life and I owe you big time. Yes, your right but we are a hard headed lot who aren't used to being around those who know more than we do. Yes, I'll remember that from now on. Okay, and thanks. I'm sure we'll be in touch."

He looked up at Van. "That was a one sided conversation, wasn't it?"

"No problem, sir. We all have the same set up and it works well for us. I'm sure in time, it will be just like a second sense and always there when you need it."

Van departed and a short while later, the president had his lunch. He thought, as he was enjoying it.

"If I had ordered this from my office, I would have never heard the end of it. Always got to be something healthy and nourishing and must taste like crap."

He finished his meal and a few moments later someone was by to pick up the tray. "Thanks," he said. "I enjoyed that."

"Our pleasure sir, now can I get you something else or would you like to see your press secretary and doctor."

"I suppose you best send them in," he replied, "but after they're gone, do you think it possible I could have a bowl of ice cream?"

"Not a problem, sir. Would you like some pie with that ice cream?"

"You have pecan?" he asked.

"You want vanilla or chocolate with that?"

"Why, vanilla if you don't mind," smiling to himself as he realized he was moving his arms and it was getting easier already.

A few minutes later, the press secretary and his presidential doctor were ushered in.

"How are you feeling sir?" his doctor asked as he walked up to the side of the bed. The secretary was shuffling through some papers and making his way to the other side of the bed.

"I'm feeling better by the minute," the president replied. "Nothing like some forced bed rest to get your body re-established."

"Yes sir, I suppose if you put it that way, it makes good sense."

He paused then asked if the president minded if he looked at the stitches for the transplants?

"Well, knock yourself out doctor but you won't find any stitches, just a slight redness where they made the connections."

The doctor looked both arms over, then moved down to his legs. As the president had said, there were no stitches, only the slight red areas which would, according to Van, eventually blend in.

"This is astounding," the doctor said. "I have never seen work like this."

About then, Captain Todd joined them. Van had notified him that the president had visitors who might need to have a few questions answered. He walked up, observing at the same time the doctor examining the president's legs.

"Good work, don't you think?"

"How did you get them to bond without stitches? There are no scars either."

"It's a bonding adhesive," Todd replied. "We have an adhesive that bonds the bones together and you can't even tell where they were reattached when they are done properly."

"Well, it's simply amazing," the doctor said.

The press secretary interrupted.

"Mr. President, sir. I have some papers perhaps you could take a few minutes to look at."

"Will they wait a few more days, John?" he asked.

"Well, yes, but I just thought you might give them a glance and if anything, peaked your interest, you could let me know."

"John, I appreciate your work ethic but is our Vice President handling the day to day chores okay for you?"

"Yes, sir but these are more relevant to you," he said.

"Okay, I tell you what. Leave them here on the side table and I will look them over later and you can pick them up tomorrow."

"Some of this is sensitive, sir."

"I suspected as much but you are in a secure facility and I trust those around me with my life and I am not worried about wrong eyes seeing those papers so just leave them here and we will have them ready tomorrow."

"Very well, sir. Now, how soon before you think you will be able to hold a press conference announcing your return to office."

"Let's give it two more weeks and if all is progressing like I am expecting, I will be ready to move back to the Whitehouse."

"That long, well okay sir. I will be glad when you are back to your old self and we can resume business as usual."

"John, it will never be business as usual. From here forward we are going to start working with a new set of ground rules. Just like this," and he indicated his body. "This is what happens when you ignore good counsel and listen to those who only have self-serving interests. I am fortunate to have friends in very high places, who put my wellbeing to the forefront of our relationship. Otherwise, I would not be here."

"Your right sir, I will keep that in mind and see you tomorrow for those papers. Now, if you don't mind, I will take my leave."

"Very good," the president replied. "I will look forward to your return tomorrow. Anything else you need doc," he said to the white house doctor.

"No sir. I'll check back with you later," and he turned and left with the press secretary.

The president looked up at Captain Todd.

"Thanks for showing up when you did. I'm beginning to think my old circle of friends don't have my best interests in mind."

"A few months back, Mr. President, I might have sided with them but now, I see where you're going and I am totally onboard with it. Common sense and good judgment can never be hurried."

"Well said," the president remarked.

"Now, I wonder where that ice cream and pecan pie is."

Smiling as he turned to leave, Captain Todd replied.

"I'll have it sent right in, sir."

Chapter 28 – Valley Ambush

The soldiers were manning their lookout point from their solitary outpost overlooking the valley. Across the way was a ridge that was similar to theirs. It was a trafficking area for locals and occasionally enemy insurgents. They maintained a well-fortified position and had done so for several years now. Always, before today they had been able to deter the Taliban from taking positions that would compromise theirs.

The soldier manning the spy glass for the ridge had just looked down at his watch when the sniper round came through the lens of his equipment. It only missed hitting him by a fraction of an inch. His spy glass was out of commission and he had nothing to replace it with.

The other men in the post with him heard the shot and moved into the enclosed and fortified porch of the outpost. As they did, multi shots fired from several positions entered their outposts through the firing ports. Two men were hit in their upper bodies. Neither was killed outright but their wounds were serious.

They began calling for medical assistance. The only problem with that was that they would have to leave the outpost and trek across their ridge to a clearing where helicopters could land. Multiple rounds continued to enter their outpost, entering the firing ports from three different directions. Someone had gone to a lot of trouble and it appeared a lot of training to be able to make such accurate shots.

Their radio calls were heard at their base at Kandahar and a medevac chopper and several gunships were dispatched to assist them. In thirty minutes' time the choppers began to come in range.

Almost immediately they began to take fire from multiple locations requiring the choppers to turn back. The insurgents were well dug in and obviously prepared for this as they now had the soldiers boxed in. Even if a helicopter could have landed, they would have been right in the middle of a firefight with no sense of direction as to where the enemy was.

Getting the wounded out was going to be a problem for the Army. Today's activities had coincided with multiple attacks on army camps all across the area. A drone was sent in to see if they could locate the firing positions of the Taliban snipers. Almost as if they knew it was coming, the firing stopped while the drone overflew the area. As soon as it had passed over a position, the sniper there resumed firing into the outpost.

According to the soldiers, the snipers must have hundreds of rounds as there was no letup in the frequency of the shots coming from various locations across the valley. They couldn't tell if the shots were coming from five hundred yards or a thousand yards away or anywhere in between.

As the day turned into night, the wounded soldiers began to get weaker, their bodies in shock from the damage the large caliber rounds had done to them. The outpost was in constant contact with their base but for now nothing could be done to help.

After a very long night, it began to get light as the beginning of another day began. The snipers resumed firing into the outpost, and except for a limited time during the night when they had been able to use their night scopes, the soldiers were yet to locate their attackers.

During the night and now early morning, the officers back at the base tried to come up with any solution that wouldn't end up getting a lot of their people killed. One man suggested they go outside the loop and see if an intervention team could help.

"What do you mean?" a senior officer asked.

"Sir, I had an opportunity to spend some time at Area 51 before I was reassigned here. They have craft there that are nothing like we have ever seen and they are bullet proof. The enemy here has nothing to touch them. It is just a matter of reaching the right person to authorize their assistance."

"Any idea, who we can call?" the senior officer asked.

"No sir. The only person I remember was a General Neagle. He works at Area 51 but before that he was a foot soldiers general. I do remember that the man who coordinates the other activities is called Trainer. I overheard two specialists talking but I don't know what his job title is but he apparently coordinates everything related to the special equipment."

"I don't recognize the name but I may know a few people that might."

He got with a communications officer and gave him some names of people to call. Then he had a thought.

"Google this," he said. "Army needs help from Trainer. See if you get a hit."

As he walked away he thought.

"You can get anything off the internet now days. Who knows, maybe this trainer person was paying attention."

The communications officer did as the officer asked, typing in "Army Unit needs help from Trainer." then added, "Wounded men trapped in outpost overlooking afghan valley. It couldn't hurt," he thought, "and it just might help."

Funny thing is, there are few google requests for someone named trainer so when the request went through one of his many search engine servers looking for keywords here and there, that one was picked up and sent to him.

Trainer read the message then initiated a search for the sender. In a few seconds, he had it and sent a message to the man's inbox.

The communications officer was getting no response from the google search, only the suggestions that the internet offered like do you mean help with training aids and other such help suggestions.

As he continued to work, he saw the yellow block at the bottom of the screen say you've got mail. Clicking on it, he saw a message from someone named Trainer. Odd, he thought, that he had received it but there was no return address. He opened the message. The request was simple.

"Type in what you need or the nature of the problem, if in fact there is one, and I will respond."

He called the senior officer over, showing him what he had received.

"I'll be damned," the officer said.

"Send him this," and began to dictate the message relating how they had severely wounded soldiers in a remote outpost currently cut off from support by enemy insurgents using sniper rifles and positions that prevented them from reaching the pickup point.

The communications officer finished typing the message. Before he could hit send, a reply began to appear below what he had typed. Good enough he thought, since there was no mail box to send it too.

The message asked what was the latitude and longitude of the outpost.

The senior officer, looking over the communications officers shoulder and told him to standby. He quickly walked over to his work station, remarking to another officer sitting there.

"You're not going to believe what we have here," and he turned and went back to the communications station. "Here's the location," he said. "Type it in."

The location was typed out and immediately there was another reply.

"Very good, advise your soldiers in the outpost that help is on the way. Please tell them this is unconventional help, so they shouldn't be surprised by what they see."

"Just type in, thank you sir and sign off," the officer instructed.

"You think it's legitimate," the communications officer asked.

"We don't have anything else. Get in contact with the outpost. Tell them we may have some help coming their way. Just expect the unexpected.

The radio man at the outpost received the message and told his fellow soldiers what was said.

"What did they mean by the unexpected?" The ranking officer asked from where he lay. He was propped up on sandbags and was the least injured of the two men who had been shot.

"I have no idea, sir," the radio man replied.

#

Trainer spoke to Brad who was currently in his office following a day on the spaceship. He told him what he had, and Brad asked him did they really contact him via the internet.

"Desperate situations call for desperate ways to solve a problem. I think someone there heard about our operations and thought it was worth a chance to try it. They have nothing to lose and everything to gain."

"Alright sir," Brad replied. "I agree. I'm sending a team in now with two Hawks and one shuttle."

Brad contacted those ready for action. At the base, for the moment, that was Colin and his team. In ten minutes they were assembled in the tunnel ready to board the shuttle. Brad gave Colin a quick brief on what they knew and what he had regarding the injured. He also instructed them that they were to drop the injured off at Walter Reed here in the U.S. I will alert them of incoming once you're close.

"I thought that place was closing?" Colin stated.

"It's more of a re-alignment and consolidation of services," Brad replied.

"I will provide you with the landing coordinate for the emergency care facility there."

The soldiers waited expectantly for help to arrive. They just didn't have any idea when it was coming or how. As they huddled out of reach of the sniper rounds, they heard an explosion and could see bright flashes every few seconds. They were afraid to look through the ports, fearing another sniper round would take one of them. The only place they weren't taking any shots from was the rear entrance.

A silent shadow passed overhead and seemed to hang there. They knew something was there because of the shadow but as it was above them they couldn't see what it was.

Briant and Mack were manning the two Hawks. They had no trouble finding the snipers as their heat signatures gave them away. There were seven of them and then there were none. They found two pits with combatants in them who had been responsible for keeping the helicopters at bay and eliminated that threat as well. Briant maintained a position above the outpost while Mack ran a search pattern around the valley perimeter.

At the army base in Kandahar, the communications officer received a new email message. It stated simply that insurgents were eliminated and they could send in replacements. The wounded would be transported directly to the Walter Reed Medical Facility in the U.S.

He immediately alerted his senior officer who directed the army helicopter unit to approach the outpost with caution. A new squad of soldiers was to be ferried in as well.

Another officer working with him asked who was coordinating the evacuation and was told that it was someone named trainer.

"Are they army?" he asked.

The senior officer replied. "I have no idea who he is. We googled him for help and he answered."

"You what?"

"You heard me. We googled him and he responded."

"That's a hell of a way to run the army," the other said.

"Yeah, your right but if it works and saves lives, then I'm all for it."

They stood there waiting for the next report.

It had grown quiet on the ridge. One man was watching the entranceway. Moments before the shadow hovering above them disappeared. Then hovering in the air a few yards from the doorway was the Hawk.

"What the hell," the soldier watching the opening said, "what is that?"

Another soldier joined him. It was at that moment that they detected movement near the door. Both readied their weapons.

"Hello, in the fort," they heard someone say. "Did someone call for help?"

"Yes, we did," one of them said. "Can you identify yourself?"

"Well, who were you expecting? Bob Hope."

The two men looked at each other and one replied.

"Yeah, you're okay, just come in slow."

A black gloved hand reached out into the doorway. Then Colin spoke. "Okay guys, let's not shoot the cavalry and stepped into the doorway."

Both men were surprised. He wasn't kitted in standard army wear. He was dressed in black armor with headgear and all. As he stepped in, he removed the head gear.

"Okay gentlemen, I am told you have wounded."

"Oh, yeah," they replied, still taken back by how he was dressed.

"Forgive the outfit," Colin said. "I was in church and didn't have time to change."

Both men laughed.

Colin whistled and two more men followed him in. They too, were dressed in the black gear and carried a stretcher with them. As soon as they were in the outpost, they began to check out the two wounded men. One was now unconscious, the officer was alert but in a lot of pain. They took the most injured first and some few minutes later were back for the officer.

Helicopters could be heard in the background. It was the other cavalry. The two wounded men were now loaded onto the shuttle.

"Alright gentlemen, helicopters are approaching with your replacements. We're out of here now. The wounded will be dropped off at Walter Reed Medical center."

"But that's in the U.S." one man said.

"Right," Colin replied as he exited the outpost.

The men began gathering their gear while one walked out the rear door expecting to see the men in black loading up. As he looked around, he could find no sign of them.

"Where did they go," the man following him out, asked.

As they stood there, a shadow passed over them but looking up, they couldn't see anything.

"Beats me," the first soldier out said. "The only thing I saw was the shadow passing over us."

A few minutes later the medevac chopper landed and the two gunships were positioned nearby. Two medics and the relief squad exited the chopper headed for the outpost.

"Where are the wounded," one of the medics asked.

"They've been loaded onto something and are gone," one of the men said as he began to talk to his relief.

"What do you mean loaded onto something and gone," the medic asked

"Brother," the soldier said. "Some kind of intervention team was here. They silenced the Taliban snipers and the positions that kept you away earlier. All we saw were three men and a large shadow overhead. They took the wounded men out and said they were going to drop them off at Walter Reed and they left."

"Walter reed is in the U.S."

"I know that and that's where they said they were taking them."

The medics headed back to the chopper while they waited for the soldiers to do their handover.

"It's been a strange day," one said to the other.

"You're telling me. I would be interested to hear the rest of this story when we get back to base."

Trainer contacted the emergency reception at Walter Reed. The party answering the call asked how they could help him.

"Aircraft coming in to offload wounded in four minutes," he said. "Please have a team at the door to assist."

"What do you mean, aircraft coming in with wounded?"

"Just be ready," Trainer said and hung up.

The receptionist called the emergency switchboard and told them that someone had called in and told her that an aircraft would be there in four minutes with wounded and they were to be ready.

"Must be army," the woman answering said. "We'll be ready."

By the time, a team was exiting Walter Reeds emergency entrance, the shuttle was sitting on their helicopter landing pad. Two stretchers were out and the team was waiting on the hospital staff.

One man shouted out, asking how many they had.

"Two," was the reply. "We need two gurneys."

The medical teams quickly responded with the first one arriving in seconds. When they got close, Colin's team lifted the wounded soldier from their stretcher and laid him on the hospitals gurney.

"What is that thing?" asked a medical attendant.

"It's a stretcher," Graham told him. "It stabilized the soldier, now the rest is up to you."

They quickly wheeled the soldier away as the other gurney arrived. This time they didn't ask any questions, just helped load the wounded officer and followed those before them.

As they wheeled him away, the officer lifted his hand to Colin and said, "Thanks Man."

"Our pleasure," Colin replied and joined his team in the shuttle which quickly lifted off and headed back to their base.

Back at the base in Kandahar, the communications office received another notice that he had mail. He opened it up. It was from Trainer and stated.

"Your wounded are at Walter Reed. You may want to have someone liaise with them as we don't handle those things."

The communications officer typed in the space below the message.

"Thanks to you, Trainer, you saved the day for us. I hope that we can work together in the future."

There was a one word reply.

"Perhaps."

Chapter 29 – World Changes

It took two weeks to organize and prepare for the first visitors to the Eden Paradise 7. By then the media had been given full access along with specialist in all the fields of antiquities, history and theology with many others to follow, as they broadcast their daily findings to the world public.

On one occasion, individuals with the intent of either trying to destroy or make off with some of the items on display learned the hard way that one couldn't just walk up and touch, or strike the displays. They didn't know the nature of protective force fields and pretty much got the shock of their lives.

So many private tours had to be arranged that three days a week were designated for those with the remaining four designated for the general public. Any time the private tours were for short periods, anyone wishing to visit was allowed to do so.

It didn't take long for Brad and General Neagle to realize that it would be better if they had the spaceship move to other selected countries for short periods of time as being at the Dugway proving grounds full time was keeping a lot of other people from other nations from seeing it.

After three months, they announced that the ship would be moving for a three month period to other countries. After sorting out the logistics, France was chosen as the first location allowing two weeks there. Many people were on hand as it powered up and lifted off from the Dugway Proving Grounds. It took all of a half hour from lift off to landing to move it to a location near Paris. Paris was chosen as it was not that far from England and convenient to much of the rest of Europe.

Following France, they moved to Dubai. After two weeks there, they moved to Indonesia then China. They spent three weeks in China then two weeks in India and two weeks in South Africa. It was obvious that the planned three months was not long enough so they decided to continue on and return to the U.S. when they had provided sufficient time for the most people. Their next stop was Brazil followed by Mexico. After a two week trip to Australia, they returned to Dugway. It was as if they had never left.

The number of people pouring in to see the displays seemed to double over the next few weeks and they soon discovered that as it was summer the number of European and Africans visiting the Ark as many now called it, had increased. They were still being besieged with requests to visit other countries.

It took a year and a half for the government to complete the showing of the Arks displays and prepare the storage facilities for them. Once the displays were safely removed from the Ark, it became once again, Eden Paradise 7. It remained in the pit where it had rested for so many years but under military guard.

There was a national debate over where the facility to house the displays would be built. Many were against placing it in Washington or the bigger cities like New York, San Francisco, Chicago or Houston citing traffic grids and other similar issues not tourist friendly. After much wrangling, it was decided that a replica of the ship would be built where the ship had been lying all those years.

General Neagle and his team having completed their preparations for travel from Earth moved onto the ship. Personnel from the two nearby Black Hawk Warships watching over Earth were transferred to the Eden Paradise 7 as she needed a larger crew for the trip to the planet Eden 2.

Once the ship arrived near to Eden 2 and personnel change outs were completed, the ship would go to a nearby facility for refurbishment and upgrades. The old crew would do likewise. Circuit and exterior upgrades and the latest in android technology would be transferred to them and they would then be returned to their ship or reassigned as needed.

As the day for the Eden Paradise 7 to depart drew near, the President, now fully recovered was finally given a tour of the vessel. Due to the assassination attempt and presidential duties, he hadn't had an opportunity to tour the displays but would be on hand to open up the new display facility now renamed the Ark, when construction was completed in another year or so.

Presidential polls almost all guaranteed he would still be in office following the next election. He hadn't campaigned since the attempt on his life but his public approval rating was as high as any prior presidents had ever been.

He had a long meeting with General Neagle and his team and was shown the stasis chambers where they would sleep during the journey. It was all a marvel, he told them and he looked forward to hearing back from the General and his team once they were settled in on Eden 2. He expressed his hope that soon, they would have a greater interaction with the Council of Planets including a greater transfer of technologies to Earth as they moved forward towards less dependence on the planets natural resources.

General Neagle assured him that as soon as he could work out the details he would be spending all his available time working towards that goal. By the time the President's visit was almost over, Brad joined them. They had lunch onboard and then Brad and the President made their goodbyes to Neagle and his team.

The next few days saw the removal of all external ramps and railings previously installed to make access easier. During that process, Neagle and his team were given quarters that would be theirs prior to entering the stasis chambers and available when they came out.

He had a team consisting of three men and three women, each of them a specialist in their own fields and while none knew if they would be of any value on Eden 2, they were for the most part valuable to the team.

The media were on hand as the Eden Paradise 7 began to power up for departure. Brad and his team were on hand to see the departure but rather than see it from the ground, they chose to witness it in groups onboard the Hawks that were now available from the Area 51 base.

The flight wing there had recently been increased by another ten provided by the two Black Falcon vessels now on station nearby. As they no longer needed to be positioned between the earth and the sun, they maintained a position much closer.

At exactly 1200 hour's mid-day, the spaceship lifted up off its landing pads. The pads were retracted and the ship continued its slow climb straight upwards. At what onlookers would later estimate was 3000 feet, the ship then appeared to rotate, veer off in an upward direction and shoot up into and out of the earth's atmosphere. The Hawks followed it up into near space and stopped as it stopped.

Onboard, General Neagle and his team were on the bridge as the ship exited earth's atmosphere. Once well clear, the ship stopped and for the benefit of those who wanted to see Earth one last time, the bridge rotated and there she was.

After one minute, the bridge rotated towards outer space and the ship accelerated until she was out of range of the Hawks sensors. The journey for the Eden Paradise 7 had finally come full circle as she departed Earth to return to those who had built her and their new home planet.

Brad and the teams onboard the Hawks returned to the Area 51 base. As the pilot flew Brad near to the Dugway Proving Grounds, he could see heavy equipment moving in to begin the preparation phase for the construction of the Ark and facilities for the soon to be Museum of Earth and Man's Beginnings.

The base of the bottom of the pit would be concreted in and the sides sealed to prevent sand slides. It was determined there was enough sand beneath the site that drainage would not be an issue.

During the time period while the facility was being built, the Army would warehouse the displays under armed guard and only after contractors had fabricated and completed the replica of the Ark would the displays be returned. The site was designated as a national landmark and the park services would eventually operate the facility.

No one could contest the proof that had been provided and was still being provided as there were over a dozen sites undergoing different phases of excavation to uncover further proof of man's introduction to Earth by the Edenites. Of course, there were fringe groups that insisted it was all a massive hoax but theirs was a voice pretty much falling on deaf ears.

The war on crime, with the assistance of the quick response teams was beginning to take a toll on organized crime syndicates and gangs with so many arrests that the current prison systems couldn't contain them. Large strides were being made against terrorist groups and rogue governments.

The world was fast becoming a one nation society with calls for a world government. Some nations saw the benefits while others would resist for years. It was one thing that would not be forced on them as long as they remained a cooperating nation.

Chapter 30 – Meanwhile

On Bara, life went on. The Princess Alexis had given birth to a healthy baby boy named Mathew Trainer Farmer just before the real Prince Mathew departed. Only a few were aware of the change and all seemed well with the princes and the new Prince Mathew.

In truth, she had accepted the transfer and opened her heart to the new prince, knowing that Mathew had done the best he could in the circumstances and knowing as well that the new prince was turning into a very attentive husband and father.

Princess Alexis remembered Mathew saying that the ship could possibly do something for Tina's husband, Randall. His leg injured in a previous war gave him a lot of trouble, so she mentioned it to Logan.

A few days later, Logan informed her that all was in readiness for Randall's surgery. Once she had informed Tina, arrangements were made and Randall was transferred to the Phoenix.

It would be some months before he was fully healed and in the pre operation meeting on the Phoenix, the doctors showed him the advantage of getting both legs done as he had damaged the other knee over the years and it would be a hindrance in a few more years.

Once the healing period was complete, he was like a new man and began part time work as an advisor to the warrior forces. That of course was when he and Tina were not sitting on their pier fishing. She had finally retired after training another young woman named Kacie to replace her.

It was a few weeks before Queen Marie was due. She told Logan she was ready and as soon as his son was born, she wanted to start getting out more with him. Logan himself was already trying to come up with a name for the son they would soon share as the queen had insisted it was his right and duty.

Maxim and Kieran were joined as one. She too gave birth to a son. She asked Maxim if he cared if she named him after the two men most recent in her life. He said it was certainly fine with him and so she chose Carlos Mathew but wanted a third name. As was the custom on Bara, most people only had the one name but Prince Mathew had changed that and she saw it as something everyone would be doing soon.

She asked him to choose a last name for him, her and their family. After a day, he told her he had chosen Prince, as that is what their son would be and also the ones to come.

"I like that," she said, so the young lad became Carlos Mathew Prince.

Two delegations were formed to travel to Tomar and Waardin. They were delivered and both planets sent delegations back to Bara. With the help of the Edenites, ships capable of space travel were being constructed with the guidance and technical expertise Logan was able to arrange with the Council of Planets on Eden 2. In the near future further delegations were to be arranged for the Council of Planets.

\#

For the former Prince Mathew of Bara, a new life filled with many adventures was beginning. In time, the chronicles of his life would be written, but for now, the here and now were real. The new Shadow Prince has been chosen and his thousand year journey has begun.

The Beginning.

Made in the USA
Columbia, SC
30 September 2023

23582845R10126